EARI

MW01092544

GREENWICH

"A DARK, LUSH, COMPLEX TALE about the ways in which perception can be manipulated and privilege rules all. **URGENT AND GORGEOUS."**

—Lindsay Hunter, author of *Hot Springs Drive*

"An engrossing tale of a family tragedy layered against class and racial rifts in an upscale Connecticut suburb . . . it's **A RIVETING READ AND NOT-TO-BE-MISSED DEBUT."**

—Vibhuti Jain, author of *Our Best Intentions*

"AT ONCE A TENDER COMING-OF-AGE AND A CHILLING PORTRAYAL OF PRIVILEGE, *Greenwich* gets at the heart of how wealth confers protection. The stakes are as high as the net worths in this haunting debut."

—Avery Carpenter Forrey, author of *Social Engagement*

"More than just a compelling coming-of-age story, *Greenwich* takes a hard look at class, race, and privilege in one of the country's most affluent suburbs. NOBODY GETS OFF THE HOOK IN THIS BRAVE AND UNFLINCHING NOVEL OF PENANCE AND PLACE."

—Christina Clancy, author of *Shoulder Season*

"PREPARE FOR AN INTENSE READING EXPERIENCE . . . Book clubs will find themselves immersed in lengthy discussions about whether accidents just happen—or is someone always responsible. Get ready to have your opinions challenged and your emotions heightened."

—Pamela Klinger-Horn, Valley Bookseller

"A BEAUTIFULLY WRITTEN, UNFLINCHING, AND HARROWING TALE."

—Liz Harmer, author of *The Amateurs*

GREENWICH

KATE BROAD

ST. MARTIN'S PRESS
NEW YORK

This is a work of fiction. All of the characters, organizations, and events portrayed in this novel are either products of the author's imagination or are used fictitiously.

First published in the United States by St. Martin's Press, an imprint of St. Martin's Publishing Group

www.stmartins.com

Designed by Gabriel Guma

Library of Congress Cataloging-in-Publication Data (TK)

ISBN 978-1-250-36304-6 (hardcover)
ISBN 978-1-250-36305-3 (ebook)

Our books may be purchased in bulk for promotional, educational, or business use. Please contact your local bookseller or the Macmillan Corporate and Premium Sales Department at 1-800-221-7945, extension 5442, or by email at MacmillanSpecialMarkets@macmillan.com.

First Edition: 2025

10 9 8 7 6 5 4 3 2 1

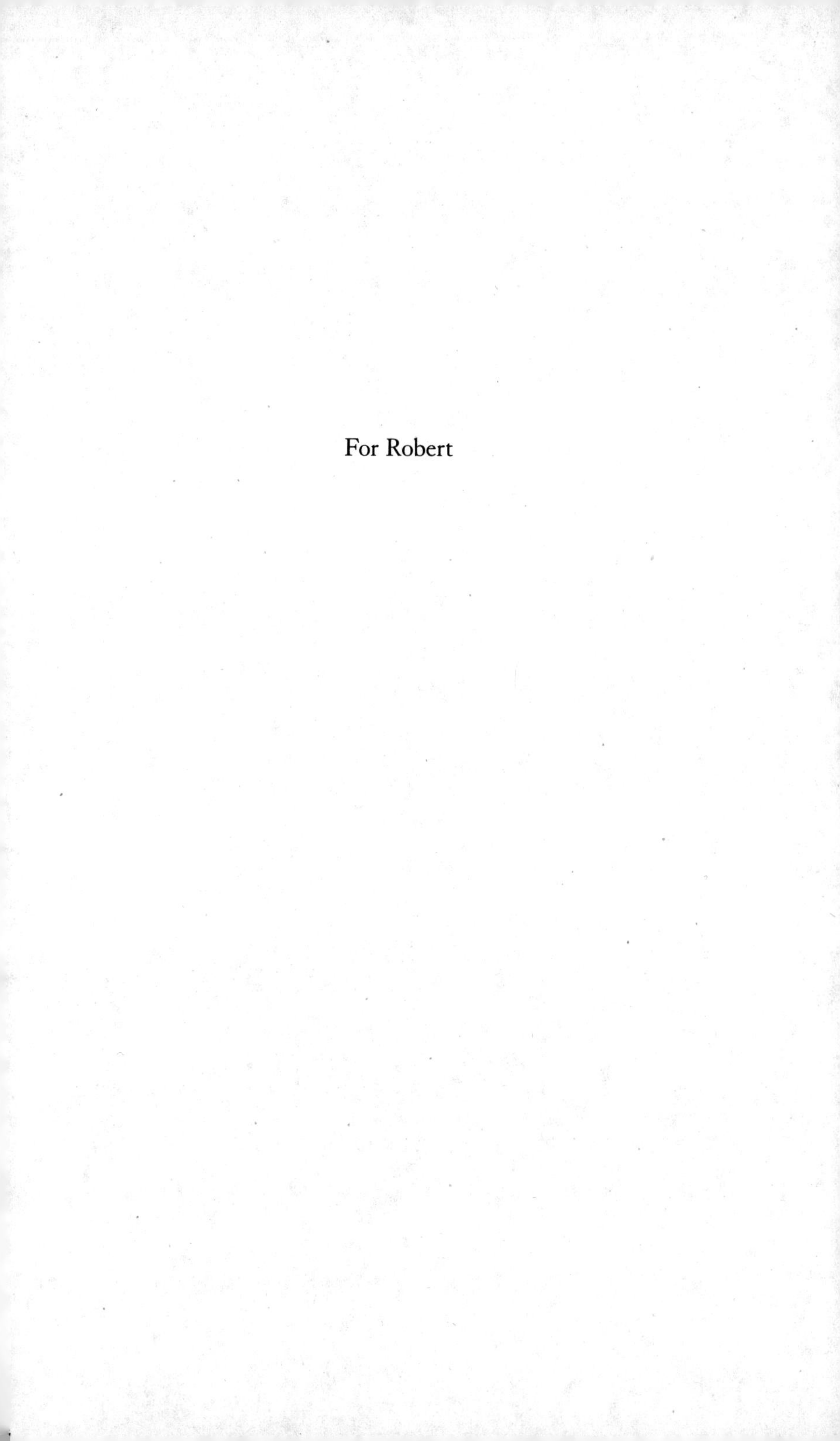

For Robert

One deed, and sometimes one word, suffices to change every constellation.

HANNAH ARENDT, *The Human Condition*

GREENWICH

I

ONE

I went to Greenwich at the last minute, to do what I thought would be some good. It was the summer before college, and I needed a fresh start, a clean slate, the chance to atone for some mistakes my seventeen-year-old self had made.

But I left my aunt and uncle's house early, before the summer was over, stuffing my clothes into garbage bags. I was crying too hard to pack. The mistakes had only compounded—I was the same person making them all. I never got to say goodbye to Claudia, to explain myself or tell her how I felt. All I could do was practice my lines, repeating the words like a prayer: *It was nobody's fault. I didn't see anything. It was just an accident.*

I wasn't lying.

But not lying isn't the same as telling what happened. Telling what happened, I've learned, doesn't have to mean telling the truth. I stuck to partial stories, a simpler account. Carrots sliced. Baths filled and drained. As though all Claudia and I did that summer was drink coffee and wring out our bathing suits and sing *Two more minutes, Sabine!* while my cousin played magic, played fairies, dressed up like a princess, a queen. My aunt Ellen on the phone or running errands. My uncle Laurent busy at work. Everyone believed me. My parents, the police, the lawyers who said I made a perfect witness. I was finally being *good*—I was doing what they wanted. Or that's what I told myself, most of the time.

It had seemed so exciting at first, the train ride down with the late June sunlight sparkling off the coast, the money my mother had given me fat and full of promise in my purse. Aunt Ellen was a star to me then, a woman of spa trips and gifts for no occasion, partial to buttery leather and buttery cheeses both flown in from France. She was late picking me up at the train station, but that wasn't unusual. It didn't raise any alarms.

When her Jaguar finally pulled up she did seem different, somehow. But that was typical, too. Ellen always seemed a little different to me, her hair always dyed a different shade of dusky blond, a little longer, a little shorter, bangs or no bangs or teased out or totally straight. Everything she wore was black, white, or cream, a mix of fitted and draped, but then there'd be a burst of color somewhere: her nails, her purse, a broach, a belt. That day it was white denim, a white silk blouse, snakeskin boots with a heel. She looked stunning. She always did. I can still picture the teardrop opening of the neckline, her collarbone lying so neatly underneath.

Now when I think of my aunt, that blistering summer, that same silk is smeared with blood. But she never recycled an outfit—she wouldn't have reworn that blouse. And anyway, it was Claudia, not Ellen, who was with me when it happened. Memory has its gaps, its tricks and little deceptions. But it's all I have, after the fact. The ways that I remember.

"Rachel!"

My aunt called out the window and I scrambled up from the curb, turning off my Discman. "Hi, hi, sweetheart, I'm so happy to see you. You weren't waiting long, were you? You look wonderful, I wish I had your hair."

I touched the back of my neck. I'd chopped it off right before graduation, all the way up to my chin, and I couldn't tell her I hated it, that when I looked in the mirror, I wanted to cry at what I'd done.

"It's so thick," Ellen said as she got out of the car. "I've never had that kind of volume. But if I could pull it off, you know." She ran her tongue over her front teeth as though to wipe a smear of lipstick that wasn't there; the pink was impeccably set. "I'd love to be brave like you." She popped the trunk, adding that she was sorry she couldn't help with the suitcase.

"Is it still hurting?" I asked. My mother had warned me to be careful when talking about Ellen's injury. I was to be patient but not indulgent, positive but not dismissive, sensible without making her feel criticized.

It was an impossible position.

But Ellen held out her arms for a hug, awkward because I was so much taller. "You're sweet to ask." Her shoulder pressed into my breastbone. Her hair spray smelled like chemicals and fruit. "I'm fine, really. Just no heavy lifting. Which is hopeless with a three-year-old—every time I look at Sabine, I swear she's grown." A laugh, stepping away now. "And you—a high school graduate! Who can believe it?"

I gave a thin smile. I didn't want to think about it—not high school, not home. My mother had bought the Amtrak ticket for herself, a short visit, saying it'd be good to have a *check-in*, Ellen needed some *family time*. It didn't matter how long it had been or how much Ellen insisted she was fine. No one could fall off a horse and bounce back *just like that*.

But my mother couldn't take a week off now, not even a long weekend, not while my sister was—

She'd developed this new habit of no longer finishing her sentences.

While Jules was *what*? I bit the inside of my cheek when Ellen asked how the surgery went.

"Good, I think. They got everything out. Now she waits to start treatment."

I kept my voice neutral: stating the facts. I hadn't expected my mother to say yes so easily when I'd offered to come in her place, when I'd said why not make it the whole summer—I could babysit, run errands, be someone for Ellen to talk to. Whatever she needs, I'd promised. I didn't want Ellen to start thinking maybe what she needed was to send me back.

"You're so lucky to be in Boston," she said. "Such good doctors there. You're lucky you caught it so soon."

I wasn't sure it felt that way to Jules. But I nodded, sure. "We're really lucky," I echoed dutifully, careful to keep my voice upbeat. "So where's Sabine?" My sister had been sleeping when I'd gone to say goodbye, and I wondered if she missed me. But I was so much older; our lives had barely overlapped. I wanted things to be different with my cousin this summer. My aunt would see I was ready, I was excited, I'd help out right from the start.

The silence stretched for so long that I finally glanced over and found Ellen staring—just staring—strangely, in the rearview mirror. But Sabine wasn't in the car seat, quietly napping. There was nothing back there but Ellen's oversized purse.

She must not have heard me change the subject. She must have been thinking about something else, something much more important, or she was just that thorough about checking in the mirror for cars. Call me naïve, but it was the only explanation I could come up with—the pause, that vacant look, her confusion followed by my own. I turned around as though I were the one who'd been mistaken. Until she cried, out of nowhere, "The pool! The pool, it's so gorgeous there, it's what sold us on the move—"

And then she was herself again, describing the club where Claudia had taken Sabine so I'd have time to get settled, and the spa, the tennis courts, the shrimp cocktail I was going to love.

"But your back is better?" I asked. Afraid of being rude, or too obvious, too *myself*, I flashed the kind of look my aunt and I used to share behind my mother's back, say, or when she'd sneak me a hard candy but didn't have another for Jules. "I won't make a big deal of it to my mom."

"The Maureen police." Her lipsticked mouth opened wide. Teeth, tongue, all of her went into the laugh. She reached over and squeezed my hand, I felt the bones and her rings and the line where her nail nicked my skin. "I'm great, sweetheart. And I promise your sister will be, too."

"I know," I said, because I had to believe it, and then the light changed, a car honked, and my aunt took back her hand to drive.

The house was high on a hill and set so far back it was as though the driveway were its own private street. You couldn't see it from the road, not with the trees and the stone ledge and the iron gate that required a code to unlock. The chimneys, plural, appeared first as we drove up, then the windows, the pillars, the red slab of a double front door. It had once been a girls' reformatory, and although Ellen had crowed to my mother about the changes they'd made, it still had that look, an institutionalized brick, like I'd been dropped into a nineteenth-century novel: the governess's tale.

"Wow," I said as we pulled up. And then, because Ellen was looking at me expectantly, as if waiting for more: "It's beautiful."

"It still needs so much work." She clucked her tongue. But I'd said the right thing, and she was pleased.

There was a field's worth of grass, a massive front yard sloping down to the road. At its base was a pond, not large enough to be a lake but really, it was something to have it on their property, an actual pond in front of their house. They never used the front entrance, Ellen said. Or the side entrance, which was the separate entryway into Claudia's suite. It was almost disappointing to drive all the way around to the back and discover just a regular door, a pot of geraniums that looked thirsty, but what did I know.

We used to go to their old apartment in Manhattan over the holidays, Jules and my parents and me, my uncle Stephen and his wife, Anita, and my three other cousins. Before Sabine was born, before they moved and got so busy with their renovations. In Manhattan, they'd had to unfold the leaves of their dining table to squeeze everyone in, but that wouldn't be a problem when they hosted us here. Ellen led me on a tour of the living room, sitting room, family room, parlor. Everywhere Sabine smiled out from tables, bookshelves, the mantels above each fireplace: laughing in the French countryside, eating gelato in Rome. I hadn't seen her since last Christmas, when the Corbins brought her to Cambridge and kept her in a Pack 'n Play in my room. Already in the recent pictures she looked more like a person, her hair gold in the sunlight, eyes a watery gray as though the color had been leached from her gaze. It was disarming how pretty she was, how much prettier she'd wind up than me. I didn't want to think like that. But the measuring was automatic, the valuation of what mattered to me then.

I followed Ellen up polished wood stairs, past Sabine's bedroom, playroom, plus another guest room, bathroom, their bedroom, and then Laurent's study at the far end of the hall. "Which nobody needs to go into," she said, shutting the door before I caught more than brown leather and thick curtains behind. She led me on a steep climb to the third floor. I'd expected, I guess, more of the same, the rooms generous with furnishings, colors muted with just the right touch.

But the hallway was narrow and bare, nothing more than a small table with a portrait of my grandmother. Ellen herself seemed out of place as those snakeskin boots clipped past all the closed doors to the last closed door on the end. "I hope you like it," she chirped.

It smelled like old wood, a closed-in closet smell. There was only a dresser, a nightstand, a single chair sagging in a corner. Was this where she'd have stuck my mother for their *sister time*?

But I said the room was gorgeous, I was so happy I'd come. "I've missed you," I said. "I can't wait to see Sabine. And Claudia," I added, since she was the real babysitter, the one Ellen relied on the most. I didn't want Ellen to know how nervous I was about meeting her. Things hadn't gone well at the end of the school year and I couldn't shake the feeling that everyone hated me, which meant Claudia was going to hate me, too.

"Claudia's a godsend. But your mom's right, it'll be such a treat having you pitch in. Don't feel like you have to spend your whole summer taking care of us, though. We'll find a way to make it fun."

I nodded, smiled, hugged her again. Checked her gait as she turned and left—but there was no limp, no hitch, no telltale sign of anything once broken. Maybe she wasn't in pain anymore, and it was only the memory of pain, the betrayals of her body, that lingered these months later.

After she left, her footsteps echoing down the empty stairs, I unlatched the window and pushed it open, fighting against the swollen wood, its creaky resistance. The screen had a hole in it; dried ladybugs gathered on the windowsill. But I wouldn't bother Ellen about it. I wouldn't bother anyone at all. "She's great," I told my mother when I called home to say I'd made it. "She's Ellen. She dressed like a supermodel just to come to the train."

Tell me if anything's wrong, she'd said. But *wrong* wasn't Ellen being late, or a little spacey, or putting me in a small room. Anyway,

Jules had another appointment. My mother said that sounded just like Ellen and got off the phone. I'd done my job, then; I'd set her mind at ease.

I unpacked my T-shirts, shorts, and went exploring down the hall. The other rooms were even smaller, one with just a bed, others with no furniture at all. They had plans, Ellen had explained, to tear down walls. "Make it all feel less stuck." But that was for a later renovation, when Sabine had friends over and wanted more space. How many friends did they think one kid was going to have? If her social life went anything like mine, she'd just wind up rattling around on these empty floors, alone.

But I didn't ask that. And it didn't come to be—not the renovation, not the sleepovers, not the many giggling girls. By the end of that summer, media vans would already be camped out by the iron gate, sneaking shots of the mansion and its manicured grounds as everything was spruced up to sell. "They never should have bought such a place," I'd hear my mother lament to Uncle Stephen on the phone, and I'd wonder if she really thought that. If you could blame a house for what you'd done inside its walls.

TWO

By the time I figured I should come downstairs, start making myself useful, Claudia the godsend had come and gone. Sabine was sitting at the table, intent over a bowl of sliced grapes.

"Hi," I said. "Do you remember me?" She stared up at me with those lake-gray eyes, then went back to her project. She was using her teeth to peel the skin, eating the outside in strips and discarding the viscera to leak on the table. "You going to eat those?" I asked.

"Grapes," she answered, or something like that, it was hard to understand through the wet of her mouth, the smallness of her child's voice. She extended a curl of skin to me.

"Thanks," I said. I wondered what three-year-olds liked. What you were supposed to say to them. "That was really good sharing." I took the slippery piece and put it on the counter. Ellen didn't seem to notice the mess. She was humming and opening drawers, closing them like she'd forgotten what she was looking for. I tried to decide if this Ellen, shiny and unbothered, was the same Ellen my mother had been worried about. This Ellen said she wanted to show me the town. Was I up for it? Laurent was at the office.

"On a Sunday?" I popped a grape into my mouth, as if to show Sabine how it was done.

"It's this project." She banged a drawer shut. "He never should have gotten into real estate. I told him—"

She got Sabine's sandals, a little denim jacket too warm for the day. "Told him what?" I asked, when enough time had passed that I wasn't sure if she'd forgotten, or was checking to make sure I was listening, or maybe I was supposed to do more to help get Sabine out the door.

"The end of River Point has nothing, I mean honestly nothing there. A storage facility and a municipal lot. And it's right on the water! All that wasted land. Can you imagine? No, you can't, I'll take you—we'll drive by and you'll see how bleak it is."

I nodded. I had no idea what she was talking about. My uncle was a hedge fund manager, which as far as I could tell meant he made money for other people and that resulted in more money for himself.

"So what's the problem?" I asked. Sabine had stripped her jacket off, and I grabbed it from the floor to hang on the back of a chair. Unless Ellen wanted me to bring it? But she was picking up her keys and somehow misplacing them again, going on about zoning and permits and regulations that went back fifty years, a hundred. How it was enough to make you think the state didn't actually want a better business district, or attractive condos for people to live in, or a marina bigger than a postage stamp.

"You wouldn't believe the investors he's pulled in," she said knowingly. "But Laurent's always had vision." I nodded more, my head bobbing away. "It won't be an option for this goddamn state to say no."

Her voice dropped as she took Sabine's hand and we walked out to the car, all those grape skins still seeping on the table. I revised my earlier opinion. Not so shiny, then. Not all the way through.

I didn't mean to add to her problems. But at the bottom of the driveway, I told her to stop. Before the road—had it been there earlier? I was still thinking about my uncle, those investors, if you could really make Connecticut change its laws for you. But also, there was something in the pond.

"What, sweetie?" Ellen checked her lipstick while she waited for the gate to open.

"That." I pointed.

It was an antler. An antler was sticking up out of the water.

Ellen leaned over to peer through my window and I caught her scent again, something like pear. "Oh my god," she said, finally seeing it. "Oh my god, oh my god." She snapped upright in her seat, clutching the steering wheel tighter.

"I'll go look," I said, and opened the door.

The pond smelled of spongy ground and old, forgotten rot. There was a copse of trees, and from the road and the house the effect was bucolic, some perfect pastoral scene with the hill and the grass and the pond, hedges lining the driveway; a glimpse, across the road, of the next hill extending up. But maybe it only looked like that from far away; maybe up close everything was like this, the fetid water, the slippery rocks, the same way that, as she'd leaned over, I'd seen the layers where Ellen's makeup clumped in her pores and along her lashes, making her look not luminous but cakey and strange.

The deer's head lolled to the side. It must have been hit by a car and punched through the hedges before landing in the water. Its eyes were open—could it still be alive? But a river of blood ran from its nose, more gummed on its haunches and in the divot where its ribs had smashed. Up close I saw the antlers were new, young, softened by velvety down. One had cracked open and blood matted the velvet, pooling in the cup of split bone.

It should have been frightening. I heard it like a voice in my ear: *You should be afraid of this.*

But I stood there, looking. Looking for so long that I worried Ellen would wonder what was wrong with me. Earlier that year my best friends had stopped speaking to me, three bitchy dominoes falling in a row, and I felt the strangest kinship with that deer, that it knew me. That it knew from a place beyond knowledge what it was to be alone.

A flash of periwinkle caught my eye, and I turned to find the girl racing toward me. Her car door was wide open, but my aunt was still sitting in the driver's seat. I was the only thing standing between Sabine and the road and the pond and the dark, gummy deer, and I saw all at once the terrible ways it could happen. A rock, a root. Tires screeching too late. What if she fell in the water or ran through the open gate into the road? What if she saw all that blood?

Did Ellen know where she had gone?

The panic was raw, new. I must have had some kind of instinct after all. I ran to intercept her and picked her up under her armpits. She let out a yelp, as though I'd been too rough with her—

So I laughed. I laughed and twirled her in the grass, like it was only a game.

"You're such a fast runner!" I cried.

She wrapped her arms around my neck. "You went away."

"Just for a minute, silly." I was surprised by her sudden attachment, that she'd followed me at all. Surprised, too, by how flattering it was. "Let's go find your mom, okay?"

I carried her back, thinking Ellen was right. She wasn't so light anymore.

My aunt called through the window: "Sabine?" The way she said it and looked over her shoulder, searching, I knew the answer to my question. She hadn't let Sabine out of the car.

Had she known Sabine could undo her buckles? Open the door? "Aunt Ellen," I started, sliding into the passenger seat once Sabine was secured. But I'd only just arrived; I couldn't sound too critical.

"What is it?" She craned to look through the window. "Did you see?"

I said, treading carefully: "I should remember to keep an eye out, right? If Sabine won't stay in the back seat?"

"Do you need me to go look?"

"No, it's not that. But Sabine—"

"We've had so much to do with the house, I've barely started on the landscaping down here."

I should have pushed harder. I should have made her focus.

"It's dead," I finally told her. "It's a dead deer."

"Dead deer," Sabine echoed from the back seat, and I wondered if she knew what that word meant. If I'd overreacted by trying to shield her. If I was overreacting now. Ellen wasn't worried, and Ellen knew children better than I did. She knew her own child best of all.

"Sorry," I said. "I don't think she saw it, though."

"I'd better call Laurent."

She dialed on the car phone. The Corbins were the first people I'd known to get one. My uncle's voice through the speaker as he picked up was nothing like I remembered, or maybe I didn't know how I remembered it. People could change, after all, in not a lot of time.

"What is it?" he said, quick, even his voice agile, no time to waste on hellos.

"There's a deer," Ellen said. "There's a dead deer in the pond. Here, can you—"

She was driving by now, one hand waving, and I realized she was pointing me toward Sabine, who had picked up on her father's voice and was shouting, "Papa, Papa!" from the back seat.

"Hey, little strawberry." I reached around and grabbed Sabine's toes through her sandals, whispering: "Mama's on the phone."

I wiggled her foot. She giggled and kicked, so I unbuckled my seatbelt to reach the other one, grabbing with little gobbling noises in the back of my throat. She laughed harder, and I couldn't believe that those feet belonged to a person, that the skin could be so soft, that this was all it took for her to like me.

"It's in the pond and it's dead," Ellen was saying. We hit a turn and my stomach lurched with it, but I didn't let go.

"What are you telling me for?" Laurent's voice crackled through the speaker. Ellen explained it all over again, her voice rising, until he cut her off. "Call someone to get rid of it. I'm meeting Harry at Belle's, you know I can't be late."

Ellen said who, who was she supposed to call for a thing like that, what was she supposed to do with a dead deer in the pond, and my chest turned hot with shame. That Laurent would talk to her this way. That she could be so put together, so perfectly coiffed, and also so foolish.

"Just take care of it, El." He hung up without saying goodbye.

Belle's, or Bellebrook to the rest of us, was a private golf club, invitation only. I'd look it up later; and Harold Singer, who was in a foursome with the governor's chief of staff and knew when another in their party was away on a cruise down the Rhône. I didn't have to guess what my uncle was after. The way Laurent said it, I could see the men in chinos, pressed linen, the kind of pants you could only call *trousers*. At what point would he bring it up, whatever favor he needed from people like that? I squeezed Sabine's foot and spun back around. I was thinking.

"I can find someone," I said. "In the yellow pages, or—"

"Not you." Ellen seemed appalled.

"But he's busy."

She flicked her wrist as if to brush me away. Her engagement ring was enormous; it must have snagged on everything, plus there were gold bands inset with diamonds and an emerald catching the light. My mother claimed she'd never wear so much jewelry at once, even if she had it. But I didn't believe her.

I believed Ellen, though. Maybe she wasn't so foolish after all.

"Let me tell you something, the most useful advice I've ever received. Men are all bluster, all of them. The kind of storm that passes through but never rains."

Leather squeaked on the backs of my thighs as I shifted. (My father: "They charge you half price for those shorts?") Ellen tapped a fingernail against the steering wheel in time with the turn signal, but I knew she wouldn't break it, she'd always use just the right force. "That poor deer will be gone by morning. Mark my words."

THREE

I'd thought it would all be like that: window-shopping in the boutique stores on Greenwich Avenue, Ellen insisting I try on a yellow blouse, new sunglasses—a hundred and eighty dollars pretax but Ellen said it could be my graduation present, my coming to Connecticut present, a present just because.

But when I came downstairs on Monday morning, I froze. Ellen wasn't up yet. In the kitchen stood a stranger, tall, barefoot, holding a dish towel as she dried Sabine's Minnie Mouse cup.

Yolanda, I realized—the housekeeper Ellen had said came twice a week and sent most of her wages back home. "Hi," I said cheerfully. "I'm—"

"Rachel!" she cried. "You're up, I hope we didn't make too much noise. I'm Claudia. Or *Caw-dee*, if you're Sabine." She scrunched her nose and I managed, barely, to choke down my horrendous mistake.

Ellen had said Claudia's sister worked in her office, and I'd pictured Denise as someone like Ellen, an Ellen-in-training, which meant Claudia would be the same.

But Claudia was younger than I'd been expecting, and Black, and no one had mentioned either of those details. Not that they needed to, but I was embarrassed by my jolt of surprise. My (former) best friend Dana was half-Chilean, enough to check Hispanic on her college applications even though she looked white and my mother, when she found out, had paused and said, "Really? She can do that?"

But I wasn't my mother. I wasn't like that. "I'm so excited," I said, tripping on my pajama bottoms as I rushed over. "I've been dying to meet you, I know Sabine is obsessed."

Was I laying it on too thick? But Claudia smiled, revealing two deep dimples and the sliver of a gap between her front teeth. She was pretty. Really pretty. How had I not noticed that first? She was almost as tall as me but nowhere near so plain. Her hair was short and tightly coiled, springing around a strip of yellow fabric she'd tied into a headband. The fabric matched the metallic swoop of her eyelids, which matched the tiny pineapples of her tank top, which matched the glittery polish on her toes. Her skin had a smooth glow that said she never stayed up late, alone, picking at acne scabs and scrambling to cover up the damage. "Coffee?" she asked, getting me a mug, and I couldn't say no, that I hated the stuff. I'd turned as childish as Sabine, who wouldn't touch her breakfast until Claudia sat with her, until Claudia assured her that their bagels were toasted exactly the same.

I was so used to telling Dana everything, I narrated it to her in my mind: the cream cheese pink with salmon, peaches sliced and dripping in a bowl. Then I remembered that Dana didn't give a shit. Dana didn't even know I was here. Claudia laughed at something Sabine said and I tilted my head back and laughed as if I'd heard her, I was part of it, too, and so we were all laughing, the three of us together, when Ellen rushed downstairs, saying just coffee, she had no time to eat. She was late for a call with her boss, Billie, some rebranding thing with shampoo, and she pulled a stack of twenties from her purse as she pressed a palm over the mouthpiece, whispering for us to have fun.

We went to the pool that day. The clubhouse, Ellen had called it. The country club, I realized, when we stopped by security to get me a pass. Claudia put in a *Sesame Street* tape for Sabine, but not before I heard she'd had the radio on, the news—I caught something about Clinton, Kosovo, and I was impressed that this was what she listened to on her own, even as she knew the words to "Rubber Duckie." The red ties of her bikini peeked out from under her tank top as she drove. She'd taken off the headband and replaced it with sunglasses and the coppery arm of the glasses matched the coppery sheen of her skin, her hair, which I saw in the sun was bleached the faintest orange at the tips. I couldn't stop that stuck feeling in my throat, like I'd swallowed too fast without chewing. "I was expecting—this is so stupid—but like another kid," Claudia said once we'd plopped down at an umbrella. "Except of course not, didn't you just graduate? It's perfect. *You're* perfect. You can watch Sabine when I pee and I don't have to feel guilty."

Her relief fed mine, or mine fed hers, the way my laugh made her laugh and her laugh only made me laugh harder. I asked how she'd gotten the job, and she explained it as we piled the table with sunscreen and Sabine's floaties and the club's starchy towels. How her sister worked with Ellen at the advertising firm, before Ellen moved and switched to part-time, and I had to face all over again how stupid I'd been. Denise wasn't an assistant, a secretary, whatever I'd assumed. She'd gone to Columbia, which had waitlisted me.

One time they needed babysitters for their company holiday party, Claudia said, and Denise pulled some strings to get her hired. "I was so lucky to have the connection. They covered a hotel for spending the night in New York, plus a ton of free champagne. When the kids were gone, don't worry." I smiled. I wasn't worried. "So Mrs. Corbin came to get this little Bean." She nodded toward Sabine, who was ankle-deep in the kiddie pool, calculating if she wanted to play with the two little boys in there or pretend they didn't exist. "And she was all, I've never seen her this happy with a stranger, Denise says such great things, can we hire you through the agency. I had to explain that I wasn't with some group, but when they added that they'd include an apartment, and guarantee enough hours that I wouldn't need a second job, how could I say no? I worked at the childcare center at UConn," she added, as though I might protest her lack of credentials.

The nannies clustered on one side, the moms on the other. There wasn't a single man who wasn't a club employee. The nannies were all Black, older than us, and the moms all white and just like Ellen, their hair dyed and artfully arranged, their one-piece bathing suits suctioning everything in. I wanted to find out where Claudia sat when I wasn't there. But it would have meant naming something I shouldn't have noticed, like pointing out a pimple, a rash. "What'd you major in?" I asked.

"French and studio art. I know, real marketable." She rolled her eyes. "Monsieur Corbin lost his mind over the French, though. I think he was skeptical about the whole full-time thing, but I brought him around."

Her mother, she said, was still anxious. Was this a real job? Was there any kind of future? She'd graduated early, through an accelerated high school program that gave her college credits, so at least she'd saved on tuition. But Denise had claimed there was no way to get health insurance with an art degree, and now look at her: full salary, benefits, and all her housing and most of her food was paid for. "Crazy, right? If I were paying rent in the city, you know they'd be complaining all the same."

My friends didn't talk about rent. Health insurance. Claudia seemed so worldly to me then, even though she was only twenty-one and I was going to be eighteen in September, as soon as I started at Swarthmore. We could have overlapped—in my mind we were overlapping already, she the senior and I the freshman nestled under her wing. "What do you want to study?" she asked, then crossed her fingers. "Please say Play-Doh, because I'm a pro."

"Premed is basically the same thing, right? Slicing, dicing, smooshing things together?"

The knot of worry wasn't there, the usual one that said what if I got there and couldn't hack it, what if I failed out or had to change careers altogether, and everyone would know.

"Oh shit," she said. "Shoot. That's Advanced Play-Doh. I'm going to have to up my curriculum."

Claudia grinned around the straw of the Banana Slam smoothie she'd ordered, one for each of us, and what a prize it was to win her smile, to think that it might be because of me.

"Sabine's the best kid in the world," she said. "You'll see. But I can't believe how much I've missed having an actual person to talk to."

I wondered what Ellen shared with her, if they talked about her move or the injury or Laurent's job, their stress over his investors and whatever regulations were blocking the River Point deal. But Claudia wasn't Ellen's friend, not the way she could be mine. I passed her the sunscreen. "Will you?"

I didn't need it. We were in the shade, I could have put a T-shirt on. But I turned my back and slid down the chaise to make room. She came up close and drew aside the straps of my bikini, running her hands across my shoulder blades. Her skin was soft, her fingers strong. It took too long to remember I still had to breathe.

"Dr. Fiske," she said, and when I turned in surprise, she smiled. "Just getting you used to how it sounds."

FOUR

In the other version of my life, the one where I didn't kiss Jonathan Savino senior year and then lose all my friends—in the version that was supposed to have happened—I never went to Connecticut that summer. I never met Claudia Meadows. And maybe Sabine and I wouldn't have been close as she grew up, not with fourteen years between us. But maybe she'd have texted me sometimes, too late at night, saying, hey cuz, how r u, i miss u, u coming for xmas?

And I'd have said, Of course, I miss you, too! I'd have stayed by my family's side all this time.

In that parallel world, I would have spent that summer inseparable from my friends. My friends who were still my friends, in my life that I still recognized. That year was the first time we didn't have to worry about college applications, and we were too old for scrimmages at lacrosse camp, sharing a cabin with all the other girls. We'd considered what job would hire four of us together, but on a spring day with our toes in Morgan's pool, sharing the warm vodka Morgan's brother had bought us, Dana said fuck it, guys. Let's spend every second just like this.

We started a checklist of everything we'd do together: Dana, Morgan, Ilana, and me. Make piña coladas and get our belly buttons pierced and tailgate before the Tori Amos/Alanis Morissette double header at Great Woods. My last real summer, or so I thought of it, before I'd have internships and research programs and clinical practice. The best summer, we declared, still young enough to make that kind of promise.

And then right at the end of finals, turning in my last exam, I felt the scratching in my throat. A scratching that became a knife, a fever that set in so quickly the school nurse took one look at the thermometer and shook her head. "You must be friends with that boy Jonathan," she said. "I just sent him home, too."

But it wasn't friendship that had given me Jonathan Savino's case of streptococcal pharyngitis. It was making out with him in the school auditorium after dark, and in his car, and sucking his dick in the woods while Natasha McNally, his girlfriend, was out sick. Out sick with a sore throat, I only remembered when it was too late.

It must have taken Dana only seconds to make the connection. She and Natasha weren't even that close, yet the news spread faster than the virus blistering inside me. Jonathan was mad at me, Natasha was mad at me, Dana and Morgan and Ilana were mad at me for the same reasons and for others, too. At graduation I walked across the stage, collected my diploma, and told my parents I still didn't feel well and wanted to go home. "No pictures with your friends?" my mother asked, feeling my forehead, and I couldn't say I didn't have any friends, that half the grade wouldn't speak to me now.

Some part of me knew I deserved it. I couldn't deny having done something wrong. But then how to account for my sister when she announced her throat felt funny, too?

Copying me, our parents said at first, because Jules wasn't acting sick—she had ballet and piano and when Mom said to get the zoomies out before dinner, Jules did jumping jacks in the living room while I watched TV and groaned for her to shut up. When the phone rang—

Ellen, again—I heard my mother saying we were great, both her girls were doing so well, before she ducked out of the living room to ask how Ellen was feeling.

Except then Jules kept complaining, even after my illness was over and I had no excuse to sit around watching movies all day.

"It's just a cold," my father said. "A ten-year-old can't have strep without a fever."

"No, not a *sore* throat," Jules said when my mother told Ellen she had to go, she'd call back soon, she promised, and brought out the thermometer again. "Just a funny throat."

What, they wanted to know, was a funny throat?

"It feels like I got a seed stuck in it. There's a sesame seed in my throat and it won't go down."

A week passed, then two. I was losing my whole summer. Bored on the couch, bored in my room, hating Jonathan and Natasha and my so-called friends who never called. The phone rang only to taunt me: my aunt needing my mother, no one ever needing me. I'd seen Dana punish other girls for their transgressions, but not me. Not like this. There'd been another incident before the Jonathan thing, at a school dance before the year ended. But it was hard to believe she was still that angry.

I didn't go to Morgan's pool. I didn't swipe lip gloss from Urban Outfitters or perfect that colada recipe. I logged online but Dana was never there. hey, I wrote. are we meeting up or what?

"Maybe it's a peanut," Jules amended. "Maybe it's not a seed. Maybe it's bigger than that."

Someone finally touched Jules's neck. Someone finally took her to the doctor.

"El," my mother said on the phone, and there was a catch in her voice I'd never heard before. "I don't have time right now."

danes, I wrote.

can't we talk???
it's important
i have to tell u something.

My parents had bought me a cellular biology textbook to get a head start on next year, and I stayed up reading about nodular sclerosis, Reed-Sternberg cells. "Rachel," my dad said, loading the dishwasher so loudly the plates clattered with the bite of his voice. "I don't know, okay? We don't know yet. Can you cool it with the questions?"

How useless I'd become.

At the CVS in Harvard Square, strolling the aisles for crap I didn't need, I heard a laugh followed by a stream of louder shrieks, and somehow I knew as I peered around the corner what three heads I was going to find bent together with three sets of newly highlighted hair. Dana in the middle, beneath the FAMILY PLANNING sign, holding up the Trojans like a medal she'd won.

I dropped my basket in front of a Kleenex display and walked out. At home, I found Jules rereading *Little Women* in bed. Her tumor had been removed with clear margins, but the red gash across her throat made her look like she'd been partially beheaded. I picked up her raggedy stuffed elephant. It was warm, like she'd been hugging it. "How are you feeling?" I asked.

She shrugged and kept reading, and I understood. What was she supposed to say? She was my sister. The only one I'd ever have. But I knew I couldn't stay in Cambridge all summer, afraid of running into my friends who were perfectly happy without me, every weekend another party I wouldn't be invited to. I needed something better to do. A reason to be gone, so that when my absence was noted and dissected and discussed, it wouldn't look like I'd gone slinking away.

Downstairs, my mother stood in the kitchen gripping a box of Funfetti cake mix, my sister's favorite, as though it were her birthday.

She was just staring at it, not even reading the instructions. "Mom," I said. It took a long time for her to put the box down.

I told her I'd had an idea for how I could help Aunt Ellen while she stayed with Jules. "This is more important than me hanging out with Dana and them all summer," I insisted, like it was a sacrifice but I was ready to step up. I promised to tell my parents if it was too much—if Ellen needed more than just another set of hands. Nobody thought I wouldn't be able to handle it, though. Nobody said maybe I should spend those months at home.

I wanted to tell my sister I wasn't deserting her. But maybe I was. I had money, a train ticket, instructions, a plan.

I logged into AIM one last time before leaving, still thinking there was some way to explain it. I hate bitches, Dana's away message said. And then, in the white space where I knew to highlight the hidden text:

this means u

FIVE

I don't google Dana anymore. I don't hate myself that much. Although I still look up Claudia sometimes, so maybe I do.

She has the same dip of her chin when she's focusing, the same sliver of a gap between her teeth. Her hair is longer, but so is mine. I dye it dark now, not just for the grays but because there came a time when I needed to be a different person, I needed to become someone I wouldn't recognize if I passed myself on the street.

I think Claudia would understand that, Claudia more than anyone I know. "How do we have the exact same taste?" she exclaimed when we went out for lunch on the waterfront and both ordered Bacon Burger Bombs with extra pickles. "My sister hates them, so I always eat hers." She snorted as she crunched into a pickle spear. My sister still slept with Fuzzles the elephant, and I felt guilty, briefly, that I had a basket of french fries the size of my head while she was in bed drinking smoothies. But already the world outside Greenwich was fading away.

"How about a bite of carrot to go with that chicken?" Claudia asked Sabine.

"The carrot sticks will be sad if they're all left out," I said when she shook her head no. And then Claudia made up a story about

Nuggetland, and I added in the family of Carrotheads, and Sabine laughed so hard she forgot her own resistance. When Claudia said I was great at this, Sabine never ate this many veggies for her (Sabine: "Wedgies!"), I felt as warm as if I were baking right under the sun. We took Sabine home for her nap, and Claudia said she had laundry to do and owed her mom a phone call. But we stayed in the kitchen still talking, even when I told her I didn't mind hanging out by myself, she should go.

She was lonely, I sensed. Or not lonely but she missed her college friends. Unless I was the one who was lonely, who'd gone to the same private school with the same small cohort and finally got to start over. Claudia said oh, she had this great recipe for limeade with muddled mint that she'd been meaning to make for Mrs. Corbin, and it'd go faster with two sets of hands. We stood side by side at the counter squeezing limes, picking mint leaves, laughing when we squirted each other. Simple syrup bubbling on the stove.

"I learned this from my best friend, Kelly. We were roommates off campus and it was a staple in our house. With vodka and a cherry on top," she added in a stage whisper, even though Sabine was sleeping and no one else was home.

"We can put it in our sippy cups," I joked. And then, buoyed by her laughter: "Some special limeade might be exactly what my aunt needs."

I waited for her to ask what I meant, or to say yeah, she'd noticed the Corbins both seemed stressed, uptight. What was that about?

But she didn't, and I made a mental note that I probably shouldn't talk about Ellen that way, or hint that my mom was concerned. "Where's Kelly now?" I asked.

"She's got this internship for the summer in London, something to do with banking—don't tell her that I barely understand it. How I wound up friends with an econ major." She made a face. "But she'll be back at UConn in the fall. We made a pact with our other friend Justine to try to wind up in the same area for grad school, so." She crossed her fingers.

"Grad school for what? French?"

Claudia had her public smile—we all do. But that moment was the first time I saw her lips press into something that was all for her. "Art school," she said. "Not for a while, though. I can't even think about leaving that little Bean! Plus it's crazy hard to get in, and my sister can't go five seconds without reminding me not to go into debt to be a painter."

I shouldn't have been surprised. Claudia wouldn't want to live in someone's basement forever, no matter how good an arrangement it was. We'd been cutting lime wheels for garnishes and I picked up a thin slice and peered through the small hole in its center so she was framed in a circle of green. "I can see your future," I gasped.

She rolled her eyes and tried to snatch the slice from me.

"I can see your future," I persisted, "and in it you're famous and fabulous—"

"I don't want to be famous! Just fabulous."

"You're extra fabulous but just the right level of famous—"

This time she grabbed the lime slice and stuck her tongue through the middle, sucking out the pulp. "How can you do that?" I cried, as if it were my own mouth puckering. When she stirred the limeade and held up a spoon for me to taste, I said more sugar, more sugar, until she teased me that I sounded like Sabine. She liked sour, spicy, salt. I'd never had fried pickles and she promised to take me out for a basket sometime. It was just an afternoon making mint syrup and dreaming. But it wasn't. It was a future. Plans. The kind of friendship I'd always longed for.

The next day, Ellen bought twice as many limes, more mint, and asked Claudia to make a double batch. She was on the board for a local Greenwich charity and just *had* to bring it to their meeting that night. The exact same way, she said. But in a nicer, cut glass pitcher with even more lime wheels floating with the ice.

"I'll help," I promised as soon as my aunt went out again. Claudia rested her forehead on my shoulder.

"You're a lifesaver," she groaned. But when she lifted her head, she was smiling. She smiled, looked me right in the eye, and said I was the best.

Every day we had a new destination: the country club, the playground, the private beach for residents only. We took Sabine to downtown Greenwich for ice cream. Bought picture books to fill up her shelves. Claudia knew how to make paint out of food coloring, string buttons onto bracelets, turn egg cartons into caterpillars and popsicle sticks into crowns.

When my mother asked how Ellen was doing, I said good, better, because that was how it seemed. She had fundraisers, events. The library in downtown Greenwich honored her for her support of their new children's wing. And she was busy with work. Sometimes we'd hear her phone calls from the kitchen: "Yes, darling, *exactly*!" Or: "*This* is what you think you get paid for?" in a tone that gave me goose bumps, a tone I use now, guiltily, on my own residents, it's so horrifically effective. Other days the ad firm sent a car to take her to Manhattan to make pitches for makeup and fruit juice and a brand of slip-on shoes she swore (correctly) was about to explode. But she projected a sense of purpose even when that purpose was getting a manicure, her roots dyed, snapping her fingers at the men who mowed the lawn and trimmed the hedges and planted mock orange along the patio, the patio she'd gotten rebricked, with a new gas grill and furniture with cream cushions to stay out in the rain.

Later I'd think, of course I would, about the days when she said she had a headache, she hadn't slept, and there'd be no snapping her fingers, no saying what had to be done. Once she spent so long in her room that I took three messages from her boss, Billie, thinking she wasn't home.

"Do you think she's okay?" I whispered to Claudia after that, but she asked what I meant and I didn't want to elaborate. She'd met my aunt only months ago—she wouldn't know if something was different. And was it? Or was I only stirring up trouble? Anyone could get a headache. Barometric pressure, a flickering light; my mother herself was especially prone. "I've got it, sweetheart," Ellen said when I offered to put away the groceries or drag the hose across the yard. "Doctor's orders to rebuild my strength."

It was a week of this, maybe more, before Claudia and I came home from Sabine's Music and Me class to the largest SUV I'd ever seen parked in the driveway. I'd spied Laurent's coffee mugs left on the counter; a glass tumbler with a puddle of melted ice from the night before. But I hadn't seen him, my own uncle, the whole time I'd been under his roof.

Only there he was, standing in the kitchen chopping mushrooms, shallots, like that was normal, like he was home for dinner all the time. He tossed a piece of cheese to what I suddenly realized was a tawny brown mass at his heels. Sabine, who'd been running toward him, stopped in her tracks and screamed.

Laurent picked her up as though she weighed nothing. Her small foot kicked against his stomach. His arms were dark, tanned, matted with what looked like fur—a contrast to his knobby head, which was bald and shining in the ceiling lights.

"Meet Tucker," he said, but as soon as he set Sabine down, she started to cry. "You don't want a puppy?"

She shook her head.

"She's really tired," Claudia offered. "We didn't get in a great nap today, did we, Bean?"

I didn't know much about dog breeds, but this was no shelter mutt. He was a lustrous chestnut with a chocolate nose and long, silky ears still too big for his body. I'd thought Laurent would say something like it was wonderful to see me, he was sorry he'd been so busy. Sorry, too, about my sister—but he ignored me entirely and frowned at Sabine.

"You love puppies," he told her.

"Kitty." Even I knew that. Sabine was always asking if the neighbors had cats, if there'd be a cat at the playground, the pool, the park.

"Puppies are better. You'll see."

The dog jerked toward her with his curious energy, his snout trembling, those ridiculous ears. Claudia grabbed Sabine's hand—"Let's get you ready for dinner, yeah?"—and led her upstairs before the crying started up again.

Laurent turned back to the cutting board. I assumed I too had been dismissed, until he said, "You like dogs?"

I curled the edge of a place mat left out on the table. "Sure."

"You know anything about training them?"

"Not really."

He thew another piece of cheese to the floor.

"Guess we'll have to find someone who does."

I was trying to come up with some response to this when his BlackBerry rang. "Peter!" he barked, and turned his back to me. I sat there fiddling with the place mat. There was a long pause as he wedged the phone against his shoulder and kept chopping. My mother would have called this eavesdropping, but I didn't move.

"The Harbor Commission?" The knife hovered. "I'm sure of it. Never been more certain."

Another pause. The knife hit hard against the cutting board.

"Absolutely not—don't know where you'd have heard that. I've got the drainage specs right here, I'll have Fran send them over so you can confirm. They talk about watersheds but you know how those commissions are, the whole city's a goddamn watershed. Listen, Pete—"

I learned he'd hired a new engineer, something similar had happened in Stamford, but there were ways to expedite the permits. "No, no, it's not expensive, you won't notice any delay. By the time this all goes through, I'm telling you, Pete." Laughter. "Exactly." Another laugh. "You don't say?"

I got a glass of water, but I shouldn't have—Laurent finally seemed to remember I was there. "You mean Whittier?" he asked. "Brad?" He glanced toward me and put the knife down. I walked slowly into the living room, as though I weren't paying any attention. But he put the dog on a leash and brought him out to the patio, where there was no excuse for me to follow.

"I know how to get him" was the last thing I heard my uncle say before the glass doors clicked shut.

He was still out there when Claudia brought Sabine down for dinner. Still there when Claudia said she was super sorry but actually she was off tonight and had a date—or not a date, maybe, but dinner plans, and she had to go. Should she get Ellen? In case Laurent took a while?

The way she said it, I sensed these calls had happened before.

"I've got it. Have fun." I even managed a smile.

The first time I'd sat behind the wheel of a car with my learner's permit, my father had said, "Don't be nervous. Stupid people do this." How long had I spent with Sabine by then? Not alone—but I wasn't alone now, either. Ellen and Laurent were home. One of them, both of them, would come back soon for their daughter.

"Thank you, thank you, thank you," Claudia said. "Normally I'd stay for the overtime, but this guy is seriously hot."

I waved my hand, the kind of thing I imagined Ellen might do. "Go," I insisted, that Ellen voice swelling inside me. "And then come back and tell me everything."

Claudia kissed Sabine on the forehead and told her to be good.

And then she kissed my forehead, right at my hairline, and laughed and told me to be good, too.

"Some guy named Peter called," I explained when Ellen finally came downstairs, asking where was Laurent, what happened to dinner, how had it gotten so late.

"Again? That man makes a transfer on Monday, I swear by Friday he wants to know where his return is." She looked pale, or maybe just exhausted—I wondered if she was coming down with a cold.

She unwrapped slick, pink pieces of chicken from the fridge and got them heating in a pan. But there were still the mushrooms half uncut, the minced shallot pungent and weeping on the counter. She took out a bottle of wine, a pint of heavy cream. I was glad to see her add a pat of butter, but later I'd second-guess whether I ever actually saw her eat any of the food she prepared. The fridge was always full, and sometimes she'd ask Claudia to store something in her freezer downstairs, apologizing for the imposition even though it was clear she liked it, the signs of an abundance she hadn't grown up with. My grandfather had died when my mother was young and Ellen was younger and Uncle Stephen was a baby, and my mother had to watch her younger siblings while my grandmother taught piano lessons after school. Once Ellen got caught stealing boxes of Kleenex, the good kind, from the church bathroom—it was a story she'd tell with a laugh after a few glasses of sparkling wine. But my mother would always snap at her to be quiet, saying it wasn't something to joke about. Those years weren't funny at all.

Ellen flipped the chicken and went upstairs, leaving the flame on high. I waited for her to come back—she hadn't asked if I was okay to stay watching Sabine, if I'd keep an eye on the stove. I wasn't sure if she even remembered that Claudia had the night off and was gone.

But then I didn't hear her footsteps, I didn't hear anything from upstairs or outside. Sabine was hungry, whining for a snack. I closed my eyes and pretended Claudia was here. That I was Claudia and knew what to do.

"Papa's going to finish cooking soon. What if we make him a drawing for when he comes back?"

Sabine scrunched up her face. "Want noodles," she said. "Want now."

I brought her construction paper, crayons. "How about a nice house with everyone in it? How about a big, bright sun?"

And she did start scribbling, long enough for me to finish slicing the pile of mushrooms. But I didn't know how Laurent wanted them cooked, or what to do with the wine and the cream and how long the chicken should stay searing in that pan—I turned off the heat, it was starting to burn. Make yourself at home, Ellen had said. But it wasn't really like that. Every so often I caught a glimpse of Laurent pacing on the patio, running a hand over his scalp or flinging a stick for the dog while his call dragged on. He had large hands, a thick neck, shoulders that strained against his starched shirt when he moved. It was impossible to imagine my aunt and uncle meeting, even harder to think what they'd have talked about. He'd been married, I'd gleaned that much, but no one told me any more than that.

"Hungry," Sabine said again, and threw down the crayon.

"How about some cheese?"

"Yuck."

"You like this kind."

"Don't want."

"You ate it yesterday."

I put a plate in front of her and she shoved it away.

"Sabine!"

"Caw-dee make noodle," she declared, kicking the table legs, cracking the yellow crayon in two. If she screamed loud enough, would someone remember we were here? Would they say what are you doing, how is this helping, why are you letting her scream?

In the end she barely ate any of the noodles I made her, soft and buttered the way (I thought) she liked. It was too late for a bath, it took forever to get her into her pajamas, brush her teeth. But at least I'd tried. And her skin was so soft. Her scalp still had its baby smell. In bed she rested her head on my chest and asked for one more story, just one more, and every time I said that's it and every time I caved and let her pick another.

Still I waited for someone to tiptoe in, to find us. When she was finally sleeping, I slipped out of her bed and went down the hall. Their bedroom door was closed. I pressed my ear: silence. What was my aunt doing in there? Downstairs, Laurent's car was gone but all the lights were blazing. The chicken had congealed in the pan, the mushrooms starting to shrivel. I didn't understand why he'd left it all sitting there; I didn't know yet that doing nothing is a form of action, too. Was I supposed to cook it? Clean up? Was I supposed to knock on Ellen's door, or leave her alone?

I took the phone out to the patio the way Laurent had done and the motion lights burst on, luring the moths. The phone rang and rang. My mother's voice was groggy, slow, when she finally answered.

"Sorry," I said. "Were you sleeping?"

"What happened?"

I pictured her sitting up, turning on the lamp, squinting as she forced herself awake.

"I shouldn't have called."

"Just tell me."

"It's nothing. I don't know." I walked away from the house, even though the windows were closed and no one would hear. "Ellen didn't eat dinner, at least I don't think so. Laurent started making it, then he left, then Ellen came in, but then she left—"

"Rachel." She was rubbing her face, I could tell. She was pinching the bridge of her nose in that way she did when she got annoyed. "Where was Sabine?"

"In the kitchen with me. But they just left me with her, even though they were both home. They didn't even ask. I fed her, obviously, while she threw a fit. I put her to bed. I just—" I sounded ridiculous. I couldn't explain. "I thought you should know. Claudia had the night off, so what would they have done if I hadn't been there?"

There was a pause. I heard her saying to my father, turning from the mouthpiece so she sounded even farther away: "She's fine, she's just calling."

"I know it's not an emergency. I just wanted to—"

Talk, I could have said. But I felt like Sabine banging on the table, begging for what she couldn't have.

My mother yawned. "They trusted you with Sabine because you're responsible, sweetheart. It sounds like you did a great job."

"I know, but it was—"

"I'm sure Ellen needed the rest."

"Okay."

"We spent four hours downtown waiting for the specialist, only to find out they hadn't gotten approval for the test your sister needs and we'll have to go back."

The motion light clicked off. There was no grass, no pond, no gate, no road. Just the halo of a distant neighbor's window, and then that, too, was gone. Guys in a truck had shown up just as Ellen promised, but I wondered if there were parts of the deer they might have missed. Blood pooled in a crevice. A lost splinter of bone. I waited for my mother to say I should keep her posted or keep an eye out or keep calling whenever I needed, but it was quiet. It was always so quiet. "Okay," I said again. "Goodnight."

I waited out on the patio for Claudia to come home from her date and fill me in, for Laurent to return from wherever he'd gone—work, probably, but what was he doing at the office so late? Had he gone to see Peter? Or that other guy, Brad? It was hard to think of what could be so urgent. But the mosquitos were vicious, and I went back inside.

SIX

It was almost midnight when headlights turned up the driveway. Claudia's car, not Laurent's. I was in my bedroom, watching the street while telling myself I wasn't watching the street, I just happened to be awake by the window. I'd been finding excuses to walk past Ellen's door, but in all those hours I hadn't heard her stir.

I went downstairs. I thought Claudia would come in through the back door like she usually did. But she parked and then I didn't see her. The door down to her suite from the kitchen was closed; after a moment, light seeped under the crack. She'd gone in through her private entrance, not knowing I'd been waiting.

I knocked softly. Why not? We could make a snack and sit together in the kitchen, gush about the juicy details of her evening the way Dana and I used to—even though the dates were always hers, not mine, and sometimes I'd wanted to shake her and ask why she went for these guys she'd only wind up crying over, later. Claudia didn't answer. I told myself I shouldn't bang any louder. I was being responsible—I didn't want to disturb Sabine or Ellen upstairs. I was doing the right thing as I slowly, quietly, turned the knob and opened her door.

I heard her right away. Laughing. At first I thought she was calling to me. She knew I was there and that's why she sounded so happy.

Then she said, "—like, *slobbering*," and I stopped at the top of the stairs.

"Because!" That laughter again. "I didn't know he had a salivary disorder when I met him—no, not literally! Kells, stop!"

She was on the phone with Kelly. Her best friend from UConn, who had the internship in London for the summer. What time was it in London? Late. Or early, depending on your perspective. The stairs were carpeted and plush, the rest of the suite around a corner so I couldn't see her and she, I hoped, couldn't see me. She must not have heard the creak of the door, like she hadn't heard me knocking. I took a silent step down.

"At least this one's still in college. There's no way that other guy was twenty-five, and if he was lying about his age I'm pretty sure he was lying about having a job, too. I'm sorry, but no. Remember when Justine met that guy who tried to move into the dorms?" A pause. Claudia snorted at whatever Kelly had said. They talked more about Justine, about was it anti-feminist to feel like if you'd bought the makeup and put on more than your same ratty tennis shoes, you shouldn't also have to pay for your meal. I wondered how many dates she usually went on. How hot this guy really was. I tiptoed farther down until I could peer around the sloped ceiling and through the banister.

I was ready to say I'd heard her come in. That I'd knocked first (true) and wanted to see how it had gone (also true). But her back was to me as she sat on the cream-colored couch. She'd gone out in a skirt but had already changed into blue-and-white shorts and a tank top that was sliding off one shoulder. She leaned against a pillow—polka dots—as she listened to whatever Kelly was saying. Then she stood. I stepped back quickly, which killed any hope I had of telling myself it had been an accident, I wasn't trying to listen.

"Objectively speaking, I don't know how someone can be that good-looking and there's still no chemistry. I can't even tell you how bad it was, Kells. His tongue was like—"

She walked around a corner, I couldn't hear what it was like. Furtively, as though I were the one being watched, I pressed the back of my hand to my mouth and licked my warm skin. Dana had insisted we practice when we were younger, and we'd tongued the flesh of our fists to evaluate motion, pressure. Too wet? Too much? I bit my hand. I was being stupid.

"I have no idea. I told him the family needs me up early tomorrow. But what do I do if he calls again? I couldn't say anything right then, you know?"

I heard the hiss of a can opening. Seltzer, I saw when I dared to peek again.

"I know, I know. But do you ever feel like you'll spend your whole life just waiting around, being patient?"

Waiting for what? I wished I could ask her. And how will you know when it finds you?

"Yeah, totally." She sipped the seltzer. Listened more. Laughed sometimes, but the laughter had changed. I should have gone back upstairs. I never should have listened in the first place. But if you get away with something the first time, you keep wanting to try it again. Claudia would go on three more dates that summer: one with a postdoc in New Haven, one with a friend of a friend in Bridgeport, and one with a guy who picked her up at a Starbucks and turned out to be thirty-two and hadn't finalized his divorce. I'd learn about each one as she talked to Kelly while I listened breathlessly, above. And then I'd ask her in the morning how it went, as though I knew nothing at all. "Remind me why I bother," she'd groan over coffee, and I'd tell her, truthfully, "I really don't know."

I didn't get caught until the last date. It was late, and the rain had turned heavy. I didn't like knowing she'd been out for so long.

I snuck down to the kitchen as soon as I saw her car pass through the gate. My aunt was in her bedroom with the door closed; Laurent wasn't home. Rain hit the driveway, the windows, the roof, and the sound covered me as I opened the door to her suite. I was so sure I was safe, as though I'd forgotten what I was doing, what it actually meant.

But when I peered around the corner, Claudia wasn't lounging on the couch or strolling toward her bedroom. She was standing in the living room, turning away from the mantel. Turning at just the right moment so that she faced the stairs.

Our eyes locked. She jumped—that's how much I'd startled her. I stammered that I'd been worried about the rain, I'd just wanted to make sure she'd gotten back okay. The more I talked the more plausible it sounded, and her face softened.

"I didn't mean to interrupt—I'll see you tomorrow!" I smiled and headed up the stairs. I was closing the door behind me, making sure she knew I was closing the door behind me, when I heard her say to Kelly: "Mrs. Corbin's niece. I told you about Rachel, right? Yeah, she's great."

I paused for the longest I could get away with waiting before I had to cross the kitchen and go back to my room.

"We had some thunderstorms," Claudia went on. "They weren't too bad, but it was sweet of her to check."

SEVEN

Whatever Laurent did the night Peter called, whomever else he talked to while Ellen was in her bedroom and Claudia was off with her slobbery kisser and I was watching Sabine, it must have worked. Or maybe it wasn't like that—maybe he just went for a drive to clear his head. Maybe he stayed alone in his office reviewing environmental regulations, the details of that *goddamn watershed* he'd huffed about on the phone. Maybe it was all thanks to Harry in the governor's office and Laurent's golf game at Belle's. Maybe there was more, a lot more, I wasn't privy to then and could only speculate about later.

What I did know was that it wasn't long after that the Corbins got their phone call. The chief of staff was throwing the governor a birthday party in New Britain, and my aunt and uncle were invited.

Ellen bought a new dress, heels, a matching clutch and shawl. "It is too much?" she asked as she came downstairs and caught her reflection in the hall mirror. "It seemed like I should buy something new, something I could be sure no one'd seen before. But maybe that's ostentatious? I can't overdo it for Lori."

The governor's wife. Laurent may have been the face of the River Point deal, but Ellen had her role to play. She'd immediately tasked Laurent's secretary with finding out everything about the First Lady: hometown, school mascot, kids' birthdays. There was no telling what you could use.

Sabine raced around the kitchen island, telling Mama to put on more sparklies, more sparklies. She meant the diamonds in Ellen's ears, on her wrists, around her neck. I did think it was a lot on top of the sequins shimmering down the dress, but this wasn't for her usual nights out to celebrate a kids' charity or a new parking garage. "It's perfect," I assured her. "But maybe just one of the bracelets? So the necklace has a chance to shine?"

Ellen pressed a hand to her chest. "You're so right. You've got such a good eye. If you change your mind on med school, we could use you, you know. Next summer, if you want an internship, let me know and I'll speak to Billie. She'd hire you in a heartbeat."

She was already taking off the tennis bracelet, dropping it next to a basket of fruit. "These gifts from Laurent—I've had so little excuse to wear them. Hopefully that's all about to change!" She laughed. "What do you think, Bean. Is that better?"

I tried to picture elevator rides up a towering skyscraper, sliding off my pumps at the end of the day. Could I be like Ellen? Would I want to? It was hard enough to picture nine weeks from then, moving into a dorm room with Alexandra Harkness from Kentucky who loved Russian lit.

Before moving in with Laurent, Ellen had lived in one of those Manhattan apartments with a bathtub wedged between the sink and the undersized fridge. She gave up her bed for my parents to sleep in and we'd have a slumber party with cushions on the living room floor. My memories from before Jules was born appeared in sharp, scattered fragments. Sleeping in Ellen's novelty T-shirt from her trip to Miami. Pretending not to look at the neon signs in the video store window at the end of her street. Did Ellen remember that video store? Did she ever go back to her old neighborhood, wherever it was?

I picked up the tennis bracelet and draped it over my wrist while Ellen went to touch up her lipstick. I wondered what else she kept in her bedroom, how many dresses and shoes and purses and god only knew what else she owned. "Oh, honey. That's perfect with your complexion. And the earrings, with that haircut! Try them on."

But I slid off the bracelet, mortified at having been caught.

I'd begged my mother to let me get my ears pierced, but the holes had started to close after I stopped wearing jewelry for lacrosse. And once Jules got hers done, years younger than I'd been allowed, the last of the novelty was gone. I didn't remember why I'd wanted it so badly in the first place; I'd lost all traces of that other girl I'd been. Did a person shed their former shelves like snakeskin, or did each version accumulate like the rings of a tree? I wasn't even sure when I'd decided I wanted to be a doctor, only that I heard the reverence my parents reserved for getting Dr. Goldstein's opinion, for announcing, "Dr. Cherry will know what to do." I should have been flattered Jules wanted her ears pierced like mine. I should have given her the jewelry I didn't wear. I could have spent my summer thinking more about how she was doing, and what if I'd been brave enough to stay in Cambridge instead. Some choices couldn't be undone, though, because when I tried to push the posts of Ellen's diamonds through my earlobes, the pain was searing and I had to set them down.

"I can stay here," I offered after Sabine was asleep and Tucker had been lured into his crate. "If you want to go somewhere, with that guy or whatever. I don't mind staying with Sabine."

I didn't know why I said it. Of course I minded. But then came the bloom in my chest, the pleasure uncurling as Claudia teased that I couldn't get rid of her that easily—didn't I want to hang out?

We sat outside on the patio and she stretched across the sofa so her toes tickled my thigh. I played the little piggy game as if she were Sabine, wiggling each one, laughing, and she slid farther down until she was resting her feet in my lap. "This is the life." She sighed. "Just exactly like this." There were other chairs but it never occurred to me to take one. To ask why she hadn't sat in one, either.

"You won't tell, will you?" she asked, and I thought she meant about us going outside while Sabine was sleeping, bringing with us the baby monitor and citronella candles and a box of truffles a realtor had sent Laurent from Luxembourg by way of New York.

Then she pulled a small pouch from her pocket. It looked like pencil shavings inside, but the smell was deeper, woodsy and sweet. She took out rolling paper. I couldn't stop watching how deftly she filled it. The pink of her tongue slipped out to lick the edge before she sealed the tip and lit the other end.

"We know they're going to be late, right?" she said. "Like, really late. I've been trying to cut back since you got here, but Mrs. Corbin was so frazzled. She was getting me stressed."

I mimed zipping my lips. "You don't have to worry about me."

"It's just that I told them I don't smoke."

"Obviously."

"And it's not a lot. I'd never leave Sabine to take cigarette breaks."

I'd thought it was weed; I'd never seen a cigarette hand-rolled like a joint. And I'd thought, actually, that it was pretty bad to get high on the job. What if Sabine woke up in the night?

Now that I knew it was only tobacco, I felt more sure of my agreement. I thrilled at the weight of her feet in my lap, her trust in me. That afternoon, she'd unveiled a box of magazine cutouts that we'd used to make collages, and we'd had so much fun that even Sabine pursed her lips to tell us to *shush*. I reached out a hand and she hesitated, but I snatched the cigarette before she could say no.

"I play lacrosse," I admitted. "I shouldn't smoke." I'd only tried it a few times with Dana and it had always made me nauseous, but I wasn't about to admit that.

And then: "Played." Past tense. That was important.

Claudia raised an eyebrow. Everything she did was expressive. The turn of her ankle. The way her fingers brushed mine as she took the cigarette back. "You're not going to do it next year?"

"I don't know." It was the first time I'd voiced this aloud. "I just feel like, what's the point?"

This seemed particularly clichéd, the kind of thing my mother would have told me to stop being dramatic about. But Claudia nodded. "It's different in college. You don't have to do the same things anymore."

Maybe this wasn't profound, but it was the first time someone had talked to me this way, like I had choices. I wanted to talk to her—really talk to her. To tell her what had happened in a way that I couldn't tell anyone else.

"My friends were all on the team," I confessed, edging toward it, gauging if it was safe to go on. "But that's over now."

"What's over?"

It's easy to dismiss the cruelty girls inflict on one another. The things you're told you'll grow out of, you'll forget, you'll learn from, you'll change, you'll laugh at later, you'll overcome. But I can't do that to myself, I can't pretend it didn't matter. We'd laughed at Ellen's nerves over meeting Lori, but was it really so different, our smaller lives, those training grounds for who we would become?

It wasn't about Jonathan, I knew that. I had to go back further, to the end-of-the-year dance. It was at a boys' school, Catholic but not really, and the four of us had all gone together in matching electric-blue eyeshadow, Dana, Morgan, Ilana, and me. Maybe I did feel a stab of envy, just a little, at how quickly Dana started dancing with some guy. That it was Dana, always Dana, who was chosen.

But they weren't just dancing. Morgan and Ilana twirled in circles, lost in their own world as usual. I was the only one who saw the boy thrust his hand beneath the back of her low-rise jeans and pull up the band of her underwear so anyone could see she was wearing a thong. Once, Dana had spied Jonathan tracing his fingers up my side, joking, tickling me, and she'd rolled her eyes: "Come on, Rach, have some fucking self-esteem." I waited for her to shove the guy off and run back to us, fuming.

But she didn't, and he saw that she didn't, and so he did it again, tugging harder: his marionette in peach lace, his little dancing doll. I didn't feel that envy anymore. I felt bad for her, and angry, and something else—I now think of it as shame. Guys hollered, chopping their forearms to their crotches as they egged him on. He waved as more of them noticed and joined in.

Only it wasn't a wave. He was cupping his hand, making an O with his fingers, moving his wrist back and forth as he poked his tongue out against his cheek. I did it for Claudia and she lunged across the sofa to grab my arm, her mouth dropped all the way open. "Tell me she clocked him, please don't tell me she laughed—"

But when I pulled Dana away, when I said I had to tell her something and dragged her into the hall, all she did was stare at me, her face shiny with sweat, lips stained from the fruit punch we'd spiked in the car.

Claudia stayed gripping my arm, so close I smelled the smoke on her, saw the way her cheeks puffed when she gasped.

Dana wasn't grateful. She didn't thank me for having her back. "What the ever-loving fuck is wrong with you?" she hissed, and I saw too late that I'd humiliated her, and publicly, and there was no apologizing my way out of that.

"She thought you were jealous," Claudia said.

"And meddling, and overreacting." I rattled off my sins.

Then came the Jonathan problem, and the fact that I was a hypocrite, a liar, once Dana found out I'd been sneaking around with him for months. But I didn't tell Claudia that part. I gave her instead my other secret, the bigger one: that I'd come to Greenwich not for Ellen, but because I was selfish. I couldn't stay a pariah in Cambridge, avoiding parties, stores, whole sections of the city where my friends might go. I wasn't brave enough to be on the outside, alone.

"Don't feel so bad," Claudia said. "I have a Dana. I think everybody does."

"Does Dana have a Dana? Does your Dana have a different Dana? Or what about a Dan, a Daniel—why don't boys do this?"

"They beat each other up, it's not that different." She spun around on the couch and rested her head in my lap. I spied the gap down her V-neck T-shirt, a sliver of her pale pink bra. "There was this girl in middle school who wrote anonymous letters and signed them *The Truth Teller.* Three full pages in pink cursive telling me I was ugly. Plus deodorant left outside my locker, but that might have been somebody else."

"Jesus. Claudia."

Down by the pond the fireflies blinked on and off, hovering where a deer had once lain but now wasn't. I touched the place on her neck where the smallest hairs curled soft against her skin.

"Every week some poor girl would get a new one. Cute envelope. Little heart sticker on the outside. I came early to school, did a whole stakeout, caught her red-handed. Tracey fucking Weston. Guess which one of us the principal forced to apologize."

My legs stiffened underneath her. "No."

"She was blond and cried and her parents were getting a divorce. Meanwhile I'd *confronted her* and made her upset."

"They can't do that!"

But of course they could, they already had. "I'm sorry," I said.

"That was stupid of me." Which was so small, so easy to give, when the words were just words and cost me nothing.

"I wanted to change schools. Beat her up. Anything but give that bullshit apology. But Denise would have killed me if I got in any more trouble."

"It's not like they could make you mean it."

Claudia closed her eyes. "That's not the point, Rachel. They just want to prove that they can make you jump."

"I know," I said, as if I did. "But they don't know me. I'll go up there and beat her up myself."

She laughed and found my hand in the dark—but it was only to pass me the small nub of the cigarette. I'd had too much; I was afraid of coughing. I only pretended to inhale before I gave it back to her to finish.

EIGHT

Ellen was up early after the governor's party; circles under her eyes said she might not have slept. She stood at the counter with a pen and pad of paper covered with notes. A garden party, she'd decided. For the Fourth of July. That was their next move.

"Nothing flashy," she reminded the decorator each time she called to check in. "Family friendly," she informed the caterers.

She fretted about rain, and what if Lori couldn't make it. Or what if Lori came but no one else did? Why hadn't she thought of this sooner, before the night—an incredible success—when Lori said if only she had a reason to come to Greenwich, and it had blurted from her mouth?

"I thought she'd be more of a cocktail party person," Claudia whispered to me when Ellen was on the phone with the florist, confirming they had the Peruvian lilies in white and red—not pink—and could they promise the blue hydrangeas weren't too pale?

But I saw my aunt's reasoning. They weren't just any newcomers, bulldozing their way in. Nor were they competing with the governor's soiree. They were good, regular people with friends and neighbors and colleagues, kids playing together, a family committed to bettering its town. My mom always said Ellen could have gone to law school if she hadn't needed to start working straight out of college. She'd been president of the student council, ran her sorority's social calendar, expanded their philanthropy reach. Everything was a popularity contest, but that was the point—she knew how to win. She saw how the chessboard was conquered, how success in business wasn't just what happened in a boardroom and politics didn't only mean tallying the votes. If their friends and neighbors just so happened to be investors, politicians, some of the most influential people in the state—who could fault her for having good taste?

The day bloomed bright, the hottest of the summer so far. The caterers came early to set up the bar, the waffle station, eggs and fruit and toast points with herbed oils and bright pearls of roe. Ellen complained that the salads looked small, the bowls were cramped. She sent the manager himself to buy more rib eye with better marbling, please. This was no time to skimp.

When the gate opened and the cars began to arrive, she stopped in front of the hall mirror and pressed two fingers to the crease between her brows, as though she could smooth it away. "You look beautiful," I said. She turned, surprised that I'd stolen up on her.

"Just touching up my lipstick," she said brightly, and we both pretended I believed her.

The women streamed through the yard in sundresses and white linens, wearing mules and strappy sandals and straw hats. They had sun-kissed layers and chestnut layers perfectly sprayed into place. In the mirror I caught sight of my hair blunted and already frizzing, my tank top ringed with sweat stains I hadn't noticed upstairs. But it was too late to change. Ellen greeted everyone with a hand in theirs and her other hand cupped just so on top, and I imagined the bite of her rings, her perfume that graced each woman she air-kissed and the tanned, broad men to whom she gave her cheek.

"How wonderful!" the women said when they heard I was here

for the summer. And: "You're so lucky, I'd kill to have an aunt like Ellen." And: "Swarthmore? Lucky, lucky you." As though I had some good fortune they'd missed out on, when anyone could see it was the other way around.

Ellen had lured them with the promise of the governor's wife, maybe the governor himself if he could get away, and their boys, twins—what a playdate that would be! But they hadn't arrived yet. Would it be enough, without them? Ellen explained in a low voice that the men Laurent had gone to greet were some of his investors, and I skirted closer to listen. "Yachts," I reported back the next time I found her. "Someone's new gel coat is damaged." She nodded crisply. Even small talk could show who belonged.

On the patio the woman drank pinkish wine spritzers while their children went careening on the lawn with Tucker. He kept tripping over his paws and peeing himself in excitement, and Sabine screamed when the dog ran after her, when some of the pee splashed on her leg. There was a sprinkler Ellen used for the flower beds and Claudia dragged it out onto the lawn. Once the big kids were running in it Sabine did too, and that ended the crying and hid the dog's crimes. "You're a genius," I told her. "Seriously. How do you always know what to do?"

Ellen hovered among the guests, steering them toward the grill, the bar, the mounds of lemon pound cake pillowed with whipped cream. She was letting me sip a wine spritzer with extra Sprite when a boy ran from the sprinkler to his mother, dripping on the patio, tugging on her arm—he had to go to the bathroom. I watched Ellen's eyes tighten, the way she paused before saying, brightly, that she'd get him dried off and take him inside.

Her hand landed on my forearm, her skin cool despite the warm day. "We need more towels. They're upstairs. I can't leave, what if Lori arrives?" She looked across the yard as if imagining the mass of children racing through the sitting room, the parlor, their hair and T-shirts dripping on the floor. There was family friendly—Lori would approve of that—and then there was the zoo. I started to go but Ellen held on. "Not the white ones. Or maybe, because then I can bleach them?" She slid her thumbnail across her bottom lip. She'd never bite her nails, that was unseemly. But the idea was the same. "No," she decided. "The old ones upstairs with the linens, they're not in such bad shape."

I didn't know which towels she meant, which closet, what linens—the housekeeper took care of those things. But the caterers needed to get by, and the boy was dripping all over the patio (although wasn't that what a patio was for—to be dripped on?) and it was too much for Ellen, I could see it was too much. I told her I'd find them. I put down the drink and dashed upstairs feeling purposeful. I couldn't do what Claudia did with those kids, but I could help my aunt.

On the second floor, I opened all the closet doors. There were sheets, comforters, extra pillows. Boxes of Dove soap and Band-Aids as though Ellen were stocking a store. I found white bath towels, the nice ones with stitching on the edges, but that wasn't what she'd meant. In Sabine's playroom were bins for dress-up, winter sweaters, a third closet just for toys. So it wasn't in there, and it wasn't in the hallway. It couldn't be in Laurent's study, although that was tempting. And I'd already combed through the rooms on the third floor when I arrived.

I paused outside the master bedroom. I didn't know where else to look.

Laurent was in a circle reliving a deep-sea fishing trip to the Caymans. Ellen had just told me she couldn't leave her guests, not for something as pedestrian as towels, as though she were the help. I spent all of my days with Claudia, Sabine, while Ellen was in her bedroom or coming from her bedroom or could at any moment come home or come inside and head up to her bedroom. What did she do in there for so many hours when no one was watching? It was the first time I had a chance to find out.

I opened the door. It was bigger than I'd even imagined, more than my room at home and Jules's room and my parents' room combined. The bed was made perfectly, as though to give the illusion it had never been slept on. I'd expected books on the nightstand, magazines, piles of work she had to do. But every surface was spotless. I opened an armoire and found a large TV hidden inside. I was sure I'd never heard it play.

I went into their closets, two separate walk-ins organized by color and style and season. How many brown loafers did one man need? Did she really wear all those pumps? The Saks dresses still had their tags on, a price that shot saliva straight into my mouth. In their bathroom I found a soaking tub with jets, a shower stall with two showerheads. It was hideous to think of them together in there, Laurent's slick scalp, my aunt's rail-thin arms. But there were two sinks, two vanities, and that did make it better. They had their separate sides of the shower, like they had their separate toothpastes, their mirrors, their private sides of the bed.

From outside I heard the kids shrieking with Claudia, the rumble of men's laughter as it swelled and faded away. I should have hurried, but the bathroom held me there: the intimacy of other people's lives. It always seemed like Ellen simply appeared how she did every morning, with her hair teased and her brows shaped and even her linen shorts pressed. But now I saw the work it took; even Laurent had his spiced deodorant and his shaving kit and his creams. It wasn't magic, then. Anyone could do it. I opened an undercabinet to find toilet paper and tissues and makeup wipes and bottles and bottles of hair spray, mousse, styling gel. I knocked one over, turning it to see the brand, how much it cost, and the bottle hit another, which hit another, which hit something that didn't clink the way the others did but rattled.

I wasn't trying to snoop. But mousse didn't rattle. Lotion, creams. I groped under the cabinet. I had to put everything back how it had been.

And I was curious, of course I was, to know what in Ellen's vast array of self-improvement tools would make that kind of noise. I reached around and pulled out a toiletry bag, small, black, zippered, wedged behind the U-bend under the sink.

Something misplaced from a trip, lost in their move. I'd slide it back, she wouldn't care.

But there was no bristly toothbrush, no travel-sized tube of toothpaste recalling the long-ago press of her thumb. Inside was an orange prescription bottle.

I pulled it out and gave it a shake: there was the source of my rattle. ELLEN BRYCE CORBIN. TAKE ONE TABLET BY MOUTH EVERY FOUR TO SIX HOURS AS NEEDED FOR PAIN. Yellow stickies warned not to drink alcoholic beverages. May cause drowsiness. Use only as directed. It felt hot up there in their bathroom, even as the AC raised a prickle up my ankles, tightening the skin of my calves. I tried to remember what I'd been given after my wisdom tooth surgery, if it was oxycodone hydrochloride that my parents had allowed me only two pills of before switching me to Tylenol. Even if it wasn't, though—even if I was thinking of something else. I obviously knew the word *pain*.

It must have been forgotten. Old medicine from after her fall. I'd leave it somewhere just a little more obvious, so when she used the last roll of toilet paper, when she finally got around to finishing that scrunch-n-set gel, she'd see it and, shocked, remember. She'd dispose of it properly, never knowing she had me to thank.

But the date.

I saw it before I registered it. I registered it and the fantasy sputtered out and went dark. The prescription had been filled on June 28, just under a week ago. I tipped the bottle—it wasn't full. How many had she taken since then?

I tried to think back, but the days were so similar. Sabine and Claudia and I were at the park, probably. At the pool or stealing bites of each other's fruit popsicles or hunting for fairies in the yard while Ellen was swinging by the pharmacy, saying thanks so much. Saying have a nice day. Coming home only to disappear into her bedroom, trusting that Claudia was watching Sabine and no one would come knocking.

Because she only took them in hiding, right? That was why she didn't store the bottle in her medicine cabinet, her nightstand, her closet, downstairs in the kitchen where she kept magnesium for her headaches, capsules of psyllium husk, gummy chewables for Sabine. Or wherever else people kept the pills they took. Places that weren't usually buried quite so deep, where she could still reach them but Laurent and the housekeeper wouldn't think to search.

"There you are!" she exclaimed as I came downstairs, towels piled high in my arms—I'd finally found them in the second guest bathroom, in a cabinet slotted next to the tub. "I thought maybe I hadn't sent you after all. Leave those outside and let me show off my gorgeous niece to Lori. Thank God she was able to make it."

I must have shaken Lori's hand, said something nice to her, I can't remember how it went. My heart was beating so hard I could feel it, the physical thrum in my chest. Lori was called away, her boys insisting she watch some trick in the yard. It did look like fun, the kids wet and laughing, the men on the patio in their chinos and their tanned, hairy legs, their hands around beer bottles and plastic cups filled with whiskey and ice cubes, each with a fat watch heavy on his wrist (that was all I saw, my head down; I couldn't stand to look at their faces, I could barely meet Ellen's eyes). The women had slipped off their sandals and walked barefoot in the grass in their sundresses, legs smooth and shiny as seals. I hadn't shaved that morning; I'd run out of time. I hadn't brought any sundresses. They drank their wine spritzers with fresh fruit wedged on the rims but no whiskey, none of them. Why didn't women drink whiskey? I liked the smell of it, caramelly. Like candy that burned. But that was harder to steal. I didn't want some fake drink watered down with Sprite. When the caterer's back was turned, I walked by quickly, as though on my way inside, and grabbed a beer sticking out of the ice bucket, the first thing my hand landed on as I darted past, wishing I could dunk my hand all the way inside the freezing water. My whole arm, all my skin. Pour it over my head and feel the ice cubes tumble down my spine.

The only beer I'd ever drunk was from kegs, the kind boys got for parties after their basketball games. And cans. The boys bought a lot of cans, light stuff, fizzy and sour. I hid the dark bottle, dripping, up the front of my shirt and kept walking. The wet spread on my tank top, trickled down my stomach and to the waistband of my shorts. I hurried inside.

In the downstairs bathroom I locked the door. The beer was cold and sharp and bitter. I drank half the bottle without stopping, until in the shock of the cold ice and cold beer and cold air-conditioning, I felt flushed all over. I was going to be sick. Was this why my aunt had so many headaches? Why she spent so much time in her room?

Or were the pills meant to help—her back, her hip, her head?

But then why keep secret what was supposed to make her feel better?

I finished the beer and covered the bottle with tissues in the trash. Back outside the glove of hot air tightened around my throat, so thick it made me shiver.

"You okay?" Claudia was somehow beside me, touching my arm.

"It's freezing inside," I said. "I think I felt a little weird going back and forth with the heat." And then, gesturing toward the wet patch over my stomach: "Plus I lost a fight with the bathroom sink."

"Brutal," she said. "It does that sometimes."

I ran in the yard with Sabine, toweled her off, brought her crackers and carrot sticks but no white, she said, meaning no hummus, no dips. I played and made conversation and tried to be a good cousin, a good niece, someone who'd help ensure my family was well-liked. Well-liked people were more likely to get favors from their councilmen, receive patience from their investors, have their governors make the right phone calls to the right people on their behalf.

But I kept checking my pockets, certain everyone could see what I'd done. They'd fall out, or Sabine would ask, "What's this?" Lori would tell her husband and Laurent's project, the house, their standing, their lives—everything they were working for would vanish. All over the two pills I'd swiped from the bottle in the bathroom cabinet and stuffed into the small slot for pennies in the front of my shorts.

NINE

After the caterers packed up, after the last beers were dried off from the ice water and put in the fridge. After the tent was empty but before the caterers returned the next day to take it down. After Sabine was sitting tired in front of the TV with her thumb plugged in her mouth. After Ellen said she had a headache, all that sun, and disappeared upstairs. After Laurent finished scrubbing furiously at the grill, the mustard smears on the brickwork, the wine stains on the weatherproof cushions Yolanda, the housekeeper, had already wiped with club soda and salt. After I went inside and looked in the pantry, the fridge, uncertain what I was hungry for.

Claudia came up from her suite, keys in hand. I asked where she was going and she said she didn't know, just that she was starving, she hadn't eaten all day. "Same," I said. "Everything was so busy." Even though I'd had plenty of time for steak and salad and chips and oniony guacamole and cheese cubes soft and sweating from the sun, and the beer I'd drunk too fast and that had only made me sleepy. "Can I come? Or, sorry." I closed the refrigerator door. "Are you off? Like officially? This is probably your time to do whatever."

But she said of course, and I raced upstairs to change my shirt, roll on fresh deodorant, get my hair to do something besides flop there. I had to think for a moment about where I'd left my wallet—I never needed it when Ellen left stacks of twenties for when we went out with Sabine. This was the first time Claudia and I had gone out alone, no Sabine in the back seat or walking hand in hand between us. No Ellen calling the cell phone they'd given her for emergencies to say "What time—?" or "One more thing—!"

She suggested a taqueria in Stamford. "You have to get out of Greenwich to find anywhere that hasn't been turned into a condo," she said with an eye roll. "Or a million dollars a plate." I nodded, totally, as though I had this same complaint. But Stamford was different from Greenwich, I could tell as soon as we got there. We sat outside at a picnic table perched above a dock, strings of chili lights winding down to the small marina where the dinghies rocked. The menus were plastic, the forks as well. I could practically taste the diesel in the air.

Claudia ordered a margarita. The waitress said, "Same for you?" Only then she asked for IDs, and I had to stammer that I'd lost mine. When she left, I snatched up Claudia's license before she could put it away. The girl in the photograph was some grainier idea of Claudia rather than Claudia herself. "Five eight," I read. "Eye color: Brown. Hartford," and then I recited her address. I'd only driven through Hartford without stopping. I wondered if she'd take me sometime. "Give me that," she said. "I look like a troll."

But she didn't look like a troll. That was what was so unfair about it. She had the same perfect smile, only her hair was past her shoulders in thin braids—or that was what it looked like; in the tiny picture it was hard to tell. Would we have been friends if we'd met some other time, in some other place? For spirit week, Dana and I had ordered matching nude tights for the lacrosse team to wear, but when I passed them out there was this girl Eryn who looked Indian, or South American, I wasn't sure, only that she'd stuck her arm in the tights and announced loudly, in front of the whole team, "What about this looks *nude* to you?"

But Eryn didn't know me like Claudia did. When the drink came, Claudia said sorry, it was such bullshit. "You're practically in college, and anyone who thinks college students don't drink until twenty-one is living under a rock." I put my thumb over her straw, pulled it out, and sucked the liquid into my mouth. It tasted like sour candy, like the SweeTarts we used to share on the bus to away games. Claudia glanced around, but the picnic tables were spread out and no one was watching. When she picked up the frosted glass she said, "Your aunt gave you wine earlier, right? She doesn't mind?" And set it down closer to me.

We shared the drink and then we shared another. I kept eating the free chips and salsa, even though I'd had so many chips that afternoon. I didn't want her to think I was ungrateful, that I'd have rather stayed in Greenwich. I didn't want Eryn to have been right about me.

"What'd you think of Lori?" I asked.

She squinted at me. "Who?" And then, "Oh, right! With the twins? The boys in matching stripes?"

I nodded.

"I always find it weird when parents do that. Don't they know their kids are different people?"

"She had a Jennifer Aniston haircut," I prodded. "Red nails. Espadrilles."

"That's like, all of them."

"She was in a blue dress with white flowers, the nails were her patriotic flourish. I barely talked to her," I added quickly. "But at least she showed up. For Ellen."

"Part of me is like, fuck yeah. I should email my friends that I just got a wicked bonus to keep the governor's kids from killing each other. Another part is like, is this why I went to college? What my loans are for? It just sort of hit me today, what Denise keeps bugging me about. What if I wind up asking who needs to go potty for the rest of my life?"

I laughed, my cheeks warm from tequila and hot sauce and the way she was confiding in me. "It's not your whole life, though. Just until you go back to school."

She made a face, the kind of thing that meant *yes* and *no* all at once, so that I wanted to reach across the table and take her hand and tell her not to worry.

"My friend Kelly, the one with the fellowship in London?" I nodded like I remembered from Claudia mentioning her before and not from hearing Claudia's laughter drift up the stairs as they talked on the phone. "We'd made all these plans for how I'd come visit her, and then we'd take the Eurostar to Paris. Paris! But when do I have that kind of time off? What if I missed my shot? I used to pore over these books of Impressionists when I was a kid, I got obsessed with learning everything about them. I begged my mom to pay for French lessons even before they offered it at school. I guess I still can't believe I wound up a French major who's never been anywhere Francophone."

I confessed that my parents had taken us to Paris four years ago, when my sister was six. She was so afraid of heights that we waited in line for over an hour to get to the top of the Eiffel Tower, only to turn around and leave. "Gardens and carousels," I said. "That's basically all I know of the place."

"Those gardens are literally world-famous. Plus there's the Louvre, the Musée d'Orsay. The Pompidou—I could spend days there. And what's the one with all the Monets?" She snapped her fingers. "The Musée de l'Orangerie." Even I could tell how good her accent was.

Years later I'd finally go, alone, on a weeklong splurge before I started residency, and I'd stand surrounded by Monet's famous water lilies and wonder if she ever made it. If she'd have had the same feeling I did in that same oval room, or if our experiences would always be too different. I'd linger in the gift shop, thinking what if I sent her a postcard. Would she remember this conversation? That she was the reason I'd come all this way? But I left without buying anything. It was a relief when the week ended and I flew back to New York to start work.

The me that sat outside in Stamford drinking Claudia's drink, stealing bites of Claudia's fajitas, couldn't have imagined what would become of my own future, let alone hers. "You'll go there," I proclaimed, like saying something was enough to make it true.

Claudia swirled the straw in her glass and shook her head at me. "Maybe. You're lucky you have an actual life plan."

"If I do well enough in undergrad, get into med school, survive it, match for residency, figure out a specialization, pay off all the debt, get a job a million years from now." I rattled off each obstacle on my fingertips. "If I like it," I added, which was somehow always easy to forget. "At least you know you want to paint."

She sipped from the straw, more like a gulp. "Do you think the Corbins like their jobs? When they were in their twenties, or almost twenty, did they sit around talking like this?"

Almost twenty. I let a piece of ice melt on my tongue, sucking out the margarita taste.

"I think Ellen wanted a way out of western Pennsylvania. And Laurent wanted the kind of business school they don't have in rural France. Neither of them came from money, they made it themselves."

Claudia snorted. "No one makes anything themselves."

It was the way she made those proclamations. How she could take what I knew—what I knew to be true, because everyone said it—and change it just like that. No matter what she said, I never saw her as uncertain. She knew who she was. Who she wanted to be. I felt guilty all over again for how full I was when she'd barely had time to eat all day. For what might happen to this restaurant, her hangouts, if it wasn't just River Point, probably, but more of the coastline that transformed into luxury shopping, luxury living, places for the men like Laurent's investors to store their ever-growing collection of yachts. "I take my iced coffee the color of my nanny, not yours," one of the women had told Ellen, laughing as she'd stirred skim milk into her glass, and I'd whipped my head around, hoping Claudia wasn't close enough to hear.

But of course she hadn't been idling on the patio, meeting Ellen's friends, Laurent's colleagues—the ones, probably, behind the very condos she'd rolled her eyes about. Lori was never going to grip her hand and say, "What a treat to meet you," and, "You have such a special aunt." Anyone who'd looked across the lawn that day at the guests and the staff would have already decided where she belonged.

But I thought I could transcend it, this world we lived in even if it wasn't one we'd made. I made myself eat more of my dinner than I wanted, made myself keep drinking from her margaritas when I should have stopped. On the drive back we rolled down all four windows and Claudia put in a mixtape, Ricky Martin, the Vengaboys going *Boom! Boom! Boom!* When we drove through the gate and up the long driveway to the house, she turned down the volume and closed the windows. She waved a hand over her face: "Serious time." But we were laughing too hard to stop, the weightiness of all that future talk forgotten. The ringing in my ears from the music was still in me after we hugged a whispered good night in the kitchen, before she went down to her suite and I tiptoed upstairs past the Corbins' room.

I lay on the bed still in my clothes, the room spinning, everything in my head muffled as though shouted from too far away.

Up there the AC didn't penetrate and I'd kept a window open but it wasn't enough. I got up and pushed it higher, not caring if the mosquitos got in through the rip in the screen. I needed the air; I was sweating. How stifling it was in that room. I'd wanted to tell Claudia about the pills I'd discovered that afternoon—twice at dinner I'd opened my mouth to say she'd never guess what I'd found.

But I didn't. I couldn't.

It was one thing to make fun of how Laurent exaggerated his stuffy accent to seem extra French for his colleagues, or how nervously Ellen flitted about to everyone, like she needed Lori's endorsement for City Councilwoman of her Backyard.

But the Corbins were my family. I couldn't hurt them in front of everyone.

And probably I'd misunderstood. There'd been some confusion and I'd only make it worse. Back in bed I rolled onto my side and a tide within me rolled, too. Very quietly I went to the bathroom and threw up.

I'd seen the light on in Laurent's study when I'd slid up the stairs, but he hadn't come out to say goodnight or demand to know where I'd been, and now no one came upstairs to ask if I was all right, to smell the sour margarita mix and bottom-shelf tequila on me. I wondered if Claudia was okay, if we shouldn't have driven. But I couldn't go downstairs to find her—she'd remember I wasn't *almost twenty*, she'd think I couldn't keep up. Could anyone on the second floor hear me? It was a question that came up when the trial started; Laurent would go so far as to hire a sound expert for eight thousand dollars to prove the answer was no. But then the expert was disputed—it depended on so many factors, and there was no way to recreate exactly how loudly or at what pitch or for how long Sabine spent screaming in my room.

Which meant that even later, after it was all, supposedly, decided, I was never entirely sure. Maybe no one heard me up there being sick that night.

Or they had too much on their minds to care.

TEN

I watched Ellen more closely after that. When she seemed tired. When she went upstairs and closed the bedroom door. Was she reaching into the cabinet, under the sink, behind her bottles and sprays?

Or was it on the days when she was answering the phone and running to the store and faxing pages to Billie and picking up the dry cleaning and putting in an order for new saplings to plant along the fence in the backyard? And also, also calling Laurent's personal assistant and calling Lori's personal assistant and calling the wife of the chief of staff to the governor, who Laurent had been playing golf with, making his inroads week by week. Would she, the wife, like to have lunch at the club while the boys were in that hot sun all afternoon?

I heard the pause on the phone, felt the strain of Ellen forcing out a smile.

"It's been a long time!" (Laugh.) "Too long." (Laugh.) "But sure, I'd love to dust off my tennis whites."

"You can't play tennis," I said when she hung up. "Tell her that you can't play tennis."

I tried to sound like my mother, what I thought she might do. Surely there was a limit to what Ellen would make herself go through just so Laurent could acquire some land.

But I wasn't about to call home again and say here was yet another thing I couldn't handle. Ellen said with her customary wave, "I'm fine," as if daring me to say it wasn't true. "Anyway," she added. "Sheryl will get her win, and before you know it, it'll be martini time."

The day of the match, I came downstairs and was surprised to find Laurent still home. Claudia was off work and her car was gone. She hadn't told me she had plans, and it felt a certain way that she hadn't asked me to come.

The air had a brittle quality, as though I'd walked into a room where an argument still clung. Ellen put her mug down on the kitchen island harder than was necessary and retreated up the stairs. I started cracking eggs, making toast, while Laurent sipped his coffee and watched me.

"Maybe we should get out of here today," I offered. It could be the break Ellen needed, a quiet house, the chance to prepare for Sheryl without so many people around. Maybe I could keep Laurent's attention before he, too, up and left me alone all day with Sabine and no car and no idea what to do.

Still, I was surprised when he agreed. He brought me a pair of Ellen's old riding boots to squeeze into, which was how I figured out that we were going to the barn. Her riding pants were out of the question. So it was jeans despite the heat, but I didn't mind; I was excited. The Corbins had two horses, and I'd ridden when I was younger but mostly they'd just put me on and walked me around on a lead while telling me that I was doing great. They used to keep them at a barn in Westchester, but Laurent said now I'd see what riding was really about.

The houses gave way to fields, the fields to trees. The barn perched on the crest of a hill with a view so beautiful it made my lungs hurt, the way some beauty could be painful to look at, knowing I could never return to the same view from the same place from the very same time in my life and see it again.

Laurent tied Tucker's leash to a fence. He strode over to the barn without looking back—had he forgotten he had a child in the car? Or maybe he hadn't meant to get Sabine yet. Maybe I was supposed to hang back while he got things sorted. Maybe he wasn't really leaving Tucker to dig in the bare patch of grass. But after a moment he called, "You coming?" as though confused by why I had to be so slow. I had to figure out the buckles for Sabine's car seat, which was different in his car than in Claudia's, and it took forever getting her out. Sabine wanted to sit in the car, then she wanted to sit in the grass. Didn't she want to look at the horsies? No, she did *not* want to look at the horsies.

"She does this," Laurent called, impatient. "She just has to get used to it, and then she'll be fine."

"Should we go see Papa?" I asked, but Sabine chanted *no* until Laurent said forget it, he'd get the horse ready without us. And I saw that even at this, the attempt to have a nice day with my uncle, I'd failed.

I picked a black-eyed Susan. "It's okay to be scared sometimes," I whispered. "It's okay to feel a lot of things."

I tried to see the barn the way the girl did. How tall the flowers above us. How big the world and how little say we all have. I made it sound fun, going to say hello to Macy when Laurent led her out, getting to stroke her soft nose. But it was painful how hard Sabine kicked against me when I picked her up to take her. Even Laurent looked stung—but Sabine was getting on the horse. She was getting on the horse because he'd said so, it was how the day was supposed to go. And because the more she refused, the more she had to do it, to prove she could conquer her fears and face challenges and do difficult things and see, in the end, they weren't really that bad.

"She's only three," I ventured, but Laurent was prepared with a lecture he'd obviously given before, about how habits of mind start young and this was the kind of mental discipline she'd be grateful for as she got older.

It didn't matter that Sabine had trusted me, that she'd wanted me to pick her up and hold her. I went ahead and passed her off to her father, who plunked her onto the saddle as she screamed.

"Look," he said. "I've got the reins. Macy isn't going anywhere. She's not even going to move."

He was right, he was holding onto the horse, he was being careful with her. He was propping Sabine up, stroking her trembling back, showing her where to hold on to the saddle, and he'd brought the stirrups all the way up so her feet could almost touch. He wasn't unkind. I formed the thought clearly. He wasn't being cruel.

But Sabine wouldn't stop crying. And didn't that mean something, too? "We don't have to—" I tried again, and Laurent whipped his head to me.

"Do you always give up this easily? Is it an American thing? Is it your family? Your women? My wife is like this, too."

I saw it then, too startled to object. They hadn't been fighting that morning about Ellen's risk of reinjury, as though she were the one dying to get back on the court, back to her life, while he urged caution. It was Laurent who must have said *You can't say no to Sheryl,* and *How long are you going to drag this out,* and *You won't get better if you don't push through.* He'd probably pressed her to see Harry's wife in the first place. All that summer my mind went straight to Ellen, Ellen's fault, Ellen's will, the reflex like a mallet to the knee. Only now do I wonder what else I missed, or overlooked, or willed away because it didn't fit my expectations.

Coltrane was a skittish horse. Macy was the gentle one, accepting Sabine's futile kicks while her soft eyelashes blinked slowly and her ears sometimes swiveled about. But Sabine wouldn't stop howling, the bib of her ruffled T-shirt wet with tears and mucus and spit, and finally Laurent rubbed his forehead, pinching the skin to make a pouch. "Forget it," he said, and stuck the child roughly in the dirt.

She's not a toy, I wanted to shout. But I stood there. I'd stood there through the whole ordeal and then I stood there after. Laurent asked if I wanted to ride and the truth was that I did. I still wanted him to like me, the way I wanted Ellen to like me, and Claudia, Sabine, even Lori and Ellen's friends and everyone I knew. I wanted him to like me even more, to prove that I was different, better. I could make him change his mind about us.

"What about Sabine?" I asked.

"Someone will watch her."

"Who?"

He tied Macy to a post. "I'll take care of it."

I didn't know what that meant. I followed him into a set of offices where a wispy blond girl sat behind a desk, playing on a Game Boy and chewing the ends of her hair. "My mom's not here yet," she lisped through a mouth full of braces.

"I was looking for you, actually. How'd you like to get a better return on your summer job?"

She paused the tinny music and looked up.

Laurent pulled a set of bills from his wallet. He didn't count them. She didn't, either, before stuffing them in the pocket of her cutoffs. "Sure," she said, and the Game Boy music started again. I couldn't leave Sabine there. I knew that. Even if they'd done this before, there were no toys, no childproofing, the girl barely looked old enough to be left alone herself.

So that was my second betrayal, that when Laurent put away his wallet and hitched up his jeans, I promised Sabine we'd be back soon and followed him out.

ELEVEN

He took off the saddle and walked Macy to a tall block, where he stood and swung his leg over. "Now it's your turn."

But with no stirrup, what was I supposed to do? I hoped Sabine was okay in there. I hoped the dog had enough shade. I hoped Laurent knew what he was doing.

"Here," he said, and held out a forearm. I had to grab at him, pawing at his waist to drag myself up. I lurched into place behind him, hair in my eyes from under the rim of the helmet. There wasn't time to swipe it back before he told me to hold on. "To what?" I said.

"Don't tell me you're afraid."

I put my hands on his waist, feeling the strap of his leather belt, the edge of his jeans below the tucked-in button-down. His butt was right in front of me. I kept thinking that—how his ass was right there. And how my legs were spread wide behind him, my crotch pressed snug against his pockets. Could he feel me there? The mare's back was broad, her bristly hairs rubbing against my jeans, friction rough along the inside of my thighs.

"Squeeze your legs tight to hold on," he said. "You can do that, can't you?"

He clicked his tongue and the horse took off. My arms slid under his and I wrapped my hands around his waist, the trunk of his torso. That was how solid he was. I pressed my head into his back, my cheek to the soft slip of his button-down, the helmet tipping off my forehead, the chin strap digging in. I imagined he was my father, he was some other man. He smelled of sweat and hay. He smelled of the outside, and the horse we were on, and the trees we were riding between, moving from the pastures into the woods, to the trails he said he preferred.

I felt his body moving with the horse's, taking me with him by virtue of how closely I gripped him. The way he held the reins, leather grazing the back of my forearm. Sabine would be fine. Hadn't that girl said her mother was coming? When Laurent covered my hand with his palm and asked, "Are you ready?" I nodded into his back as the horse picked up faster. A tear slid down my cheek, or maybe it was just from the wind.

But when I squeezed my eyes shut, the dizziness rolled up through me and I had to snap them open again, afraid I was going to slide off. And what if I fell? What if holding onto Laurent didn't keep me on the horse, what if I dragged him off with me, what if the helmet cracked, what if the horse kicked me in the face, the ribs. What if I smashed straight onto a root. I pictured myself curled in the dirt, how I'd look from above as Laurent shook me, how wonderful to feel him lifting me with all that newfound care. What if I fell like Ellen had fallen, riding Coltrane for the first time after a long break when Sabine was born, the horse different after all that time away, her body different, too. Something startled him—a hare in the woods, maybe, or was it just the rider who felt like a stranger to him then? She fell on her side. Shattered her elbow and spent weeks in a sling. But it was her hip that caused the most problems. I'd heard my mother's side of the phone calls all the times Ellen rang. Listening, nodding, saying "hmm" and "that must be awful." Giving advice about how to bathe Sabine one-handed—but not too much advice, because Ellen would grow upset, tell my mother she didn't understand. She didn't have a baby and a husband who was never home he was working so much, and a broken bone, and her hip always hurting, and then her back because of how she'd come to compensate, always this ache inside and her doctors only saying give it time, she needed time to heal, there was nothing broken but the bruising could take a long time to go down.

I tried to imagine bone on rock, the shock of it, the pain.

Would I show up at Swarthmore with a cane, the way Ellen's doctors had recommended a cane and she'd gone three days before chucking it in a closet, saying she couldn't stand to use it? People looked at her differently, spoke to her differently. At work, at meetings, even fundraisers where she was the one writing the check—as though they suddenly had doubts about her, even if they couldn't put their finger on why. It was unfair, but I knew why Ellen couldn't appear weak for too long. Why she'd rushed out just the other day to buy new tennis shoes and bright white socks.

"Is this where Aunt Ellen—" I started to say when Laurent slowed to walk us through a field and let Macy chew the tall grass. I couldn't form the rest of the question. I knew she'd been thrown in a clearing. But I couldn't make myself say the word *fall.*

And since when had my uncle and I had this time together? No Ellen, no Sabine, none of his tanned associates comparing risk-adjusted returns. Not even Claudia to get in the way. We were both breathing from the exertion; I felt the rise and fall of his torso, his stomach expanding under my palm. The tautness of his muscles and then the softer layer that said he didn't quite look the way he used to, when I'd met him fresh from his first marriage that wasn't quite over—a woman from business school who must have regretted bringing her organic pet food company to the top advertising firm in New York, and then bringing her husband along to their dinners and events where he got to meet that lovely Ellen Bryce (who wouldn't stay a Bryce for much longer).

"She needs to get back on," he said, which didn't answer my question but which I took to mean yes. I could have let go of him—the horse was idle, I didn't need to clutch him so closely. But I didn't drop my arms, and he didn't move away like he wanted me to.

"She does come here, you know." I'd seen Ellen dressed in her riding pants and tall boots, a visor and black gloves in hand.

Laurent shifted, for the first time looking back at me. "Alone?"

"She hasn't taken me."

He turned around again. Took a handkerchief from his pocket and used it to swipe under the helmet, around the folds in the back of his neck. I didn't know if this was a betrayal of my aunt or if it meant he'd see that he could trust me.

"She must come to see the horses. When she was pregnant she'd still come, even when she couldn't ride."

"Does it still hurt?" Which was close to what I wanted to know, but not exactly.

Laurent made that clicking noise with his teeth. Macy lifted her head, ears perked. Things were changing; I sensed it the same as the horse. I tightened my grip, waiting for that split second that I'd leave my body behind as the horse lurched and started up again.

"It's been over a year," he said as he tucked the handkerchief away.

I could have said it. I could have told him right then. Not that I'd snooped, but *something*.

But I pictured the closed doors of the massive house swallowing our footsteps. I wouldn't hear everything he'd say to her, but I'd know it was happening—what was wrong with her, even a seventeen-year-old had noticed, and why wasn't she getting over it. Was she even trying? Why wasn't she better by now?

Or else I'd be banished, pushed aside just like Sabine. They'd send me home for being too much, too little, too in the way, too not quite right. I could hear my mother scolding. The kids at school who'd ferret out, somehow, that I was back again and disinvited from their parties. I couldn't keep an eye on Ellen from Cambridge. Who knew what might happen to Sabine.

Still, I thought we'd keep talking; he'd at least want to know why I'd asked. I wasn't ready for it as he moved and the horse moved and we were suddenly flying.

~

"He thinks it doesn't even hurt," Ellen had told my mother on the phone one day. I'd walked into my parents' room looking for Wite-Out and my mom had mouthed *Ellen*, so I'd know to keep quiet.

After, I'd asked about the call. I liked hearing about Ellen's doctors, the things they advised. These were the people who knew what to do, and I admired that certainty—I thought that meant they'd always have the answers. My mother said something about Ellen trying a new type of pill, but mostly she was irritated by Laurent. "I don't know how that man can think a woman can fall off a galloping horse and just"—she'd snapped her fingers—"magically be fine."

But after weeks, after months had passed, my mother wasn't as snappy, and sometimes she said, "Ellen, honey. Can we talk about something else? It won't help you to dwell." It seemed everyone was growing tired of Ellen's story. Perhaps even Ellen herself.

"You've come so far," I heard my mother telling her when we hosted Christmas that year. The two of them were in the kitchen, champagne fizzing around raspberries and sugar cubes dissolving in their flutes like jewels.

I stepped into the kitchen to get more sparkling cider, and I saw Ellen nod. I heard her say, "It feels like I can breathe again. And once we finish renovating the ground floor, we'll be able to bring in more help." I thought this meant she was, if not healed, then on her way, crossing a solid line from pain into wellness that as a doctor I still find myself wanting to believe in. If she kept calling my mother after that, if something continued to linger, it was because of the move and her job and the house and Sabine and the stress from Laurent's investments, all while she was getting her strength back. Adjusting. My mother's worry at the start of the summer didn't mean that Ellen wasn't better. It was supposed to be what older sisters did.

We brought the horse in. Before Laurent could lead her to the water trough, he shoved the reigns at me. "Brad!" he called. "I can't believe it!" He trotted over to a tall man tacking up a chestnut horse at the end of the barn.

Brad. I pressed a palm to Macy's neck; she was sweaty, too warm. I tried to remember the last name Laurent had said on his phone call with Peter weeks ago—Whitaker? Whittier? I wanted to hear who Brad was, what they were saying, why Laurent was so interested in him in the first place. But the horse needed to drink—how had he simply left her? She dipped her nose eagerly down. The men laughed. There was no clock in there, I couldn't say how long we'd left Sabine in that godforsaken room. "Showing Ellen's niece—" I heard him say. Brad glanced over and I tried to smile, but his interest was already gone.

"Great running into you!" Laurent called after a time, and Brad said what a coincidence, it had been a long time. He didn't remember their schedules typically overlapping.

"I'll get you Kip's number," he added. His voice had dropped but I heard that clearly, and I filed the name away, the same way I'd held onto Brad's. "I'll tell him to expect a call soon."

Laurent said thanks, he wouldn't regret it. There were promises about grabbing drinks, the kind of thing they didn't mean. Neither of them said the words *River Point*, but it was there between them, buzzing like a neon sign. I looked around the barn. Nothing in writing, no phone record, no way to trace their contact. The only witnesses a teenage girl and a stable hand so far down the row, he'd never remember their button-downs and identical helmets. I leaned against Macy, my whole weight, knowing she would hold me. I wanted to touch her ears, her throat. To crawl inside and seize her heart and swap it, strong and muscled, for my own.

"You must run into people all the time here," I said when he finally strode back, a flush up his neck, to his ears.

He took off the helmet and rubbed a hand over the sweat on his head. He shrugged, but the smile was there. "He used to come on Sundays. Guess he still does."

I thought we'd cool down the horse, get her back in her stall like a game we'd finished playing. But there were employees for that. It was hard to walk away from her warmth and the salt of her neck and the feeling still rubbery in my legs, as though I might never find my footing. Laurent went straight to the car. Had he forgotten the dog he'd left tied? His own daughter still in that office? I made my way back and pushed open the door. She was asleep on the rug, her thumb in her mouth. Alone. It hit me all of a sudden, again or maybe for the first time, that we'd just left her there, that I'd cared more about impressing Laurent than protecting Sabine. There was no telling when the girl and her Game Boy had left, or how long my cousin had cried. She didn't stir when I picked her up, she must have exhausted herself, and I felt heavy with the dead weight of my own guilt bearing down.

I couldn't believe how close I'd come to ratting out my aunt, as though Laurent had wanted to take me here. As though we had some kind of bond. He'd never waste an entire Sunday having a nice little jaunt at the barn. He'd used me, the same way he'd used that girl in the office, except I didn't get any cash. I helped you get to Brad, I wanted to tell him. So give me a cut of whatever you get from his connection. But my uncle wouldn't get the twist to my laugh, the line between joking and not.

TWELVE

After the barn I lay naked on the bed, my wet towel leaving damp spots on the sheets.

I put on underwear, shorts. A bra but no T-shirt—it was too hot. No one from the road could see me through the window; there was only the grass and the pond and the ghost of that old dead deer to spy. I hadn't talked to my parents since the last time I'd called and I wanted to hear their voices again. Not late and clouded with sleep but the people who were still my parents, the people I was still supposed to know.

What could I tell them, though? About the deer? The horse? How frightened Sabine had been?

What about the party, Ellen's headaches, how little she ate? What about the pills?

I didn't want them going through the wash, I didn't want to forget them, so I'd put them on a saucer on my nightstand next to a glass of water smeary with ChapStick stains and the room's cordless phone. On the floor were the shorts I'd worn for the party and I picked them up, licked my finger, and pushed it into the pocket, getting up the grainy dust the pills had left. I licked my finger; it was bitter, disgusting. What was Ellen doing?

But there was something appealing about tasting her secret, knowing that I held it, it was mine. I took the phone from its cradle and turned it on and dialed.

"El?" my mom said, a higher, looser pitch that startled me—a sister-voice I didn't know.

"Mom?"

"Oh, honey. It's you." As though she'd forgotten where I was, that someone else might call her from this number. Her voice dropped into its normal register. "What's wrong?"

"I'm just calling. To say hi," I added, as though it needed explaining.

"Len," I heard. "Lenny, it's Rach. Pick up the phone."

They sounded more upbeat, my parents, and so I tried to match them. Everything was great, Ellen seemed happy, I was doing a lot for Sabine. It felt strange to talk this way, calling just to say hello from elsewhere. I made sure to say the Corbins were taking good care of me. Each week Ellen asked what groceries I wanted and went straight out and bought them.

"I hope it's not too much," my mother said.

"It's nice of her."

But they'd think I was being spoiled, like I was putting her out.

"And they had a party," I added. "For the Fourth." I thought Ellen might have already told my mother about it, but it sounded like not.

"It was a picnic in the yard, just a bunch of neighbors," I went on, making it sound effortless and low-key. I could have bragged about the governor's birthday, how even Lori knew my name. But that would have meant getting into River Point, Laurent's investors and the regulations he was up against, the fact that Ellen was still in set whatever of her match against the chief of staff's wife and I hadn't been able to stop her.

"And the nanny?" my mother asked. "You're still getting along?"

"Claudia? Yeah, she's amazing. Sabine loves her." I thought of her head in my lap. That red bikini tied behind her neck. Every time she rolled one of her cigarettes she'd say, "Thanks for not making me do this alone." What would Claudia have done if it were her at the barn?

But Laurent wouldn't take her riding just the two of them. It would never be that way.

"Mom," I said, trying again, trying the only way I knew how. "Ellen's accident—does she still see a doctor?"

I felt my mother's attention sharpen, snapping toward her sister like a band. "What did she say?"

"Nothing," I said quickly. "She hasn't complained." Which was true. Technically. "Laurent took Sabine and me to the barn today, so I was just thinking about it." I knew I'd better keep talking, rambling on about the horses and how pretty it was on the hill with such a view, prettier even than the old barn in Westchester, which didn't have all the acres of woods. If I kept talking then my mother wouldn't interrupt with more questions. She wouldn't start thinking maybe this wasn't such a good idea, maybe she should call Ellen herself. Maybe I should come home.

I left out Sabine's tears, Laurent's frustrations. Brad and the girl with the Game Boy and why Ellen hadn't come. And the ride with just the two of us, Macy's body moving beneath me, everything moving: me and Laurent and the horse. Just that we went and petted them and saw the other animals—and the puppy, I was sure to mention Tucker, how Sabine was warming up to him. Gradually, I added, so it wouldn't sound like too much of a stretch.

I wasn't lying by telling things a certain way. It wasn't like they asked if I'd ridden and I said no, or if Sabine liked the horses and I gushed about how great it all was. It was just a story. They wanted a story so I told them one, the same way Sabine asked for a story before bed and I made up a princess who liked pudding, an ant named Penelope who had such a large hill to climb.

"How's Jules?" I ventured, and I thought they'd give me a story, too—wasn't that the deal we'd struck? But I couldn't miss the pause. Not just one of them waiting for the other to talk first but something like they couldn't answer.

"Hanging in there," my father said. "She's hanging in."

"What does that mean?"

"She's sleeping right now," my mother said. "I can have her call you back."

But I didn't want to bother her, and when I said this my mother reiterated, again, that Jules was just tired, just tired all the time, and she never did call me that summer. I'd call home but my sister was never free, and maybe I should have tried harder—maybe I'd have figured out my place with her, with all of them, sooner if I did. But I had only the person I was then, and I didn't think to find a different way.

My parents talked about the doctor's office, how cold Jules was.

"Lots of soups," my mother said. "We're keeping her fed."

I'd always hated it when Jules practiced her scales. The noise was constant—and yet sometimes I found myself on the third floor of the Corbins' house humming aloud, only to realize it wasn't a song from the radio or even a mindless tune; it was those infernal warm-ups my sister played on the piano, up and down and meandering around without end. I kept blinking as though the sun were in my eyes even though it was dipping too low now past the window, I was losing that long, golden light that summer always held on to for so long. I didn't know what my sister was like as someone tired and sick. I couldn't imagine the house without her music.

"We want you to keep having a good summer," my father said,

and I understood. My parents had enough problems. I climbed off the bed and smiled even though they couldn't see me. Dana had once read in a magazine that it made a person sound happier, even on the phone. It made it easier to pretend.

I stuck my finger through the ripped part of the window screen and widened it even more. The chair in the corner was piled high with dirty clothes. I dragged it over, pushed some off, and sat on the rest. I thought maybe I shouldn't do things like that, maybe Ellen would come upstairs and suck in her breath at the mess I had made.

But Ellen wouldn't bother. "This whole floor is yours," she'd joked that first day. "What a house—I almost never make it up here."

I miss you, I could have told them. *I love you*.

But they might say, again, "What's wrong?" And I couldn't bear to make them worry.

I heard a noise in the background, faint but there nonetheless. It was nothing I recognized. Then shuffling; my father pulling away from the phone so I couldn't hear him.

"Mom?" I said.

"Hold on." I heard it again, only this time I knew what it was: my sister, somehow, even though that noise seemed to have nothing to do with her, with the only Jules I'd ever known.

"We should go, honey," my mother said, and I said sure, I'd talk to them later—but was everything all right? I asked them that twice, if they were okay, if Jules was okay. What was happening?

"We'll talk to you soon," my father said, and my mother told me to take care of Ellen and Sabine, and all I could do was say yes. I thought of Sabine on the horse, her hands balled into fists so tightly the pads of her fingertips turned white, her face red and angry and unavoidable. How funny to envy a three-year-old. Whatever she needed, everyone knew it.

THIRTEEN

It was hot in the bedroom, and stuffy, and I could have gone downstairs where it was cooler but I didn't want to. I didn't want to do anything. I got my Discman and put in my Hole CD and played it loud enough that anyone could have called for me and I never would have heard them.

But no one was calling for me. I knew that. I lay on the bed and picked up the broken pill from the saucer on the nightstand.

Courtney Love blasted through my ears. I'd always done what I was supposed to, and look where it had got me. I put the pill on my tongue.

It tasted horrible, but I didn't have any water left in the glass by my bed. I'd have to go to the bathroom and I didn't want to get up.

I chewed the pill and swallowed and stayed in bed as long as I could, until I couldn't stand it anymore, and then I went to the sink and ran the tap and washed it down.

I lay on the bed and waited to feel different. But nothing felt different. It was okay, though. I didn't mind if nothing happened. I wasn't tired but I closed my eyes. Sometimes when I was falling asleep I imagined I was lying in a small raft drifting into a broadening sea. It wasn't scary, though. Once everything had been covered in a filmy haze but then it fell clean off and there I was. Alive. I smiled at myself in the mirror. I was in the bathroom again. I didn't know how long I'd been in the bathroom, smiling at myself in the mirror. I was actually kind of pretty. I thought this clearly: that I was pretty and should remember it more often.

And anyway, fuck it. Who cared if I wasn't. How many times had Dana said I needed new highlights, a better foundation, and what about my sneakers. I drank water from the tap and thought of how easy it was not to care. I could do that, if I wanted. I could simply make it so.

Downstairs I poured almonds into my palm even though I wasn't hungry. Even though it didn't matter. Ellen wasn't home yet but that didn't matter, either. When Claudia's car rolled up the driveway, I jumped out and threw open the door, the almonds scattering over the stairs, falling into the geranium pots.

"Hey, you!" My face stretched from the grin. I could smile right out of my skin.

"Hey." Claudia stepped out of the car. "What'd I miss?"

I walked out on the gravel in my bare feet and hugged her. The gravel pinched but not in a bad way. It felt like the most natural thing in the world, rocking back and forth before I let go.

"Guess it's been a while." She laughed.

I laughed, too. "Sorry. Just got bored without you." I opened my fist, but there weren't any almonds. I wiped my palms on my shorts. "It was so crazy today."

I glanced toward the house—Laurent was probably in his study while Sabine gorged on TV, but I didn't want him hearing. Claudia must have known what I meant because she went to the back seat and took out a grocery bag. "Come with me. You can give me all the dirt."

I clapped my hands (how freeing, how funny!) and followed her through the side entrance, into the apartment downstairs. Something in the back of my mind—that I'd never been down here before, never officially invited, and so I should remember not to know where the couch was, or the fireplace mantel crowded with picture frames. "It's a mess," she said, even though it wasn't. The house cleaner picked up after her—the Corbins included it as a perk of the job.

From my perch on the stairs I'd imagined it as small, some basement hovel, but of course it was the footprint of the whole house. Claudia took me on a tour: the kitchen and bathroom and the bedroom twice the size of mine upstairs, the king-sized bed made up with a brightly patterned duvet and pillows that said Claudia had picked them for herself, none of the austere creams of the upper floors, Ellen's hotel-like choices. On the walls, a framed reprint of one of Monet's paintings of Notre-Dame Cathedral from the National Gallery of Art in D.C., and a poster of four Black women laughing that said *Waiting to Exhale*. Floor-to-ceiling bookshelves crammed with paperbacks and a collection of DVDs and VHS tapes organized by category and type, some of which I knew, like *Saved by the Bell*, most of which I didn't. I ran a finger over the titles: *Living Single, A Different World*. A bunch of stuff in black-and-white, in French, a whole shelf devoted to Robert Bresson. "Wow," I said. "Have you seen all of these?"

"More than once, if they made the cut to come with me. You should see what I left behind at my parents'."

I pictured her in a dorm room, in her apartment with Kelly and Justine. Popping in a sitcom after a party was over and laughing along as she cleaned up the red Solo cups. Asking who wanted to catch an art film off campus, eyes alit as she dissected it after. There was a quilt at the foot of her bed and I hadn't realized I was stroking it until Claudia said her aunt and her grandma had made it—her mother didn't have the patience—and she wished she'd taken more time to learn.

"I know it's silly to have a quilt out all summer," she said. But I shook my head. It wasn't silly. Everything had a glaze, a bit of shine like I couldn't see it head-on. I wished I could wrap myself in the fabric, just press my face all the way in. "It's so good for Sabine," Ellen had once confided in me, "to be exposed to other people at this age." *Other people* meaning Claudia, I assumed. "She'll know it doesn't matter if you're black or purple or green," my aunt had continued, and I'd nodded even though Claudia wasn't green, she wasn't purple, Ellen couldn't have meant what she said.

"Do you want anything?" Claudia asked, and I followed her into the kitchen. She unpacked sliced cheese, canned soup. A six-pack—I picked up a bottle before thinking that might not have been what she'd meant. But she said it was okay, she wouldn't tell. And if the pill was bad, wouldn't I feel bad by now? If Claudia didn't want me here, wouldn't she ask me to leave? I opened two beers and we went into the living room. Now I could study the photos up close: Claudia at graduation, Claudia with friends, Claudia as a little kid picking strawberries, hair laden with colorful beads. It felt like wringing out a bathing suit, how I could always squeeze more from myself. She came up behind me and I gasped, "Those cheeks, oh my god!" I wanted to know everything—a wedding photo, a graduation, what must have been her brother's birthday when he'd smashed both fists into the cake. How clearly she loved her family, how close they were—but her life wasn't news to her. She flopped on the couch and asked what happened.

"What?" I said, then laughed as I remembered, laughed more as I started to tell it—Laurent's insistence, his eventual capitulation to Sabine's more powerful hand. It wasn't funny but I made it funny, I made her laugh as she prodded me for more.

Again I left out the shitty office with the nonexistent babysitter. How I'd wrapped my arms around Laurent and swallowed down my breathing. It didn't matter that he hadn't cared about taking me there, he'd just needed the excuse to run into what's-his-face. Brad. I'd seen it, I'd heard, but maybe it hadn't been that way after all. Each thought was a soap bubble rising outside my body, one of the shiny orbs that caught the light as Sabine and Tucker chased them in the yard.

"You know Mrs. Corbin never takes her there," Claudia said knowingly. "She thinks Sabine's too young, she hates when Laurent does it."

"But it'd be weird if I told her, right? To tattle on her husband?"

I was still standing by the mantel, looking at the photographs. Looking at Claudia, who'd gotten a haircut that day, or recently—the tips re-dyed a brighter orange, the line at the nape of her neck redefined.

She raised her bottle toward me. "Do *not* get mixed up in their drama. Still." She pouted. "My poor Bean."

I went upstairs and brought down chicken salad, mozzarella balls, a whole baguette, promising they wouldn't be mad at me for taking it, and truly in that moment I couldn't imagine any kind of trouble. We sat on the living room floor and spread the food out on the coffee table. I'd brought down slices of lemon cake, too, and Claudia said we were having a banquet. We were having a feast. She got two more beers from the fridge. By then I couldn't feel my fingertips. My mouth. Something came off on the beer bottle—blood? Then I remembered. Claudia touching my chin. Smearing the waxy lipstick, her instructions: "Blot." She'd gone to Manhattan, bought makeup with her sister. So she hadn't been with some guy all day! I laughed so hard my head tipped back, all of me tilted, until I was lying on the carpeted floor.

We'd been talking about her sister, how protective and careful and driven she was, how Claudia wondered if that gene had passed her by. "At least I'm in the middle. My parents can brag about Denise and focus on Reggie and I just do my thing." But it was never like that with my sister, getting brunch and lipstick and talking about life. You couldn't do that when someone was ten and possibly dying.

"Is she?" Claudia leaned over me. "Is it really that bad?"

"I don't know. No one tells me anything."

She extended a hand to help me up. She sat on the couch but I stayed on the floor, leaning back against her shins. She asked if she could braid my hair, she was trying to practice for Sabine, and I said god yes, and sank against her. I knew she wanted to say something about Jules, but how could anyone know how. I pointed to a bright framed picture on the wall, which from my angle on the floor looked massive, a swirl of colors and ink. "What's that?" I asked.

She teased out a tangle. "It's a painting."

"What's it of? Who's it by? Where'd you get it?"

"Do you like it?"

"I don't know." I let my head drop back onto her knees. "How would I know?"

"Did you like that cake?"

"Yes."

"How do you know?"

I snorted. I knew where this was going. "Because it's delicious."

"What about that beer?"

"Not really. I know, I know—" I moved to fend her off as she tried to snatch the bottle from me. "But I sort of do? I mean I know that I don't but I don't really mind that I don't. I know that doesn't make sense."

She called me crazy, but she was laughing. "The point is that you know."

"That's different. It's food. You don't have to think about whether you like chocolate. And there's a finite number of reactions. It's all along one scale. One axis." I was mixing up my words. My thoughts. I touched my lip: rubber. Another smudge of lipstick came off on my thumb. "You might hate it or you might like it or you might love it in one thing but not in another but it's all about you, really—it's your opinion, there's nothing else to consider. But that." I meant to point at the painting but it was too much work and perfectly pointless. "That doesn't ask whether you like it. It's not there to care about you. It's there whether I like it or not, and I think it's brilliant, I mean it's really in your face, and I don't know that I like it but I don't know if that should matter." I finally stopped talking, unsure about anything I'd said.

"I made it."

I swiveled on the floor. "What?"

"It was part of my thesis and I wish you'd been on my committee instead of all those stuffy old white dudes with one foot in the grave, because they kept saying they didn't like it and I kept telling them so what."

White dudes. My mouth opened. Closed. I settled back against her legs and rested a cheek on her knee. All that time I'd known she'd painted, and I'd never even asked her to show me. In the projects she'd done with Sabine, and in our talks about art school, Paris, life. I hadn't seen her, the real her, separate from all that—separate from us. She'd layered cut paper and pastels with thick, dark outlines, watercolors bleeding behind. There was a mountain, or maybe a woman, or maybe that wasn't right, either. Her hands found my hair again, weaving the strands. I didn't know why I was sitting like that, why she tolerated me at all.

The people I knew had always appeared fully formed to me: my uncle the hedge fund manager, my father the orthodontist, my mother the college librarian. Even seeing the changes to Ellen's life didn't connect to me then: that people could be one thing and become another, slowly, step by step, or all at once in one great ladder. One great slide. Claudia's painting was incredible—it was unbelievable, actually, to know it had come from the hands of the person who was right that second running her fingers through my hair, this person I'd grown closer to than anyone else in the world.

Maybe destiny had forgotten about me. Maybe I wasn't meant for anything good. I'd always been proud to give my answer when adults asked, "What do you want to be when you grow up?" But that was nothing in comparison. If Claudia worried about how to build a career, a plan, how to use her talent for something that would last, I didn't have any of her doubts. In that moment, leaning against her, I knew it better than I knew my own pulse. She was going places I would never know.

FOURTEEN

It was late when I climbed the stairs from Claudia's apartment. The lights were off. Had anyone wondered where I was? If I'd eaten dinner? Had Sabine asked about me?

I was careful on the steps up to the second floor, feeling my way in the dark. Probably they thought I was asleep. Probably they hadn't noticed either way. I couldn't tell if I was walking normally or very slowly or maybe it was all going so fast and only felt slow to me then. Whatever I'd taken had worked its way through me, leaving a heavy tiredness behind. I'd felt it slipping away from me lying there half on Claudia's lap, feeling the stir of Claudia's fingers, squinting at the painting Claudia had made. Some euphoria, only I couldn't remember what it was or why I'd felt it, just that I'd begun to miss it as soon as she hugged me goodnight. When I got to the landing, I saw a single light coming from the far end of the hall. Laurent's study, the door cracked open, the yellowed glow making a frame.

I could have turned to keep going upstairs. I could have headed straight to my room. But I crept down the hallway, inching toward the study and the murmur of his voice. I'd never seen him in there without the door pulled all the way shut. He was always stepping away when his BlackBerry rang and there was no way to hear what he was saying, I mean specifically, not some vague pitch about investments and *revitalization*. Even hearing him talk to Peter, or Brad—there was always something out of reach. Who was he talking to this late, his voice so low that I couldn't make out the words until I was almost to the door? I leaned against the wall to steady myself, hoping he couldn't see my shadow. I didn't want him to come out and smell the beer on me. He might know I'd taken something, something I shouldn't have, and it would get me in trouble and Ellen, too. Claudia hadn't noticed, I didn't think, but that didn't mean no one else would.

"No, no, we've got the perfect location already scouted. After we clear this one hurdle, we'll be ready to go." His voice was different, not his usual booming but hushed and thick, a midnight voice. I strained closer to listen.

"It's nothing, really. We've found the right engineer to get the regulations sorted—they've done the same thing down in Stamford. You know how these commissions are. They make you sweat for it, but that's why the return is what it is."

I held my breath through his faint laugh. Heard the creak of his chair as he leaned back, even the scratch of his pen.

"Exactly. The watershed makes it a state matter, but you're a smart man, you can see why that's better for us." A pause. "Once the governor says this is the direction to go in—no one wants that empty land to go to waste." His voice rose, then dipped again. "You understand there'll have to be a bidding process, for appearances. But I've been assured I can trust you, so I'll say it right now: I can make sure the marina is yours." Another pause. "As long as you give me that extra help along the way."

I should have turned then and run up the stairs. Backed down the hall and started walking up it louder than was necessary—not enough to wake Sabine, or Ellen, but their doors were shut. Just enough that

Laurent could hear me and know I was walking down the hall normally, the way a normal person would when going normally to her room upstairs. I wasn't near his private study and I wasn't listening in but it would remind him to close the door or quiet his voice or end the call or maybe it was fine, what I was hearing. Maybe it only had the sound of shadows because it was late and I was tired and didn't understand. He'd poke his head out and say goodnight the same way he'd sauntered back to me after pretending he'd just happened to run into Brad. Nothing hidden, for the simple fact that there was nothing to hide.

But I didn't do that.

I stood in the darkened hallway, holding my breath for so long my heart began to thump its wild questions and I had to let it out slow and shallow through my nose, not wanting the sound of myself to drown out the sound of him saying "He's up for reelection next year, and it's going to be tight. So here's what we're going to do, Kip. Are you with me? Listen. We're going to set it up so your donations—he's going to get a great donation from you. You let him know now that he can count on you, and I'll make sure that donation comes through in your name. There won't be any regulations standing in our way after that."

I closed my eyes. I didn't want to stand there and I didn't know what else to do and also—I knew this, even then—I wanted to hear everything, every single word he was giving away. I wanted to be inside something, something important. I want to *know*. What marina? What donations? Was this reputation-damaging illegal, hefty-fine illegal, jail-time illegal? Or did men like my uncle not wind up in places like that? I considered what Claudia would say but I knew I could never, ever ask her. Or Ellen. My parents. I couldn't repeat this to anyone.

"It'll come off the construction costs, I'll have it all covered. You don't need to do a thing. You need any work on your house, though? You won't be the only guy getting a new hot tub this fall. Landscaping all around. It's beautiful—your wife will love it. She'll ask why you didn't get one years ago. Let me make a few calls for you." A chuckle, though not the kind where anything was funny. "Nothing's going to compete with a marina of this size, Kip. They'll be using River Point as a model for the state—Stamford, Norwalk, they're all going to be next. And your name will be top of the list."

Laurent repeated that this was his private line, it was safe to talk here, Kip should feel free to call anytime. "I was told you were the person to contact," he said. "And I can tell. You have a—what's the expression? A nose for opportunity."

My toes pressed down against the wood. My heels. I may not have known how real estate worked, the hedge fund world. But I was pretty sure it was illegal to give someone a free hot tub in exchange for lobbying the governor. To make a donation using someone else's name, skimming from someone else's money, because you'd exceeded your limit or needed to apply more pressure or both. And how could you say there'd be a bidding process if you already knew who would win? Laurent must not have realized the door had slid open, that anyone could hear him if they came close enough.

Or else he was just that arrogant, untouchable, to think nothing of engaging in a little casual corruption late at night while his family was supposed to be sleeping. Maybe this was how the world worked, and I'd better get on board if I wanted to find my place in it.

The phone clicked back into its cradle and I waited for him to do something—start typing, maybe, and then I'd have the sound of the computer for cover. At least he could get up and close the door.

But what if now that he was finished, he left the study? What if he came down the hall to bed? The thought sent razors up my skin. Holding my breath, I tiptoed backward down the hallway. Slow.

Steady. I pressed my palm to my chest to hold the shuddering in. I was overreacting or it was just the pill, the drinking, I couldn't make myself stop. I went partway down the stairs, to where he couldn't see me. And then I sat down, head in my hand, curled up as tight as I could. The braid was already slipping away, my hair wasn't long enough, and I wished I could ask Claudia to do it again, make me beautiful but make it last. From the end of the hall I heard the roll of his desk chair, click of the light. The door swung all the way open, then all the way shut. Laurent wasn't quiet with his footsteps. Every one of them jammed against my heart. What if he came downstairs? What if he saw me on the stairs like this, what if he turned on all the lights and demanded to know what I'd heard?

Another door opened and closed. The bedroom. Running water—it was safe to stand. I tiptoed down the hall. There came a shiver of . . . it wasn't fear anymore. My feelings from before were already shifting. As I turned up the stairs to the third floor, I let my heel's thud against the wood. I wanted him to hear me up there. I wanted him to know I was awake with him, and I knew things. Or I could know things. I could be someone to worry about. I could be worth his attention, his concern, after all.

FIFTEEN

On a day when Laurent was at work and Ellen had to be in Manhattan and Claudia had plans to take Sabine to the dentist and then, as a treat, out to lunch, I didn't set my alarm. I showed up downstairs still in my pajamas. I gave them no choice but to leave me behind.

I was afraid I'd misjudged and I'd push open the door to find him sitting at his desk, pen in hand, and he'd look up with that frown wrinkling his forehead, furious at me for interrupting.

But of course Laurent wasn't in his study. I sat at his desk, careful not to adjust the seat, not to touch anything I couldn't put back. There were large sheets of paper by the keyboard and those I unfolded panel by panel, making sure the pages wouldn't wrinkle. It took me a moment to resolve the lines into a map. The south Connecticut coastline, with a layer of tracing paper showing color-coded zones. Each color corresponded to a range: One million to ten million dollars, one hundred million or more. I looked for River Point. I wasn't sure exactly where it was, but there were lines extending out into the harbor, more in an adjacent cove—which one was Kip's new marina? I tried to work out where in Stamford Claudia and I had gone. Those picnic tables, the dock lit up with chili lights. It was hard to know how long they'd last once all this land was bought up.

Laurent had made it seem so normal, like anything could become something else if he did enough convincing. Or maybe it wouldn't work out, no matter who he lobbied or bribed or cajoled—and then how would Ellen face their friends and neighbors and colleagues and Lori again?

I opened the desk drawer and picked up a stapler, extra staplers, Doublemint gum. An engraved pen, *LJC*, heavy and perfectly proportioned. I put it in my mouth. I ran my tongue over the whole thing, even the inky blue tip. I woke the computer from sleep.

There was nothing in my inbox. My high school email would be phased out in August and I didn't have a Swarthmore address yet. And who would write to me? My only friend was Claudia. I logged into AIM but Dana and Morgan and Ilana were offline. It was a perverse torture to imagine what they were up to, how even the most boring tasks, buying tampons, nursing a hangover, took on a shimmer when I was on the outside peering in.

I logged out before I could type something I'd regret. Opened Yahoo and put in Laurent's name. Maybe I shouldn't have cared. But I wanted to know what he was doing, what was happening, what no one else, perhaps, was even aware of—not even his wife.

I found his company, his graduation year. I looked up Harry, who was on the board of the golf club and easy to find. But all that showed were more headshots, dull biographical facts. There were too many Brad Whittiers to sift through. For Peter and Kip I had only their first names, I didn't know if Kip was a nickname or what, and *Kip + marina* brought me somewhere in Scotland. There was news, though. Way more than I'd expected. Op-eds in the *Connecticut Post* saying rezoning served corporate interests, not communities. A website called Fairfield County for Sustainable Growth with a petition hundreds of residents had signed. A whole group had formed with the mission to *Save River Point*, seeking local input on development ideas. The area, I learned, could become a park. A community center. Normal housing for normal people commuting to their jobs in Greenwich from over an hour away. The land didn't even have to be sold in the first place. "Empty," Laurent had called it. "Bleak," Ellen had said. But a storage facility isn't empty if people use it. The opposition was vocal but fractured. Did they want more environmental regulations, or different ones? And the groups fretting about *the character of the village*. What were they after?

I closed the page. It wouldn't matter once the governor weighed in. Once he suddenly and inexplicably found himself strongly in favor of loosening restrictions and ensuring undervalued areas like River Point became profitable again. I went into the browser history to see what Laurent searched for when he was in here late at night and planning.

That was when I saw the list of websites.

He always made a big deal about no one touching his computer, and I'd thought it was for the business sites and sensitive accounts. But really it was for this: page after page of every porn site he'd visited, day after day after day.

I scrolled back through the last seven days, the last month, as far back as the record went. I didn't have to worry about someone calling the house and getting the squeak and pop of the dial-up and wondering what I was doing. Laurent had his own dedicated line for the computer—Ellen said you had to when someone worked that much, it made her crazy to miss so many calls.

I deleted the sites I'd visited myself. Then I went into the previous history and clicked on the first page, the one at the top, not the architectural firm but the one before it. Big Bunnies, the website said. The next site he'd visited was a subset with the word *insertions* in the title and I clicked that, too.

A woman appeared on the screen. She had soft legs shiny with oil and they were spread in front of the camera, her fingernails long and chiseled nearly to points. Something in my chest flattened, pounded down. It wasn't that I'd never seen porn before. But I'd never seen it like this. The woman had some giant glass triangle that was all the wrong shape but she stuck it inside her anyway, her bunny ears wiggling as her face wrenched somewhere between a grimace and a grin. She pushed it deeper: pink nails, pink bunny ears, the frosted pink flesh of her distorted through the glass.

I closed the page quickly, as though it could erase the image of those insides. It wasn't that I couldn't stand blood, marrow. Like Claudia's painting, it didn't matter how I felt. It was there whether I liked it or not.

But the stretching. That gaping hole. Jonathan had tried only a finger and even then I'd faltered. "It'll be different when you actually do it," Dana had said with a smirk when I'd drunkenly admitted this fear to her—that there was no way a dick would fit inside me, and didn't it seem excruciating. "You'll see."

But I still didn't know, it felt like I'd never know, and there was no one to ask anymore. How childish my pawing about with Jonathan had been. Even Dana at that dance, whatever she'd wound up doing with that guy who'd bragged about getting her mouth. Claudia had been right to roll her eyes. This was what adults did. This was what they wanted.

Laurent must have gotten bored with the bunny thing because there weren't more of them. The rest were from another website he visited, from the looks of it, almost every day. *Ebony Teens*, it said. *Cum and Play.*

I told myself to stop it even as I couldn't stop clicking through the pages. Each one had a different woman, and they weren't costumed playthings with fake tails. There were girls in bikinis. Girls with their bikini tops off. Girls bent over. Girls on their knees. Girls at a party touching each other's breasts, one girl with the other's nipple in her mouth, looking up and smiling . . .

I crossed my legs. Pinched my thighs together. It was horrible, it was so horrible. I clicked a video to see a hairy white man thrusting into a slender Black girl's mouth, instructing her to look at the camera. Teens, the website said, but how many were lying about their age because some of them were clearly older, even thirty, dressed like stupid schoolgirls with plaid skirts and knee socks, rolling sticky lollipops over their fat nipples as though anyone were fooled.

But then there were the ones who must have been lying the other way because they looked younger than me, they looked—

I had to click those away, I couldn't think about it. It was one thing to be almost eighteen, so close I was basically already there.

But it was different seeing those girls on the screen. Knowing the men—my uncle—who saw them this way. Laurent had clicked through page after page of the same one, the same—should I call her a model? He clearly liked her the best. I sucked in my bottom lip, dragged my teeth across it. My legs hurt. Everything hurt. The woman's cheekbones shimmered, her eyelids, her painted lips. Her hair was long and straightened, jet-black but for the electric highlights streaked against her skin. One time I'd been chatting on AOL and a boy I'd thought was sixteen sent me a picture of his erection, only it wasn't a sixteen-year-old boy; it was a middle-aged man with the swell of a hairy potbelly I could clearly see in the photo and I'd deleted it so fast I'd barely had time to register the shock. We only had one computer, right there in the kitchen, and I was afraid to go into a chat room after that, knowing what would happen if somebody caught me.

When Jonathan first pushed my shoulders down and said, "Would you?" it wasn't anything like that photograph. Jonathan had a smooth, flat stomach, hip bones that jutted out like a girl's. He ran cross-country and his legs were skinny, his arms, he seemed so light, like there was so little of him. Until I'd felt the pressure of his hand on the back of my head and knew that wasn't true, he was stronger than he looked. He was a lot stronger than me.

Sitting in Laurent's chair, looking at the tissue box on Laurent's desk, the pile of crumpled tissues in the wastebasket by my feet, it was all getting jumbled together—the press of my palm against Jonathan's stomach, my legs spread wide on the horse. The stranger's picture still seared in the back of my brain, his cock thick, purple, jutting through the mass of dark hair. Jonathan's moan—how I'd felt that shiver when he said my name. When he said I was amazing, so much better than Natasha, right before I'd bent over to spit him into the grass.

And then there were the girls, the one on the computer cupping her breasts, the nipples dark as cherries and just as round and shining, as though they'd been licked clean.

It was over so soon. The whole thing, my own body, was outside my control. It had nothing to do with me in that chair, suddenly finding that I'd shoved across the leg of my shorts, my underwear, that I'd pushed my fingers there and now they were sticky, so much that I had to take one of those tissues—just exactly, I kept thinking, like Laurent did every time he was in there—and wipe at my hand, at the crotch of my underwear. At the damp I had left on the wood.

SIXTEEN

"Hope you don't mind we abandoned you." Ellen seemed brighter when she got home, more cheerful as she opened a bottle of Evian and sucked the whole thing down.

"I just read on the couch." But my heart was pounding. The taste in my mouth was all wrong. I'd triple-checked the browser history but what if I'd left a tab open or the blueprints askew or something so awful, I couldn't imagine yet what it would be.

And then Claudia walked in.

My insides shifted, a cascade of falling sand. I'd seen it but I hadn't seen it, I'd pretended it was possible not to see it that way. Claudia's hair wasn't long or sleek or straightened, but of course there were her cheekbones, her lips shiny with what I knew was strawberry gloss. I rushed to take the bag from her shoulder, Sabine's sippy cup, her toys that were left in the car. What was Laurent thinking? What had I—

"I've got it," I said quickly. "Let me help."

I hadn't hurt anyone. Not intentionally, not directly. I hadn't—myself—been cruel.

But my stomach had its doubts. It was supposed to matter what a person did when no one was watching, when it was just you alone in your mind. Ellen claimed she had a ton of work to finish, so

Claudia and I cut the crusts off Sabine's sandwich, Claudia and I walked her upstairs for her nap. Everything was a song: kissing the stuffed animals, turning down the covers. Sabine said stay, stay, and why shouldn't she get what she wanted? Childhood only lasted so long. Claudia lay down next to her and I perched at the foot of the bed, sucking in breath after breath to slow down my skittering thoughts.

Claudia sang quietly: "Close your eyes, close your eyes sweet girl."

And I did.

Until something brushed my calf and my eyes flew open—

It was only Claudia draping a leg over mine, stretching out in the small bed. How young she suddenly seemed. How much younger than Laurent, who had silver in his stubble and wasn't young at all.

"Shh," she whispered again, and I wanted to tell her I was sorry, I was so fucking sorry. But it would take years, so much more of my life, to understand what for.

A heat wave hit after that. At the pool, Sabine complained that the bricks were too hot on her feet. We were tired of the house, the country club—everything felt like a chore. Tired even of popsicles on the Sound, where at least there was a breeze from the water.

We decided on the aquarium in Norwalk. It was something to do with AC that wasn't the movies, which Ellen said Sabine was too young for. Every other family in southern Connecticut must have had the same idea. Sabine fidgeted in the lines, crying that she couldn't see. Kids raced down the corridors, their faces eerie in the underwater glow. They left smears on the tanks, everywhere they pressed their palms and wiped hot breath against the glass. I'd remembered it as magical, school trips to the New England Aquarium on the Boston seaport, the show with the sea lions leaping to raucous applause. My favorite had been the sea turtles, how they floated in slow, graceful arcs, following rules that were certain, innate. But when I carried Sabine to the tank, muscling past the bigger kids who'd only push her out of the way, the turtle curved toward us and she screamed. She wouldn't stop until I hurried her away, making apologetic faces at the mothers who inched back as if crying were contagious and they might catch what I'd brought into their midst.

"No," Sabine whimpered into the crook of my neck. "No, no, no."

It was no to the jellyfish, too. And the seals. The coral exhibit wasn't scary, but even Sabine found it boring.

"Wow," Claudia said. "I've never had an entire day be such a total bust."

I'd imagined the three of us strolling the exhibits together, Sabine enraptured by the wonders we'd exposed her to, eyes lit up with joy.

I'd even thought about the trinkets we'd buy after at the gift shop, how I'd keep the plush whale with me throughout college and say with quiet pride, "Oh, that? My best friend got it for me when we took my cousin to the aquarium, it was so cute." Or else I'd pick a key chain, something to carry with me always. Maybe Claudia would surprise me by choosing something first and we'd each keep it with us, remembering. Whatever we'd get for Sabine, she'd fall asleep with it under her arm. I'd tease her about it later, when she was older, when we were all older: "Claudia and I got you that when you were three, and you never let it go."

"Let's get out of here," Claudia said. "There's no point staying."

Walking over the hot asphalt to get to the car, I heard the music before I spotted the kids blasting it from a boom box in their open trunk. I thought kids but they weren't, they were my age or probably older, the girls in tiny shirts they'd cropped with scissors, the boys in shorts so low they were practically pants, their boxers billowing out the back. The bass of the music reverberated; every other word sounded like pussy and other things I couldn't even repeat in my head. The kids were shouting, calling each other that unrepeatable thing, and they could do what they wanted when it was just them but it wasn't just them, not here across from the aquarium where families went. If they said that at my school they'd be suspended, it didn't matter that they themselves were Black and laughing. I turned to share a look with Claudia. I wasn't afraid, but I was thinking of Sabine.

And then through the open door, I heard Claudia humming. She was humming the exact—I couldn't call it a melody because there wasn't one—but it was obvious she knew the song. She'd heard it before, enough to sing along as she buckled in Sabine, and she liked it. I touched the back of my neck; I found my reflection in the car window and it was nothing like how I'd seen myself in the mirror that morning. The distorted bass of the music, the distorted way we both seemed to me then. Claudia rolled down the window and the image of my stranger's face was replaced with her eyebrows stitching together. "You okay, hon?" she asked, and I couldn't say no, I couldn't say who are you. The shock was private and it was mine alone.

SEVENTEEN

Back at the house, I went upstairs. I said it was to change after the aquarium. But Ellen wasn't home and Sabine was downstairs with Claudia eating string cheese and I'd been thinking about it, I hadn't been able to stop thinking about it ever since Sabine had started her screaming and then that music had ruined it all. I stopped on the second-floor landing and listened to them downstairs counting strings of cheese. As quietly as I could, I slipped into my aunt and uncle's bedroom and closed the door.

Probably it was nothing, some forgotten thing like I'd first thought. I wasn't going to do anything. I just wanted to check.

In the bathroom, I reached under the sink. Laurent would never think to do this. He'd see hair products and think *woman*. It'd be out of his head just like that.

There was another bottle in the black toiletries bag. A fuller one. The old bottle had only a few pills left, but this was dated the day before, when Ellen had gotten her hair done and met some women—from the July fourth party, she'd said, waving a hand as though I were supposed to remember—for iced coffee in the afternoon.

But also. She'd had time to go pick up more pills.

After Sabine's nap she'd said she would come to the pool with us but then when we were in our bathing suits, waiting, she'd said, Oh! She'd forgotten—she had other things to do. But did she have other things to do? Or was this how she filled the hours when she was alone?

The cotton wad was still in the bottle. I pulled it out and tipped two pills into my palm. Ellen wouldn't notice. She had no reason to suspect.

I could have swallowed the pill but the last time I'd chewed it and I wanted it to be exactly the same: the brightness and the way it drenched me in a wave. I cracked it hard between my teeth, and then I tiptoed across the hall to the other bathroom and flushed. If Claudia heard me on the second floor, it'd seem like I'd stopped there to pee. But there was no sign of them yet. I climbed back to my bedroom and closed the door. I remembered to change my tank top Sabine had spilled juice on. And then I lay in bed and waited for the feeling, the nothing that was nothing like nothing at all. I didn't want the day on me; I didn't want to take it with me anymore. A shark could lose thirty thousand teeth in a lifetime, I'd learned that on one of the placards while Sabine was crying. Imagine losing that much of yourself and calling it living. If I could peel off my skin I'd start at my temples and work my way down. You look different, someone might say. And I'd smile and say thank you, because it was important to know how to take a compliment. That was the kind of thing Ellen might say.

A sound from the hall. How much time had passed? I knew I should get up but also I couldn't get up. "Yeah?" My voice didn't sound like my voice anymore. It didn't come from inside me at all.

"Knock knock?"

A smile stretched my skin. Claudia had come for me. How could I have thought she might not?

There came a second voice, a higher, lilting echo of the first, calling my name as the door opened. I unpeeled one eye and then the other, carefully and separately, as though each one were on opposite sides of my head. I wondered if this was a dream and if so what type of dream it would turn out to be.

"We couldn't sleep until we saw Cousin Rachel. Who I told you, Bean, was napping too and not playing without you."

"Napping, too," I repeated to the ceiling. "Definitely not playing." How did a person learn how to breathe? If I had gills, would everything be easy?

Claudia said, "See? It's nap time for everybody."

I liked the idea of this: a school of fish in sync with one another. Sabine didn't care about things like rumpled sheets or laundry. She came in and climbed on the bed.

"Back to your room, Bean. Remember? We had a deal that once we saw Rachel—"

"It's okay." I rolled to the side.

I wasn't supposed to say that—there was something Ellen wanted, something about keeping Sabine in her bed so she stopped climbing into the Corbins' at night. But it was just an afternoon, just one time and Sabine was already patting the pillow and telling Claudia to come nap with her and Cousin Rachel. It was a new game we could play and the rules were easy, you just had to lie there. Claudia made a show of yawning, saying how glad she was to have her nap time, and lay down next to Sabine, who had commandeered my pillow. The only space for me was next to Claudia. It wasn't my fault I had to press so close.

Claudia took my arm and draped it across her. "Thank you," she mouthed, then settled back on the pillow. Sabine's eyes had finally closed.

"Whatever it takes," I murmured into her ear, her neck, right against her skin.

"Let's wait a minute, so she doesn't wake up."

We lay there, quiet. Quiet for more than a minute; quiet for long enough that Claudia closed her eyes, too. My gills kept working, filtering. I pictured the capillaries like lace. In honors bio we'd dissected an earthworm and in AP it was a grass frog and a fetal pig. Earthworms breathed through their skin and frogs grew lungs once they were no longer tadpoles. They could breathe anywhere. I wanted to breathe anywhere, too. It was amazing to see such harmony: heart and lungs and liver. Dana was a vegetarian and thought the whole thing barbaric; she'd done a computer program and taken a test. I tried to picture Dana's face but all that came was the glitter of her makeup on the night of the dance. I closed my eyes and made a wish and when I opened them, my wish was granted. I could see Claudia's closed eyelids, her lashes, the small hairs she hadn't plucked under her brow. The freckle at the bottom of her earlobe. If I uncoiled my frog tongue, I could reach out and lick it.

EIGHTEEN

At the end of July, Ellen announced that she wanted to get out of Greenwich. It was a trip that should have changed everything. If I'd been paying attention. If I'd known what to do.

It started off simple enough: an invitation to Block Island to stay at a friend's house that was empty. "It's too hot to stay here," she said, as though we didn't have the house and the country club with a pool and air-conditioning and an endless stream of icy cool drinks.

"Doesn't that sound like fun?" Claudia asked Sabine, who was lying on a long piece of construction paper while Claudia traced an outline around her.

"Is the puppy coming?" Sabine turned toward his crate, where he'd been banished for chewing on her markers.

"Of course he is," Ellen said. "Tucker's part of the family, right?"

Sabine wiggled her toes where she lay. "Is Claudia coming?"

"Of course," Ellen repeated.

"Because she's part of the family?" Sabine scrambled up and looked at the outline of her, ten fingers and the shape of her hair. I thought nervously: now what? But Ellen only smiled. "Claudia's very special to us."

Claudia pulled out Sabine's favorite markers, all different shades of pink. They were going to fill in the outline with drawings, flowers, and hang it on her wall. "And *you're* very special to me." She bopped Sabine on the nose. "Where should we start, Bean? What do you want to draw first?"

"Is Rachel coming?" Sabine continued her questions as she lined up her choices: bubblegum, fuchsia, coral, peach.

It was a good question. I didn't think they'd just leave me here, but since when had the plan been to take me on vacation?

"Of course Rachel is coming," Ellen said.

"Because *she's* family?"

Sabine went back to the set of markers and selected a green that surprised me, until I realized it matched Claudia's fingernails. Ellen said, "Rachel's your cousin, remember? And she's here for the summer with Claudia, which is why everyone gets to be together. Aren't you so lucky, big girl?"

Sabine shouted yes, yes! She was so lucky, so happy, she had everyone she loved. She picked up a brown marker. I didn't stop her. Neither did Claudia. She was three strokes into her scribbles on the arm of her outline before Ellen swooped down to pluck the marker from her hand. "Not the mucky one, angel. Pick a pretty color that's you." She pointed to the pinks.

I wish I could say it vanished quickly, whatever flitted over Claudia's eyes. But it didn't. It was there, and I saw it. I saw it and I didn't say anything. It wasn't my place, it wasn't what my aunt really meant, it wasn't worth making a fuss. When a moment is over, don't you have to move on?

"Let's draw flowers in your hair." Claudia stepped in to stave off the meltdown while I sat there, silently. "And later we'll find real wildflowers to braid into a crown."

She passed Sabine red, yellow. Green for the stems. Sabine was excited again, she'd do anything Claudia said. And Ellen smiled, satisfied or relieved or maybe it was already forgotten as she stood, leaning into one hip, and said she'd better get ready for work.

How many times in the coming months would I pause in the middle of a problem set and think I'd found the answer, the most obvious, effortless way out of my family's predicament, and Claudia's, too. It didn't matter what had happened, that stupid marker or anything else. Claudia was special. Ellen had said so. If she remembered—even if she didn't. *I* remembered. I was there. I knew how beloved Claudia was.

But then I'd look down at the page, at my own writing from my own hand, and know that wasn't entirely true. No amount of *we can't live without you* makes a person as close as family. My aunt had been, in her roundabout way, perfectly clear about that.

Laurent was supposed to be home early from the city that Friday so we could leave, but after Sabine was packed and fed and our bags were down by the front steps, there was nothing.

Ellen called his office phone, his car phone, leaving messages to call her back, to at least say when he was on his way. "Is there news about River Point?" she demanded. "Is that what's taking so long?"

Hope radiated from her. And worry, irritation. Claudia and I took Sabine outside, but when we came back in there was still no Laurent, and also no Ellen. Claudia said, the only time I ever heard her say this, that she didn't know what to do. It was hours before Ellen emerged from her bedroom, and then there were more messages as she paced in the kitchen tapping her nails on the counter. By the time he finally pulled up, he was furious. Why had she called him so much? Didn't she understand that he was working?

"That's what you always say."

"That's what I'm always doing!"

It took forever to pack up his Escalade, even with all that time waiting Ellen had forgotten Sabine's books that Claudia had to run upstairs to pack. Laurent made another phone call and Ellen kept spitting, "Jesus Christmas—" and asking him when, really, when was this project going to be done. They kept arguing while Claudia got Sabine buckled in with her blanket and a little plastic koala she liked and Cheerios doled out one by one so they wouldn't drop and send Tucker into a frenzy.

The SUV was brand-new, the first of its kind, and it was enormous. They sat in the middle row while I pretended I was fine in the back with the dog. Traffic was terrible, there was always construction on I-95 plus the gridlock of summer Fridays at rush hour—that had been the whole point, after all, of leaving early. We were going to miss the last ferry, and then what would we do?

"We can still make it," Laurent repeated after Ellen told him again to slow down. He was weaving through traffic, bearing down on whatever car was in front of us and then swerving into the next lane if it inched even the slightest bit ahead. Tucker licked my shins, which must not have been covered in his obedience classes because I couldn't get him to stop.

Claudia and Sabine played I spy and silly games with the koala named, inexplicably, James. I looked out the window. No one had thought about dinner so Laurent conceded that he'd allow a drive-through. Sabine ate chicken nuggets with napkins spread all over the seats—Laurent was particular about the leather, nothing could spill. I had to hold Tucker by the collar as he whined, which meant I couldn't eat any of my burger. But I was too nervous anyway, with the way Laurent was driving and how it made my stomach drop.

He kept looking in the rearview mirror to rub the top of his head, as if checking that the skin was still there. For a moment, as I looked at him looking at himself in the mirror, our eyes met. I didn't look away and he didn't, either. Ellen said, hand to the dashboard, "And you say *I* don't pay attention?" His eyes jerked back to the road.

Was he happy? I wondered. Was he what could reasonably be described as a happy man?

It was growing late. Claudia hummed to Sabine, soothing her to sleep. In the darkness, in the quiet, I dug into my front pocket, still watching the rest of the car, making sure no one would notice. But Laurent wouldn't look back at me again. I fingered the small pill. Brought a hand to my mouth as though biting my nail and nibbled off the corner. It was just enough to make the lights of the highway glaze and glitter and turn to stars.

The gate was closing to the ferry as Laurent sped toward it, hitting the gas so sharply I thought for a moment that he was planning to crash right through it. He slammed the brakes and Sabine jolted awake with a cry.

"Laurent," Ellen scolded. "What in the world are you doing?"

He lowered the window. "Hey!" he called to the men ushering the cars in line onto the ferry, the cars that had gotten there before the gate closed. "Hey, you!"

"Sorry, sir." The attendant shook his head.

Laurent put the car in park and opened the door.

"What are you—" Ellen was still calling as he jogged over to the man.

"Mama?" Sabine groaned.

"She's right here," Claudia cooed, smoothing Sabine's hair until she closed her eyes again.

I watched Laurent out there talking to the guy. Arguing, really—that much was clear. Did he think they were going to change the rules just because he'd had a meeting and traffic and had to stop for chicken nuggets? Just because he wanted them to?

He jogged back to the car and slammed the door. I prepared for him to reverse angrily away. Would we find a motel, somewhere that took pets? Or would we simply turn around and drive the three hours home?

But the gate lifted. The attendant waved us through. Laurent's window was still down, bringing in salt air, diesel, and he extended his arm out the window, waving. "Thank you again," he said, his voice different, solicitous though no less in charge. I wished I knew what he'd said, how he'd done it. If he'd begged or concocted some story or simply declared how it would be. How, exactly, did a person get their way?

We were the last car to drive on. Ellen kept saying oh that was lucky, oh that was close. She went straight to the bathroom and Laurent got out of the car, putting Tucker on a leash, leaving Claudia and me behind with Sabine. "You go walk around," Claudia said. "I'll find a quiet place for her."

"I can help carry her."

"That's okay. Seriously, it's not your job."

So then I felt rebuked, because Claudia was right—I could do what I wanted, the same way Laurent and Ellen did what they wanted without a second thought. I was grateful, but it stung. That Claudia didn't need me. She was a necessary addition—the Corbins relied on her, no question. Whereas I was only brought along because they had to.

It wasn't a premonition. Nothing like that. It was just that I did think about it—how Claudia was always working. Even when the Corbins were present. Even when no one explicitly said so. If she was *on*, then her responsibilities were clear.

She was responsible for Sabine eating for Sabine drinking milk from her favorite red cup for every reminder that Sabine had to stop and pee before getting in the pool. For Sabine's happiness, for her safety, for things like not leaving her in a locked car not letting her wade into the ocean not crossing a parking lot without holding a trusted grown-up's hand.

I was, in some ways, responsible for those things, too. But I was seventeen. My age and my family's influence meant I wasn't named in the papers (although there were the journalists who'd find me later, the ones who'd keep digging as the years passed). Nothing, though—of course, oh, *honey*, nothing was my fault. I could never quite tell if the Corbins believed that. If they really believed that nothing was their fault, either. Maybe it was something they had to tell themselves because the alternative was that unbearable. Maybe anything could become true once you decided there was no other way.

On the top deck the wind assaulted me, not a cool relief but hot breath in my face, even at that hour. Passengers pointed to the lights receding from shore, the constellations blinking overhead. They were faint with the lights from the ferry and I had to squint for a long time, neck aching, before I could make out the pinpricks. I unwrapped the burger and tried to eat it leaning over the railing. It was soggy and lukewarm and the rolling of the ferry was making me seasick; it was all I could do to pick a spot on the blank horizon and stick with it. I threw the burger away and ate the rest of the pill instead. Chewing it thoughtfully, as white and brilliant as the foam the ferry left in its wake.

NINETEEN

Then came the wait to get off the ferry and the drive down the dark, winding road, the streetlamps spaced out and dim, the sense of the sea all around us. I was swimming in darkness, swimming as we found the house, floating through the long process of carrying everything in.

In the kitchen Laurent unpacked pancake mix and linguini while Ellen hefted towels, sunscreen, clothes. Only much later would I recall all the stairs, the suitcases she had to carry, how little Laurent stepped in to help. "Night swim?" he asked.

"You go on ahead," Ellen said, looking for the sheets. I'd thought he was joking but there he was heading out the back door, the beam of his flashlight bobbing along and then gone.

The house was cut into a hill so the entryway led straight up a flight of stairs to the second floor, which was really the main floor, its walls made up of windows that wrapped in all directions. More than once I turned and startled, thinking I'd come upon another room, another dimension. But it was only my reflection, my face soft and eggy in the lamplight, my limbs floating as though detached.

The master bedroom was on that second floor and was where

Laurent and Ellen would sleep, Sabine already tucked into the smaller room next door. Ellen handed me a stack of bedding and told me to pick a room, but there wasn't much choice. The other two bedrooms were downstairs, separated by a small, shared bathroom between them.

One of the rooms had a crib and a mattress still wrapped in plastic and leaning on the wall. I stood in the doorway, clutching the sheets. "I guess I'll take the couch upstairs."

Claudia took my arm before I could leave. "Don't be silly. Laurent will come back from his midnight skinny-dip and who knows how late he'll be working. Plus Sabine always gets up in the night, you know how she is."

I hoped she couldn't see my face tighten from even a joke about Laurent skinny-dipping, Laurent naked. I flashed to his study. *Ebony Teens.* I couldn't look at her then.

She took the sheets from me and marched to the other room. "Why not?" she said. "We're together all the time anyway." I was thinking about the ferry, the reminder, however subtle, that this was her job. Was it legal for her not to get her own room?

But maybe she didn't see it that way. Maybe it really was a sleepover among friends. She'd moved alone to a basement suite where she had a car and a phone and more closets than she had clothes for, and no one to talk to. She must have missed late nights, a whispered closeness, as much as I did.

"My friends and I used to basically play musical beds," she said as we tucked in the sheets. "Kelly and Justine were roommates freshman year—Kells and I bonded in this shitty sociology class, and then they were basically a package deal. Half the time I'd wind up sleeping in their room because who wants to stumble across campus when it's dark and snowing? Justine hogs the covers," she added. "So she was the one to avoid. Those beds are way smaller than this."

"It sounds like fun," I said. "Better than high school. My parents were insane about curfews."

"Everything gets better—you'll see. Even once we moved off campus, someone was always staying over. My first night at the Corbins', I couldn't sleep because of how quiet it was. I seriously considered getting some of Sabine's stuffed animals to keep me company."

"And now you have me!"

I did a *ta-da* pose, jazz hands and all. Claudia threw a pillow at me and said as long as snoring wasn't part of my routine. We laughed—or at least in my memories it feels like we were always laughing, always finding ways to be together. I know I failed her. I know that now. But I wish I could go back and remind her it wasn't all me. I wasn't the only one who made those late nights happen: curled up on couches, sharing that bed. Dana used to drape an arm over my shoulder in the hallway. Then Morgan and Ilana would find us and link their hands, too. We'd watch movies crammed four to a love seat. After big wins the whole team would pile together, arms and elbows and a chorus of screams, no telling where one person ended and another began. All I wanted was to belong again. Claudia got up to shower and I sank into the side of the bed that I supposed was mine because Claudia had set her headphones on the other nightstand. I listened to the sounds of her in the bathroom, the water that fell in different patterns as she moved.

She came out in a towel, water dripping down her shoulders, her back. I'd seen her bare feet every day of summer and yet it seemed impossibly intimate now, her ankles, the arch of her foot. The way she tucked her short hair under a silky purple cap that she said was for sleeping. She'd stripped off the last round of seafoam-green polish and painted her toes magenta at Sabine's request, and now she lifted one foot and placed it on the edge of the mattress, propping up her leg to slather on a thick, buttery lotion that came from a tub.

I rooted through my suitcase looking for a clean T-shirt to sleep in. The basketball shorts I suddenly wished weren't so ratty.

In the shower, standing in the steam Claudia had just made, using the soap she'd just rubbed on her body, I told myself to stop it. Stop being like this. We'd fallen asleep together countless times on the couch, in Sabine's bed, up in my room. Why was I acting like anything was different? I'd brought three of Ellen's pills—one for each day, if I wanted. I'd already chewed one but when I got out of the shower I crushed another, too nervous to wait. I brushed my teeth and rinsed my mouth and spat out the taste, then smiled at myself in the mirror. Smiled and hung up my towel and asked Claudia if I could borrow some of her lotion, then climbed into bed.

TWENTY

Laurent got a license from the island to go clamming. We needed to get out to the salt pond at low tide and he kept threatening to go without us if Ellen didn't hurry up and get the sunscreen on Sabine.

"Why didn't you say something sooner?" Ellen said. And: "They have clams at the store. They have restaurants. It's a specialty here—Karen and Mark will have recommendations."

But Laurent didn't want to go to a restaurant. He didn't want to wander the grocery store aisles like some ordinary man. We drove over a narrow spit of land sliced through the ocean and he unrolled the windows and stuck out his arm. The air was sharp and briny, wind blowing my hair out of the stubby ponytail I'd tied. Down in the shallows where the water pooled it was less windy, but that only meant it was hot.

Grasses sprouted in tufted clumps and in between them the water was warm. Foam along the edges; a shiny gum wrapper tangled in the grass. But if you squinted, if you didn't look too closely, it was beautiful—the grass and the blue of the water, the blue of the sky, clouds gathering along the horizon but far away, the way everything seemed far away if it wasn't right in front of me then. There were other people out, some in rubber boots up to their knees, others like us, barefoot, a pail and a net, ears turning pink in the sun. Every so often an engine started. Across the distance the white boats sped to and from the strait.

Laurent demonstrated how to dig but Sabine only wanted to splash where there weren't any waves. Claudia said she'd watch her, and Laurent turned back to his task. He used a shovel but I sank my hands into the sand, feeling the give of it and then the steady swirl as the water filled back in, displacing all my canyons. It never lasted, whatever impact I made. I pressed and pressed and still the world made its own shapes without me.

Laurent was annoyed that I wasn't finding more clams, that Ellen said her back was acting up and refused to bend down. He plunked them into the bucket of seawater and I watched them pile up, their black ridges lighter where the edges sealed, the sand and grit floating in the cloudy water. It was hard to believe they were alive, not just dark rocks clattering down. And then something would shift—an opening, a closing—a yellowed tongue probing out before the quick retreat. I bit my own tongue between my molars, feeling the flesh in my mouth. Quahogs, Laurent had said, which he'd learned in town buying the bucket and shovel and net. That was what we were supposed to call them. To be like the locals, he'd proclaimed, even though we weren't locals, anyone could see that.

Back at the house Laurent soaked the clams, rinsed them, soaked them again in salt water. In the fridge he left them in a bowl. Every time I reached for a juice box, Sabine's carrot sticks, I had to look away. Laurent had a plan for dinner: linguini in clam sauce with white wine and garlic, plain with butter for Sabine. He went running first, while Sabine was groggy waking up from her nap. "I've got her," Ellen said to Claudia. "You've done so much—go relax." So Claudia left to use the outdoor shower.

And even though Ellen was massaging her hip, even though she'd done what she never did and told us she was hurting, I left, too.

I wasn't following Claudia. I just wanted to be in the sun. I walked barefoot over the grass in the yard, the rocky sand that sloped to the edge of the cliff. Barest hint of the sea through the gaps, but it was out there. Behind me, against the house, Claudia's feet stood under the wooden stall, her magenta toes on the slats, the spray hitting.

Her bathing suit dropped: two patterned pieces at her feet. She used those bright pink toes to pick them up, and then the cascade of more water as she wrung them out. An arm draped over the edge, the fabric hung over. I made myself turn away.

Hands in my pockets, toes in the sand. Brambles clawed their way out of the dunes. I must have heard the dog barking for some time before I registered it as nearby. It was just another part of the background of things: the surf, the shower, a distant car. The dog.

And then it wasn't, but I still didn't hurry. Tucker must have gotten out. That was what I thought. Tucker was going to be running around the yard and hopefully not the road and Laurent would be furious, and how would we bring him back?

But there came a different noise, a throaty growl instead of Tucker's usual whine, and I started to run.

There was Tucker outside, straining on the leash tied to the railing. Who had put him there? The other dog was bigger, thicker, with a dark gray coat and small ears. He must have come from one of the houses up the road, who could tell—it all happened so fast. It was a cliché but it was the only thing I'd later be able to say with any certainty: how the dog had simply appeared, leaping and barking, saliva so thick it dripped from its gums. Was that a sign of rabies? The dog had a collar but that didn't make me less scared. It lunged for Tucker, and that squeal—that awful noise I'd never be able to unhear. The snap of the dog's jaw. The sound Tucker's ear made as it tore.

He howled, his tail wagging madly as though overjoyed. But there was a wild, untamed terror in his eyes as he shook his head and the blood splattered over my front, some of it warm on my chin. He strained on his leash as I yelled for my aunt—Ellen—a grown-up—she was all I could think of.

The screen door slammed. The sight turned my insides to water. Not Ellen but Sabine, calling *Rachel! Rachel!* As though we'd come outside to play.

I shouted for her to go inside, get her mama, as the other dog growled. Sabine screamed, and Tucker strained harder. The other dog jumped back, circled, lunged again, and I grabbed Sabine and turned to shield her with my body. I didn't know what made me do it. If it was even the right thing to do. My heart was the weight of a clamshell dropped through my chest. But later when I looked back it was hard to piece together: Was the dog really going to bite Sabine, or had I made it all worse? Claudia in a towel, soap on her face, running up the sharp stones in her bare feet, the shower still running.

"What's happening?" she cried, but it was obvious with the dog and with Tucker's ear bleeding. I shoved Sabine inside but she stayed calling for me, for Claudia, for her mother, who was nowhere to be found. She cried harder, kicking the door, rattling the screen.

Which was why my back was turned, why I didn't see it happen. But would I have been able to stop it, if I had? I turned and Claudia shouted, or Claudia shouted and I turned. It was Tucker, strangely, who didn't make a sound as the other dog clamped down on his neck.

He shook his head and Tucker shook with him. Blood oozed from the puncture points of his canines but mostly there was surprisingly little of it. I supposed the objective was to squeeze, not rip. The noise Claudia made—something guttural, a sputtering out. Or maybe that was the sound of my own insides. In my own, different way, torn apart.

"Mrs. Corbin!" Claudia cried, but I already knew she wasn't coming. We were alone and the dog was going to die. I was going to watch this puppy suffocate before my eyes, and Sabine was going to see it,

Sabine who was screaming and banging on the door. I pulled back on Tucker but that only broke the flesh more. I was afraid to get near the other dog's mouth, to have my hand by those glistening teeth. I was crying, I just wanted it to be over. I wanted the end to be fast.

Claudia found a stick in the yard. She shoved it in the dog's open mouth, thick with spit and froth and Tucker's jammy blood. It was her idea, and Laurent would say, later, how quick Claudia was, how she thought on her toes—

—and the defense would try to bring this up in the trial, saying it showed Claudia's dedication, the family's ongoing gratitude, her established record of outstanding care—

But I didn't want to look, I could barely comprehend what was happening. Claudia shouted at me to grab Tucker's collar as soon as the dog let go. I wanted to say no but I had to. Didn't I have to? It didn't matter how scared I was. I imagined, somehow, that it was Jules's body sweating and trembling under my hands, Jules who I alone could save.

The other dog let out a sound so human in its pain. Or maybe I was the one transformed by a fear so animal that later even my sweat would smell different to me, and I'd worry that Alexandra Harkness from Kentucky could smell me, that everyone at Swarthmore would know some part of me was starting to rot. I was so surprised by the dog's strange wail, I almost let go of Tucker. What kind of doctor would I make if I was so easily undone?

But the stick worked. The dog opened its mouth to snap at Claudia and she shoved it deeper into its mouth, she must have really hurt it, and the dog unlatched. It was enough. It had to be enough. I had my arms around Tucker, wriggling, bleeding, terrified Tucker, and managed to unhook the leash before dragging him into the house. He squirmed and thrashed, his torn ear and the side of his neck bleeding warm down my arms. I dropped him and he went racing, toenails skittering across the floor, a smear of blood trailing behind him. "Tucker," I called. "Tucker, come." But he hadn't been trained like that. And he was just a puppy. He went straight under the couch, into the far corner, bleeding on the rug. Could he die from that? I hadn't known it could come out so dark.

The first time I saw a gunshot patient, it would all come back to me: the shock, the smell. That dog and the warm slick of his blood. My hands were steady, because I'd been trained by then or because I knew uncertainty was no longer an option. But that afternoon, it was Claudia's idea—of course it was—to get salami from the fridge. She was still wrapped in the towel and had soap bubbles drying on her chin, but she got the dog to slink out, his ears pressed flat. I dropped a blanket on him, one of the blankets folded on the couch, to hold him in place. Stanch the bleeding—that much I knew. We'd have to throw out the blanket but the Corbins could buy their friends a new one. That was what I kept thinking. Better to buy a new living room than a new dog.

Sabine banged on the door to her parents' bedroom. I was about to tell her to wait, Claudia had to get dressed and then we'd find her parents. I must have misheard earlier and they were both at the beach—that was why no one had come.

And then the door opened and Ellen appeared. Standing in the bedroom doorway, blinking slowly before her mouth opened and she let out, as if a beat too late, a gurgle. A gasp.

Outside, later, I'd walk the path again, from the yard past the shower and then up to the door, to the place with the grass still matted with blood. And then inside the door, up the stairs to the second floor. I'd try to figure out if it was possible to be inside the bedroom and not have heard our shouting.

But I supposed it was; I supposed I already had my answer. Because Ellen kept crying, "What's wrong? What happened?" as she pawed at a sobbing Sabine, at the blood on her shirt that had come from my arms when I'd lifted her. I tried to explain that we needed a hospital, a vet, it had to be fast. The dog was panting, his gums turning white—didn't she see what that meant?

"Go and use the outdoor shower," she'd told Claudia. "The view of the water is heaven." That was what she'd called it, heaven, as she'd laughed in the kitchen. As she'd ushered us both out the door while Sabine played with her books on the floor.

TWENTY-ONE

"Maybe she had earplugs in."

Claudia said this as we walked on the beach. It was dark by then, and the clouds from the morning had rolled all the way in. I'd imagined what the sunsets would be like, walking down to the point, the moon shining clear off the ocean. But there was nothing, we were only lucky not to have rain.

Ellen and I had driven around that afternoon looking for a medical center; a man at a gas station finally gave us directions as Ellen clenched the wheel. I was afraid she was going to hit something, a kid or a cyclist or another dog, that was how fast she'd been driving. I carried Tucker wrapped in the blanket as I charged through the automatic doors. "Please. You have to help." I was crying all over again. At the medical center they were used to treating sunburns, boating accidents, tourists who cut themselves shucking oysters. It was nothing like where I hoped to work someday. But they stabilized the dog enough for Laurent to take him on the ferry, drugged and lying in the back seat of the car. He was in surgery at the emergency animal hospital on the mainland. Laurent would have to stay overnight.

There were calls to animal control, the local police. On the phone Laurent made me describe the dog so he could file the report, but all I knew was dark and medium-sized and short ears. "A boxer, maybe?" Claudia said when she took the phone from me. A pause, then: "Sorry. My brother had fish." The dog had a tag, it wasn't a stray, but how could we have gotten close enough to read it? Probably Laurent was cursing the dog the whole trip out. Cursing me for not doing something sooner. But maybe that's just how I feel now—angry, ashamed, replaying what I should have done, not just then but after. "It's a small island," Ellen had reassured me as she'd dabbed dish detergent on the couch and I crawled on my hands and knees with paper towels, looking for splatters we'd missed. "They'll find the owners."

Now Claudia's flashlight bobbed along the path to the water. The beam caught the edges of the dunes and then faded until there was no telling what was sand or ocean or sky. She turned off the flashlight and I said wait, I couldn't see a thing, but she said to give it a minute, our eyes would adjust.

In the darkness I skidded my toes over the sand, feeling its ridges, its shifting dips beneath me. I was afraid to step off the path, to wander into the brush or in the wrong direction. Claudia said, "Come here," and took my hand as if I were Sabine. Except not like that—it didn't feel that way at all.

Near the surf the sand turned cooler. Firmer. Damp. We'd been there just that afternoon and yet the whole beach was different. The whole world, it seemed.

At dinner, Ellen had said, "Order whatever you want, girls," and so the four of us cracked jumbo lobsters we didn't have to trap and kill and cook ourselves. And there were potato wedges, salad, crab cakes, rolls. Melted butter dripped down Sabine's chin, her tears at last forgotten. Even Ellen finished her plate, saying how glad she'd be to throw those goddamn clams away. "I don't know," I finally said to Claudia—about Ellen, the earplugs, but why would she have them? Maybe it was the heavy doors, the distance to the second floor. Maybe the dogs, our shouting, hadn't been as loud as it had seemed to us then.

I was starting to distinguish, a little bit, the ocean from the shore. The foam as it moved over my toes and then receded. Everything looked different when you weren't inside it; when you had to go back and replay it but without yourself smack in the center anymore. What would have happened if I'd said why I thought Ellen didn't hear us that afternoon, if I'd let myself face it head-on? My lobster from dinner had small red dots inside and even all these years later, I can close my eyes and taste how they'd popped and turned to liquid on my tongue. The same way, if I really want to, I can imagine the warmth of Claudia's hand still holding mine.

Five and a half years from that summer, in my first year of medical school, I'd dissect my first man—a cadaver—in anatomy. He was sixty-three. He looked like my father when he went too long without trimming his beard. It was clear no one else in the class had been around a dead body before and they were nervous. But it was possible to have seen a dead body before and still be nervous. Manny, my first and only real friend at Hopkins, said to me after that I was the only one who wasn't weird about it. "Weird how?" I asked.

"Just, you know. How nothing gets to you."

"Oh," I said, and a laugh escaped like a burp, something I should have excused myself for. He didn't ask what was so funny, but I couldn't have explained how wrong he was.

The first time I cut into live flesh was on a warm, breathing, anesthetized juvenile pig, the back of its smooth, pink head exposed. Hopkins hadn't phased that out yet, and it was one of the things I liked about the place—no matter how realistic, a simulator wasn't the same. I didn't make the first cut deep enough. The skin was springy, surprising. Different from the cadavers, which themselves were different from the slippery cuts from the butcher that Manny bought so we could practice removing the gallbladder, careful not to nick the purple liver still attached. We'd slept together a few times by then, but it was already fading. Taking off the pieces of the pig's skull, peeling back the membrane of the dura mater, I saw the brain how it was supposed to be, pulsing and intact and so alive, it was all I could do not to burst into tears.

Claudia and I walked down the beach until the lights from the houses above the bluff receded, until there was nothing but the roar of the surf in the clouds.

"Want to?" she asked, and I said, "What?" as she started peeling off her clothes. Her shirt dropped to the sand. Her shorts. She ran into the water in her bra and underwear. But even if someone came along, how would they know it wasn't our bathing suits? Technically it wasn't any different.

It was freezing, and I started to scream. I was screaming for the cold, screaming for the force of the waves that knocked me off-balance, screaming for Claudia to wait, to not go too far. Screaming to let it all out. Claudia tackled me, pulling me down with the waves, the two of us rolling through each crash as though we were drunk, or happy, or high, when really it was just the night, it was just how it felt sometimes. This thing she brought out in me, an awful elation, the way desire can come from inside you and still feel like the grip of a stranger, such unfamiliar hands around your throat.

We were walking back, dripping, my denim shorts sticking to my thighs, when she said, out of nowhere: "But where was she, Rachel? Really? I keep thinking about how much worse it could have been."

I bit my lip, licked off the salt. "She was upstairs," I said carefully, unsure where this was leading. "In the bedroom, remember? I was the one who'd gone outside."

She grabbed my forearm. That night lying next to her, I'd run my hand over the spot as though I could still feel the pressure of each fingertip, wet and cool and smelling of the sea.

"But didn't she say she'd watch Sabine?"

We arrived at the house, the car still gone, the weekend ruined. I had goose bumps up my legs but I didn't want to go in. It should have been the opening I'd been waiting for—I could whisper that Ellen might be taking pills not exactly as prescribed, and what if that was the answer to Claudia's question?

But the words wouldn't come. It would be an admission of my own guilt as much as my aunt's. And I knew what would follow. Ellen would get in trouble. No one would trust me again. And what about Sabine? This was her mother we were talking about. This was Claudia's job, which she needed to last through the summer and beyond.

"I'm not sure," I said. "It's hard to remember exactly how it happened."

Her grip on my arm tightened. "I never would have gone outside if she hadn't told me to. You know that, right?" I nodded. I felt very certain, in that moment, that I did. "So why didn't she make sure Sabine stayed inside? How did she not know what was happening?"

She kept her voice low, and in the thin porchlight I caught her glance at the windows, the darkened wall of glass blocked by curtains inside. Her eyes swung back to me. I couldn't say no, that wasn't it—Ellen had done nothing wrong.

And yet I couldn't face the intensity of her gaze, how much she wanted me to say yes. Yes, it was all Ellen's fault. Yes, what was going on with that woman that she missed an entire dogfight. That her daughter could have been seriously hurt. That she'd left it for her niece and a twenty-one-year-old in a towel to handle by themselves.

"She did say her hip was hurting," I said weakly. "Maybe she went to get an Advil or something."

I thought Claudia might be able to piece it together—Ellen's pain, her forgetfulness. I just needed someone else to do the messy work while I kept my hands clean.

But it wasn't enough.

"She must have put Tucker outside," Claudia said.

"Or Laurent did—but it wasn't like they could've predicted what would happen."

"Of course not. It was an accident, that's not what I meant."

A relief, then. She wasn't accusing anyone.

"I feel terrible," I said. "For Tucker, for Sabine. And for you—I should have done something sooner."

Her voice softened. Her grip went slack. "You can't take care of everyone, Rach. It wasn't on you."

A new stillness as we crept inside the house without Laurent awake and working, the dog whining to play. For a second I wondered if Ellen and Sabine were even there, if something had happened—but that was absurd, they were sleeping. And Claudia didn't suggest this. She didn't say we'd better not leave Sabine alone with Mrs. Corbin anymore, this is a problem and we need to decide who to tell. She left the bathroom door open while she brushed her teeth so she could keep talking. "I just assumed she must've heard something. Because she was with Sabine, and Sabine came to find you." She spat, rinsed. Wiped her mouth. "But I don't know. Like you said, it was a lot. And she seemed tired. It must have been too fast to figure out."

The last pill was in a tissue in the bottom of my toiletries bag. When it was my turn to use the bathroom I pulled out my toothbrush, face scrub, slipped the pill free when Claudia wasn't looking. Broke it in half with my teeth and let the dust fall on my tongue.

I brushed my teeth and got into bed, the sand gritty between my toes where the hose hadn't rinsed it all off. Claudia turned out the light. The darkness sank into me. I felt it like a thousand fingers dimpling my skin.

"I know she feels really bad," I whispered. My lips were soft. They might not have even been moving. "She was freaking out in the car."

Claudia turned beside me. "I bet." It wasn't said without sympathy, and I closed my eyes.

Maybe I fell asleep. Maybe I left my body altogether. Maybe I became nothing but lungs, and never needed, and never took up space, and lived on air.

Sometime later but perhaps not later at all I felt her shift again. I rolled over, rolled closer. Her eyes were closed but I knew she wasn't sleeping. I could feel her awakeness in the bed: her head too stiff, her breathing anything but shallow. I could have whispered "Hey," or "You awake?" or simply: "I know." But I was afraid. Or not afraid but uncertain, untethered, un-selfed. It's hard to remember now what it felt like, not just being young but young in that world at that time. Always, always, the careful distance you agreed to keep. Even face to face, nose to nose, two separate bodies lying in the dark.

I'd remember, of course I would, the things Claudia said that night—about Ellen, our shouting, and how she, Claudia, would never leave Sabine unless Mrs. Corbin said it was okay. Ellen had been clear that she was free to go outside. I'd told Claudia as much.

But by the time I was called to the stand, I'd be too angry to repeat it. I wasn't going to sit there in the spotlight answering questions nobody had asked.

TWENTY-TWO

And how was I supposed to tell it anyway? How to account for those days when, after the fact, I was called to make sense of them all? Some part of it still feels so simple: We drove back from Block Island. Laurent made calls behind closed doors. Ellen left sixty dollars in the kitchen each morning with notes for us girls to have fun. The dog nipped at his cone. The summer went on.

We went to story time at the library, we went to the country club, we put Shirley Temples and Arnold Palmers and french fries on the Corbins' tab, and at the end of the day the staff brought the bill for Claudia to sign. We looked for butterflies, fairies, seashells, stones. We made finger paint. We made fashion shows. We made brownies and snickerdoodles and lemon squares but those burned. We bought rainbow sprinkles that Sabine scooped from the tin when no one was looking, her teeth rainbow, her tongue orange and blue. Wondering how we'd caught her. Why we couldn't stop laughing so hard.

Even when I was in it, deep inside those August afternoons, I missed them as though memory were a solid thing, each new day a polished piece of sea glass piled up stone by stone in my heart. Those rich, sticky hours in the backyard with Claudia as Sabine finally settled down for her nap and Ellen was nowhere to interrupt us. Our legs intertwined on the couch, our shared cigarette curling its smoke to the sky. Talking, always talking. Together.

And then Laurent came home with a bottle of champagne and shouted for Ellen to get off the phone.

"It's Billie," she protested. And, after she'd gone and done it anyway: "What's gotten into you?"

"You don't need that woman anymore," he said. "You can quit if you want to. You can do anything now."

The bubbles fizzed. There was a glass for Claudia, too, and sparkling cider for Sabine in a sippy cup, and for me but at least I got a flute. Ellen said we could trade, it was too early for her, and why wouldn't he calm down.

He passed her two plane tickets. Claudia held her glass, not drinking, as if waiting to see what they'd do.

"North Carolina?" Ellen asked.

"It seems you've made quite the impression on Lori."

Ellen's hand flew to her mouth. "Oh my god," she said. "Oh my god. *No.* Please don't joke about that." But he wasn't joking. The governor had a house in the mountains, and he'd invited some friends down to golf. Some friends he hoped would include the Corbins. He wanted to know them better, to socialize. To *talk*.

Ellen dumped her cider into the sink and poured champagne until it foamed over the top. "Stop kidding," she repeated. "Stop doing this to me."

Laurent laughed. I'd never heard him laugh like that. I don't think I have, since. He tossed back the rest of his champagne, poured another, drank it down. "Time and a half," he said to Claudia. "For this weekend."

"Actually, I'd been planning to go home—"

"Double," Ellen interrupted. "Whatever you need. Please?"

Claudia put down her glass, untouched. "I'll tell my mom." She smiled. She beamed her dimples right at both of them. "Congratulations."

~

I thought Laurent couldn't become governor himself, being French. But Claudia looked it up that weekend when we were alone, speculating, and it turned out you only had to live in the state. Ellen would really be something as First Lady. "She could do it," I told Claudia. "Lori better watch out."

"The governor himself better watch out," Claudia teased. "Don't you hear the way she says the words *governor's mansion*? It's like she gets a little drool she has to suck back."

"My aunt doesn't drool!" I cried as she made slurping noises.

"Maybe it's an internal drool," she conceded. "But still. Swarthmore better teach you to expand your mind."

She wagged a finger in my face, and I laughed because I still thought we were joking—I always thought we were joking. We were sitting on the couch eating pepperoni pizza, the kind of thing we could only do with Ellen and Laurent away. We'd rented *The Little Mermaid* and Sabine was enraptured, even though Claudia kept saying it was so sexist, she'd forgotten how awful it was, we were probably warping Sabine's mind in some permanent way. When the movie was over, our greasy fingers licked clean, we built a fort in the family room with pillows and piles of sheets and used flashlights to read to her in the dark. Even Tucker slumped in there with us, the wounds in his neck faintly puckered, his small heart trembling against my thigh. We let Sabine fall asleep in the fort, she wanted to so badly. And what was the point of having your parents away if you didn't get to enjoy it?

Everything was fine. Better than fine. I said this to the Corbins, I said it to their lawyer, I said it on the stand. I raised my hand and I made the promise that was asked of me and said the words I'd practiced, the ones I believed in completely: that really, all weekend, Sabine was happy. Claudia was perfectly normal. Her *state of mind.* I didn't know whose side that helped or hurt or what it was supposed to accomplish. But it was true. Wasn't it? So what if I'd gone to look in Ellen's bathroom as soon as they'd left for the airport and found the little black case was missing. Maybe she'd brought it with her. Maybe she'd flushed it away. Who was I to speculate? Sometimes I'd stumble on the stand, forgetting what I was supposed to say and what I absolutely wasn't. But a woman on the jury would keep nodding encouragingly, a blond one in the front row who was the youngest and who I'd decided was the nicest and liked me the best. Even though they never spoke, the jurors—they just sat there listening and sometimes taking notes and sometimes making minute changes to their expressions they must have thought nobody picked up on.

The second night, Sabine fell asleep before we were even through the first story, that was how much Claudia had exhausted her dancing to Laurent's old CDs, Frank Sinatra and Elvis and funny French pop, Sabine flailing her arms, spinning in circles until she collapsed on the cushions in a pile of giggles. Claudia and I danced like I was the man and she was the girl with her hands on my shoulders. And then she was the man who led me around the living room, who dipped me extravagantly as Sabine cheered.

"She's great," Claudia said cheerfully into the phone when Ellen called. "She went crazy over the poached carrots—Mr. Corbin was right, she loves them that way."

I flashed Claudia a thumbs up. She was good. I distinctly remember thinking that: how good she was with Sabine. How deft at managing my aunt.

On the counter, the baby monitor crackled as Sabine rolled over inside the fort. I tiptoed across the kitchen, placing a finger to my lips when Claudia made a face that asked what I was doing. But she didn't falter in recounting our day as I opened the wine fridge. In their Manhattan apartment the Corbins had a little one that fit under the counter, but this one went floor to ceiling and they had more wine in a cabinet in the parlor—the overflow that didn't fit, or maybe just the kinds that weren't as good. I picked one from the bottom. Hadn't Claudia and I done enough that weekend? Didn't we deserve a Saturday night?

Claudia's eyebrows arched. I guessed this was different from drinking beers in her apartment, beers she'd bought herself on a night she wasn't working.

But she must have seen we were safe. Into the phone she said, "I'm so glad you're having a great time! Sabine was out like a light, no complaining. And the weather's supposed to be nice tomorrow, so we'll keep her busy."

I peeled off the foil. Claudia didn't stop me. She didn't shake her head or mouth *No fucking way,* things she'd never done to me but certainly she could have.

She twisted one of her curls between her fingers. "She'll be so excited to see you!" And then, after she hung up: "You sure about this?"

"Ellen won't notice. And I didn't pick a fancy one."

"They're all fancy."

"It's not one of the ones they'd pay attention to."

I was fiddling with the corkscrew, trying to remember how my parents did it, when Claudia came up close behind me and reached around on either side. Here was how to hold it, how to twist. She positioned my hands on the levers and put her own hands over them as she pressed down. Her chin rested in the crook of my shoulder. I smelled the coconut of her lotion, felt the tickly brush of her hair.

"Don't say I never taught you anything useful." Still her hands on mine as we wriggled the cork free. "Just—don't get me fired. Okay?"

But she laughed, and again I thought she was joking. The whole family loved her. Look at what they'd pay to keep her. I thought that meant we were, both of us, equally protected. Equally beloved.

"They gave me champagne, remember? Anyway, you can say I drank it by myself and you tried to stop me."

"I think it'd be better if I told them I had no idea."

"That too." I filled two wineglasses, the large goblets Ellen liked best. "Cheers." I took a sip. "Wow."

Claudia swirled her glass. Sniffed. "You have no idea how good you have it. How many bad decisions could have been avoided if I'd just had better booze?"

I made a face. "You? I don't believe it."

"The first week of college was all about alcoholic root beer and losing my virginity."

Now I was laughing, shocked but not really, eager for more. "Who was the lucky guinea pig?"

"Some poor guy in my dorm. He was cute but like, not that cute. Half the floor saw me take the walk of shame with my bra falling out of my pocket."

She took a bow as I clapped. And then I told her about Jonathan. Not about Natasha, how my friends thought I was a liar or a hypocrite or whatever it was that I'd done. Just that there'd been this guy, only it didn't go anywhere and now I didn't even know why I'd liked him.

"Maybe I only thought I was supposed to like him. Some kind of aspirational liking. Or maybe it was the idea of him. The idea of me as someone who was with him." I took a large swallow. "God. I didn't know it'd sound so depressing to say that out loud."

She refilled both glasses, fuller than I'd done. "Don't feel bad. I dated this other guy for two years—"

"Two *years*?"

"But then I dumped him last year. There wasn't anything wrong with him. He was great, actually. LeRoy. Did I tell you about him? He was older so he graduated ahead of me and moved to Palo Alto."

"He didn't want to do long-distance?"

"It was me, actually. He kept saying it was perfect timing that I'd be out of school early, like that was the only reason I'd accelerated. He'd pay for my plane tickets out there during break, I'd move in after graduation, and it was like . . ."

She sucked in a breath.

"Like he had your whole life planned for you?" I offered.

"I thought I'd miss him but the fucked-up thing is that I don't."

"That's not fucked-up. It means it's a good thing you dumped him."

"Two years," she reiterated. "Two-thirds of my college career and I didn't even care when it was over. I'm emotionally stunted. He called me incapable of love. I could be living in California right now with a guy who makes bank."

"I've known you for less than two months and I'm definitely not your boyfriend"—my exaggerated laugh—"but I call bullshit."

"Granted, he'd taken a red-eye just for me to tell him this. So, maybe that had something to do with it."

I'd been leaning against the kitchen island, and now I stood up straight. "You made him *fly out here*?"

"I thought doing it over the phone was worse. But, yeah." She raised her glass. "Given the current Connecticut market—cheers to sweet, sweet spinsterhood."

"We'll start a commune. With cats."

As though that were what it meant to not have a boyfriend. As though loneliness, mockery, were our only other choice.

We clinked glasses, laughing stupidly at ourselves and our misfortunes. After we finished the bottle I found another, and sometime after that was done, Claudia had an idea. Or was I the one who made us do it? Claudia had her version, later, but that wasn't the only account. What I remember, what I know for sure, is that upstairs in the master bedroom we found the bed as neat as ever, the only sign that anyone lived there a glass of water by Laurent's side of the bed.

She picked it up and drank the water down. "Gross," I said. "Don't move anything."

We opened their closets. Claudia tried on Ellen's snakeskin boots, draped her purses and scarves over her arm. "This one's wild," she said, pulling out the sequined dress Ellen had bought for the governor's birthday. "It'd look better on you."

"I'm too tall!"

"Nonsense, you're perfect."

I turned in front of the full-length mirror, seeing how it clung. Tighter than it was on Ellen, but Claudia insisted that was how it should be. "Mrs. Corbin's clothes swim on her," she said, and it jolted me, that the aunt who was mine was the same woman others saw, too. I thought about the pills and what they could do over time. I might have started to say something—or do I only want to think I'd found ways to keep trying? I stumbled in the heels, my ankle giving out, and Claudia caught me before I toppled—

I kicked off the shoes, they didn't fit anyway, and then there was a third bottle of wine, cherry-sweet, and no need for glasses, Claudia drank from the bottle and wiped her mouth before passing it to me. We made clumsy knots in Laurent's ties, slipped our bare feet into his calfskin loafers. A sudden, shared intake of breath when the static on the baby monitor rippled and we waited to hear what Sabine would do.

But she was only rolling over. We giggled, but quieter now. We still had to be careful.

That was what made it fun, though. Making sure the dresses were hung back where they belonged, blotting a mystery stain from a velvety shirt. Standing in the closet in our underwear, I took Claudia's hand. For a second I wished Dana were there, that we were all twirling in Ellen's diamonds with Morgan and Ilana and laughing.

But the thought was simply habit, evaporating as quickly as it had formed.

"Have you been in here?" I led her into the bathroom, the huge, opulent space with the tub perched up on a marble step, the porcelain clean and white and gleaming. I wasn't worried about the cabinet under the sink. There was nothing left in there to find.

In the large mirrors framed in light I caught my face, my mouth a purple slash stained by the wine, my eyes glassy and wet. My underwear sagged below my butt, not like the tight, cheeky lace cupping Claudia just right. My bra was equally boring, my breasts uninteresting, the nipples small but poking through the fabric. Claudia had called me perfect in the bedroom, but that was only playing dress-up, a game of pretend. I could see my pores, the sprout of hair on my upper lip, the flush of my cheeks exaggerated in the overhead light. But even Ellen had her creams and sprays and bottles, the makeup, the paint—anything was possible. You just had to decide to commit.

"Be right back," I said as Claudia began filling the tub. I wondered what kind of name LeRoy was, if he was Black, if he was as hot as I assumed—

But she'd dumped him, she didn't want him. These were our new lives, the ones we got to make now.

I wasn't sure how much more wine I could take, but someone

had gifted the Corbins a fifth of Bombay Sapphire in a bottle of swimming pool blue and I remembered Ellen saying they'd have to save it for parties, gin gave her a headache. And Laurent preferred whiskey, so it wasn't like they'd miss it if we took a little. I could fill the rest with water, the way Dana did at her house, and no one would be any wiser.

Upstairs I brought champagne flutes, the bottle of gin, fresh-squeezed tangerine juice Ellen had bought from the farmers' market and told us to finish. "Ooh," Claudia said. "Fancy." I poured too much gin into the flutes and topped the rest with juice. Claudia was sitting on the edge of the tub, her toes splashing. Every so often she reached down and ran her fingers through the stream. I tried not to stare at the swell of her breasts as they moved with her, dropping forward and then settling down against her chest. Would Dana have liked Claudia? Or would she have envied her, our friendship, the better, more interesting person she had made me?

"Whoa," I said, coughing as I swallowed the drink. "Too strong." I added more juice but it didn't make a difference.

I was ready to stay like that, sitting on the edge of the tub in our bras and underwear, but then Claudia deemed it full enough and dropped herself in.

"Don't leave me here alone."

She did it first. I only followed. Although before I got in, I swung my feet out of the tub, dripping water on the floor. In the cabinet I found what I was looking for: bath salts and lavender petals and foaming bubbles made with jojoba and vitamin C and other things that were supposed to be good for your skin, in the kind of packaging that said they cost a fortune. I dropped in the petals, fistfuls of salts, a squirt of the liquid that immediately started to foam until Claudia was laughing, calling for me to stop, we were going to drown.

The water was hot, hot on my ankles, my shins. Hot on my hips.

A burst of searing liquid at my middle as I dropped all the way in, my underwear heavy and sliding off me.

But with the bubbles, it wasn't like Claudia could tell.

I sighed, sinking deeply. "This is perfect." I reached for the champagne glass with the gin and tangerine juice gone warm and sticky in the steam.

Laughing, splashing. Claudia's voice came from across the tub, from across some great distance. But also in the close heat of the bathroom she sounded right in my ear. Our feet caught in the water as I shifted. Claudia pulled away and I mumbled, "Sorry." But afterward when we bumped again, she didn't move and so I didn't, either. Under the bubbles I couldn't see her body, not even the distorted ripple of her underwear. Just her arm reaching for the glass, trickling water and bubbles over the edge of the tub. The sheen on her face as she drank.

So I knew there were things about me that she couldn't see. My one hand on the glass. The other hand under the water, under the bubbles, sliding beneath the useless strip of fabric that couldn't hide me anymore.

"You got quiet," Claudia said, and my hand froze. But it wasn't that; she was talking about how relaxing the bath was, how she could fall asleep right there. How if this were her house she'd be in here every damn day and did I think Mrs. Corbin used it or was it one of those things that, once you had it, didn't seem so special anymore. I closed my eyes. Let my fingers move again. Softly, softly. No one else would ever have to know.

"Probably Ellen used it more when she had time," I murmured.

"What does she have now but time? Not being snarky, that's an actual question."

I must have responded; we must have kept talking then. There are flash points in my memory, places where the image is blindingly clear. And then moments when it smudges and I'm lost again. We kept drinking, I know that much, and then my heart was pounding, full in my throat, as Claudia drew near me in the bath.

She didn't have to get that close, showing me her fingertips, how they were wrinkled like prunes. Taking my hands in hers to see if they were the same. Maybe she was too old for me, maybe someone else would say it was wrong. But it didn't feel that way, not then, not ever. The bubbles made a line across her clavicle and I wanted to suck them off her skin like they were candy, billowed from spun sugar and dissolving on my tongue.

I remember the bathwater draining.

I remember the steam and her laugh and the slippery slide of her skin. Her leg, maybe, brushing mine. Or maybe that was another time, maybe that came later in the night.

I remember knocking over the carton of tangerine juice. How funny it seemed glugging out, running through the grout, making a patchwork of streams.

I don't remember how I scratched my forearm, a thin line running to my elbow.

But I remember how I bruised my back, so that for days I continued to press at it, as if to make sure I could still feel it, I could still feel something after all.

We must have climbed out of the bathtub, I don't know when. I was sitting on the counter and slid partway into the sink. I hit the faucet. Hard. Only I stayed sitting in the basin, the metal digging in, not caring because what could possibly matter besides the simple and impossible fact that my legs were wrapped around Claudia's torso and she was kissing me.

Or I was kissing her—I still can't pinpoint how it started. Maybe it started all at once, both of us together, so that there was no beginning and therefore—or so I thought—no one to point to, no one to blame. I'd been afraid of so many things. But then, just like that, I wasn't. I wasn't going to lose the night the way I'd lost the weekend in Block Island, all that closeness and still no way to touch. We'd been in the bath. And then somehow I was sitting on the counter and she was standing, her arms running up my back, into my hair. She was unhooking my bra but without any of the fumbling I was used to. I must have done the same to her. I must have slid from the counter because in the next flash of memory I know, I know, that she was lying on the bathroom floor. Her fingers curled into the towel. Those same fingers tugged at my hair. I woke up to soreness on both knees. On one elbow where I must have propped myself up. Claudia's hips moved with a particular rocking motion and I didn't know what I was doing, I'd never had it done to me before, but I pressed my palms against her thighs to keep them parted. I needed to be close, closer—

She cupped my chin, positioning my head the exact way she wanted, until her cries echoed in the steam of the bathroom, until the hum of her vibrated all the way down my throat.

TWENTY-THREE

I woke up naked.

Daylight stormed the windows; I must not have pulled the shades down. My head was pounding. I noticed that before I noticed the silk of the sheets on my skin. I was in the Corbins' bed, on Ellen's side, the pillow still damp from my hair.

And I was alone.

Nothing made sense—why I was here, where my clothes had gone. Why my arm hurt, what was wrong with my back. And Claudia—where was she? Did she know where I'd slept? How I'd gotten like this? I saw, across the bed, the imprint of another body, the top sheet thrown back and wrinkled.

And then I remembered. Not all of it.

But oh god. I remembered enough.

I pulled Laurent's pillow—Claudia's pillow—toward me and stuffed it over my mouth as if to hold in my smile, my laugh, my shout that would rattle the whole house if I—

I almost didn't make it to the mess of the bathroom before the contents of my stomach came up, a sour slurry of tangerine pulp and red wine. I didn't want Claudia to come in and see me like that, but there was no way to stop.

And the Corbins—what time would they be back? What if something happened the way it had happened on Block Island and they showed up any minute—the deal finished quickly, the deal spoiled, a flight change beyond their control? I vomited again, eyes watering, throat burning with the strain. I could tell Sabine I had a tummy ache, but no one else would buy it.

I flushed, ran cold water, splashed my face. I used Ellen's toothbrush, I didn't care. I couldn't make it upstairs and I couldn't stand the taste of my own mouth, the smell of myself. *Claudia. Sabine.* I showered in their shower, using Ellen's soaps and gels and sprays. Wrapped in Ellen's bathrobe, I used Ellen's dirty towel to soak up the sticky, spilled juice. *Claudia. Claudia.* For just a moment I lay down with my cheek pressed to the tile and realized this was it: I could trace it with my fingers. This room where all my secrets happened. This place where our bodies had lain.

I did, somehow, make it upstairs. I put on clean underwear and clothes and brushed my hair and tried not to throw up again. I had a laundry basket in my room and I didn't know if the clothes in it were clean or dirty but it didn't matter, I dumped everything onto my bed and brought the empty basket to the second floor. Into it I stuffed the towels, the bathrobe, my wet underwear, the pillowcases we'd slept on. I didn't see Claudia's bra or underwear or the rest of her clothes but she must have brought them with her when she went to get Sabine. I flushed all over again with the heat of it—what we'd done. What *I'd* done. What we must have kept doing, after, in the bed with the pillows haphazard, the comforter twisted and kicked to the floor. I almost tripped over myself in my haste to get downstairs, as if seeing her were the only way to make sure it was real.

I didn't understand how everything was so quiet. I'd thought I'd come down to coffee, cereal, Claudia pushing a glass of water in my direction. The look we'd share over Sabine's head as we whispered for her not to shout.

Our hands grazing when Sabine wouldn't notice.

Or how, sitting in the breakfast nook, I'd rest my cheek on her shoulder, the way I might have on any other day. Only it wasn't any other day—and we alone would know it.

But the car was gone, no child's sandals by the door. No Tucker, even, in his crate.

They'd left me, and for a moment the fact assaulted me with such vile jealousy I felt the vomit surge all over again—

No, I wasn't thinking, I was jumping to conclusions.

Claudia was too hungover to stand making breakfast, dealing with the dog. Sabine making a racket and banging her fork. They'd gone out for cinnamon rolls, scones, a massive coffee for Claudia that she didn't have to make herself. An excuse to keep on her sunglasses, to touch Sabine's small shoulder and tell her to be good and keep it down.

They'd come back soon with something for me, something special. "Here," she'd whisper, and everything would have that second meaning, everything would really be those other words. We'd laugh privately about how wrecked we felt. How different the world seemed now that we were different in it. Claudia would say how grateful she was that I'd taken care of things, how she'd known she could count on me to get the laundry in and refold the bedding and make sure everything was perfect. As perfect as Ellen expected. As perfect as we deserved. We'd drunk too much of the Bombay to plausibly fill the rest with water, but Claudia could buy a new one and I'd pay her back for half. No, I'd pay her back for all of it. My mother had given me four hundred dollars and I'd barely spent any of it, not with all the money Ellen left us. She'd say thank you. She'd be so relieved. She'd kiss me later, downstairs in her apartment, the second we could safely close the door.

I made toast. I got the laundry started, even though the housekeeper had always done mine and it was hard to figure out the knobs on the machine. I didn't know how the coffee maker worked; I was never the one to make it and I'd never drunk it before that summer, before the first morning Claudia had made it for me, and I'd said thanks and added milk because Claudia did, but no sugar because Claudia didn't have it out, she hadn't offered, and I hadn't wanted to look pedestrian and ask.

I took four Tylenol and made black tea because that didn't require any gizmos, there was no way of doing it wrong. I added two tea bags and didn't care how bitter it was. It was almost noon and I didn't know if the Corbins would call first or if I'd simply hear the car turn up the driveway and know our time was up.

I put the laundry in the dryer. I ate half the piece of toast and put the rest in the toaster to burn, so it wouldn't look strange if someone saw it in the trash. I scoured the bathroom floor with a spray I found in a closet with the housekeeper's supplies, on my hands and knees as my head spun. Right, again, where Claudia had gripped my hair, right where she had told me *there*. I opened all the windows, afraid the bleach would linger, afraid we'd left some permanent stain.

But there was nothing I could do to fix it. And no Claudia to help me. I missed, already, Sabine's unbridled laughter, the way Claudia was probably right now standing off to the side of the sand pit at the playground and reminding Sabine to share while Tucker sniffed in the dirt. I decided to bring the empty wine bottles down to Claudia's apartment—Claudia could put them in her car to dump them, or take them out in the bottom of her trash. But when I tried the door that led down the stairs from the kitchen, it was locked.

It had never been locked before. I'd seen her open it countless times. I'd turned that knob myself, and even if I shouldn't have, even if I'd known it was wrong, the point was that it had always been open. There was a gate so Sabine, and now Tucker, wouldn't fall down the stairs. And why worry about Sabine on the stairs if the door wouldn't open for her in the first place?

It could have been accidental. An extra precaution. Neither of us were, I knew, thinking clearly that morning.

Still.

After they'd been gone too long for coffee, too long for breakfast, lunch, the playground, for Claudia to be recovering from her headache. Too long to be giving me time to sleep in.

I couldn't stop thinking about that door. I went back to tug on it again, just to make sure it wouldn't budge.

I wanted to call Claudia's car phone, the one the Corbins had given her for emergencies. The number was there by the kitchen phone in Ellen's neat script.

But I didn't dare. It wasn't an emergency. I was simply lonely and anxious and sick to my stomach, and whose fault was that?

TWENTY-FOUR

The Corbins' black Escalade turned up the driveway late that afternoon. Panic gripped me in a vice. About their weekend, what mood they'd be in, and what if I'd folded the comforter wrong, what if there was still water in the bathtub, what if there was something obvious I'd missed that would give us away? Ellen would call my mother and my mother would—

I couldn't even imagine.

It was one thing to lecture Jules when she came home complaining that the music school's dress code for recitals was *so gay*. Or to say, offhand, that she didn't understand why other parents were up in arms about our lacrosse coach, Ms. Levin, when Ms. Levin was tasteful, she didn't flaunt it, and if an adult wanted to make her own mistakes in private then really, whose business was that?

Ms. Levin wasn't her daughter. The rules would always be different for me. Even though I wasn't like that, like her—they wouldn't understand.

Ellen hugged me like it had been a week and not two nights that they'd been away. "Bean?" she called. "Sabiney Bean? We have news, little bug!"

"She's with Claudia," I said, stomach twisting, chest hot. "They went out for the day."

Ellen dropped her purse as Laurent brought their suitcases in. "The other girls are out," she told him.

"Back soon, I hope." Although he didn't stay to hear the answer. He was already pulling out his BlackBerry, seeing what he'd missed on the drive.

"Yeah," I said. And then, backtracking: "Actually, they left before I got up. I guess I slept kind of late. So it went well?"

I didn't know if the twitch to Ellen's lips was for Claudia, or me, or the state of the kitchen as she realized no one had done the weekend shopping. Were we supposed to? But that wasn't Claudia's job, and no one had told us.

"They'll be back soon," I repeated, because truly, I had to believe it.

Her unhappiness was only a flicker. "Things are going to change around here, let me tell you. We finally got the right person's ear, and what a difference it makes! As soon as this acquisition at River Point goes through—" She wrung her hands, looking toward the patio where Laurent had taken the phone. It didn't matter that today was Sunday, I had a feeling things were about to move fast. How much money were they about to make? Was all of it legal? But I couldn't ask Ellen that. I said how exciting it was, that I hoped it was going to work out.

She crossed her fingers. "It will," she said. "It has to." She went upstairs to unpack, to make her own exuberant calls, and then I was alone again. Not really alone—I only had to walk into another room and there was my uncle, there was my aunt. But alone in all the ways that mattered.

Upstairs in my room, the music was so loud I didn't hear the footsteps up the stairs. The knock on my door. I scrambled up, heart lurching for Claudia's arrival.

But it was Ellen. I pulled off the headphones.

"Rach? Anyone in here?"

"Sorry," I said. "Sorry." What was I apologizing for? I fumbled with the Discman. Tinny sounds came from the headphones draped around my neck and for some reason this embarrassed me, that Ellen would hear it and think me adolescent, disaffected, stuck in the kind of sulking my mother deemed a rite of passage to be softly indulged, by which she meant ignored.

Ellen stepped into the room. A look crossed her face, the faintest wrinkle but it was just as quickly smoothed. "You should have said something, honey, I'll bring you up a fan. Or let's put you downstairs in another guest room—I'd just wanted you to feel like you have your own space."

"I do," I said quickly, flustered, confused. It was a reflex, this insistence I was happy, I was fine. "I love it here." Anyway, I knew it wasn't my privacy she'd wanted to maintain. She peered out the window as though looking from a room she'd never seen before, over a view she'd forgotten she had.

"We'd meant to finish this floor, but you can't imagine the expense when we moved in, all the work that had to get done." She turned back, eyes glittering. "But now." I wondered what Laurent had told her about the people he'd talked to, the promises he'd made. The private deals and secret donations that had allowed him to finally, fully lock in the governor's ear. Was it so different from her tennis matches, her garden parties that had paved the way? She'd worked hard for this, too. Nausea churned inside me. I was afraid if I spoke what might come spewing up.

Her eyes drifted over the chair piled with clothes, the laundry I'd dumped out and pushed aside. The bed wasn't made, the comforter brushing the floor—I never slept with it, not when it was so hot. Yolanda came in once a week to wash and change the sheets but I hadn't known, because nobody had told me, that I should have put my things away, I should have made it easier for her to dust in there. I could hear my mother scolding.

I didn't realize what was going to happen until it was too late to stop it. Too late to leap off the bed and steer my aunt out of the room. To get her away from me, away from the bed. Away from the bedside table. Away from the glass of old water, one small sip left, barely enough to wet my tongue. Lip stains around the rim, my smudgy fingerprints. Filthy, I was filthy. And the CDs I'd left out, they'd get scratched that way, I never took care of my things. And the small dish, the dish I should have set the water glass on. The dish that had at its center one round pill and half of another, chewed off, bearing the uneven cut of my teeth.

Ellen's eyes landed on the nightstand.

Just as quickly they turned back, and she was looking out the window again. The pause was so minute I might have imagined it. It was the hangover, the blur inside me. Excitement from last night jamming hard against my nerves. Lots of people took lots of pills for lots of harmless reasons. There was nothing so distinguishable about those.

"I just came to let you know I need to run a few errands while Laurent is on the phone. I called Claudia—they're on their way back from the zoo! Wasn't that a nice idea for the day?" I nodded in silent agreement. "She thought they'd be back sooner but Sabine had such a good time, she decided not to worry about traffic."

"That's great," I said, because I felt like I had to say something.

"It's lovely outside, if you want to sit on the patio with your music."

And then she was gone, back down the stairs. Tears pricked my eyes but they seemed to slide into my stomach rather than down my face, the world turned inside out and me still in it. Claudia and I had talked about the zoo, how we should go this summer. After the aquarium I'd said maybe polar bears would be a bigger hit and Claudia had laughed and said never mind, Sabine wasn't cut out for claws.

"Maybe when she's older," Claudia had said. "Maybe we can take her then."

I remembered it, those exact words, because of how Claudia had said them. *We.*

Only now she'd gone without me, and I didn't know why.

Bleach and tangerines. I still smelled like it, the tips of my fingers shriveled from scrubbing. Downstairs, Sabine didn't run to me when she got home. She didn't shout my name or ask where I'd been and why I hadn't come to play with them. She hadn't napped, she'd refused the whole time, and she was irritable, screaming in a way I'd never heard before—she wanted juice but not in a cup, she hated her cup, she wanted her sneakers but they were too pinchy, she wanted *Sesame Street* and was in tears that it wasn't on.

"I thought it was supposed to be the terrible twos," Ellen observed.

"I'm sorry. She wanted to stay so badly, I thought we might as well push through and see about dropping the afternoon nap."

I tried to catch Claudia's eye. What was wrong with her?

But somehow she was always busy, always just about to look away.

"She'll go to sleep early, at least. And you." Ellen touched Claudia's shoulder. "You deserve the evening off. And tomorrow—I can't thank you enough for how you saved us."

"Did everything go well? I'm sorry I didn't ask sooner!"

Ellen beamed, bursting over the gorgeousness of it all—the rolling hills, mountains in the distance, the women had gone to a spa and she'd never been so pampered. "It was divine. I can't wait until Sabine is old enough to appreciate it." As though they'd never been to France, to Italy, to three separate Caribbean resorts with a toddler who'd never remember it anyway. "Every time I see the governor, I'm surprised by how short he is." She didn't say any more about River Point. Maybe we weren't supposed to know the details yet. Maybe she didn't know herself, only that a promise had come from somewhere on the golf course, a phone number passed across the table along with the Scotch. Maybe it was uncouth to tell Claudia such things. "Sweetheart." At last she turned to me. "Tonight, you and me. Girls' night out to celebrate, what do you say? After Sabine conks out, we'll leave her with Papa and get a bite at the country club."

I opened my mouth. What about Claudia? And since when did Ellen want to go out after Sabine was in bed?

Claudia must have known by now that I'd covered for us. She could go back to normal now. I didn't care anymore that she'd left me alone all day with the cleanup and no clue where she'd gone. I'd have forgiven her anything if only she'd stop acting like I wasn't in the room.

But she reached for her keys. "I've got to grab some things from my car but have a great time tonight—and tell Mr. Corbin congrats from me." She tossed a wave over her shoulder that could have been for both of us or for no one at all. Then she headed out the door.

I wanted to run to the window and press my face against the glass like I was a child, like I was Sabine. Like I'd once done at the aquarium watching the sea turtles make their slow circles, as though if I could just get close enough, they'd whisper all their secrets. Did Claudia really have something to get from her car?

Or did she not want to give Ellen a reason to ask why, after all this time, the door leading down to her apartment was locked when I knew, I was absolutely certain now, that it had never been before.

TWENTY-FIVE

In the car on the way to the country club, Ellen reached over and patted my knee. It was sore from the tile and I hoped she couldn't see the bruising. "This whole crazy summer I feel like I've barely gotten to see you, my favorite eldest niece," she said. It was a joke on that side of the family: my favorite third cousin twice removed, my favorite uncle with a beard, my favorite youngest sibling. So they could pretend there was no such thing as favorites; that everyone was loved just the same.

It was true, though. We hadn't gone out just the two of us together, not since she'd first picked me up from the train. At the bottom of the driveway, as she turned onto the road, I thought as I always did about the deer. What had happened to its body when they took it away? Burned, probably. But where? And then what happened? Why did nobody care? I could have asked Ellen but I knew when to keep my mouth shut.

I'd never been to the country club at night. I only went during the day to the pool; we'd only ever sat under an umbrella, piling up our sunscreen and towels, leaving behind plates and chip wrappers and glasses with melting ice. Ketchup stains. Now Ellen led me into the dining room, the actual one, where the waitstaff all knew her and led her to the table she liked, in the back by the window, looking out at the tiki lamps that threw long shadows along the manicured grass and down to the glowing blue pool.

Ellen didn't need a menu. She ordered the mussels and a salad and a glass of chardonnay. I took my time reading. I'd eaten nothing but the half piece of toast all day and I was lightheaded, afraid I'd be sick if I ate more and afraid it'd be worse if I didn't.

In the end I chose the salmon special, already knowing it was wrong, I didn't even like salmon that much. But it was too late to change my mind. The waiter came back with Ellen's wine, a Coke for me. As soon as he was gone, Ellen slid the glass across the table.

"They won't say anything," she whispered. "My friend Kelsey does it with her daughter all the time."

I thought of Claudia, the margaritas I'd taken. Stammered out something about how I was fine.

"I know you liked the champagne." That smile again. What was I supposed to say? Ellen leaned closer. "I won't tell your mother."

I clenched the napkin in my lap. I tied it into a knot, then tried to do another but the cloth was too thick. Ellen had seen the missing liquor bottles. Ellen knew I'd passed out soaked and naked in her bed.

I forced a smile. "My mom would freak. She still thinks I'm such a little kid."

"She was always the uptight one." Lips pressed, a wink. Our secret. "She had to be, and I'll always be grateful. But you know I think it's important to live a little. You're a teenager! This is the time to have fun. Tell me." Her voice dropped. She made a show of scanning the restaurant but it was quiet, late on a Sunday, and we were up against the windows. No one would hear us. My stomach plummeted—this was it, the moment it would all come out. "Do you have a boyfriend? Or did you, at school? Anyone you're leaving behind?"

"No." Why were we talking about this? "Not really." Ellen

looked disappointed. Disappointed in me. I wondered what her face would do if she knew the only person I'd ever been with in any way that mattered. In her bed. On her bathroom floor.

"But there was one guy," I said quickly, and there it was again: her interest. "We were dating for a while. Like four months."

It was how long Morgan and Kevin Castleton had been together last year. And maybe about how long Jonathan had sort of flirted with me, if I pushed it a little. If I included the time he'd said he liked my sneakers, the red Converse that Dana had frowned over and said really, was I sure I was pulling that off?

"That's a long time," Ellen said. What did it matter if it wasn't true? It could have been true. We both needed it to be, for different reasons and in different ways.

"But it ended," I added. I took a sip of Ellen's wine. It was oaky, tart. My throat was sore from vomiting tangerine juice and red wine and fish sticks and gin. Everything in me had been scooped out but I kept going, kept talking, kept giving Ellen what she wanted.

"Let me guess—he wasn't grown-up enough for you. Boys that age are so far behind."

I tried to protest, guiltily, but Ellen was having none of it. Was she setting me up for something—something about (I could barely think the word) *girls*? I didn't know how I'd answer without dying. She waved the waiter over and pointed to the glass of wine. There was still half of it left but the waiter nodded and returned with another. Ellen made a show of sipping from the half-empty glass but when she put it down again it was closer to me; it was mine.

"I wish we could stuff you in our suitcases and keep you here forever." She smiled. I drank the wine. I felt like I was going to throw up all over again.

Ellen's salad came but she said no, she'd wanted it with the mussels; she'd wanted it as a meal because I hadn't ordered an appetizer.

I tried to say it was fine, she should start, really, but she sat there with her salad untouched until the mussels and my plate arrived. It was too much food, fried potatoes and ribbons of zucchini and the fish lightly poached and probably delicious, I was sure, if I could taste anything. If I wasn't so scared of what was coming.

I said what a good summer I was having in Greenwich. I said it was special (and really, it *was* special) spending this time with Sabine. And with her, Laurent, how relieved I was that his deal was going to happen.

I didn't say a word about Claudia. I didn't think I could manage her name.

Ellen smiled again. She was so glad to hear it, she said. She was so glad I was part of their lives throughout such a pivotal time.

"You know I think of you like a daughter," she said.

I looked up from the fish. I had, at various times in my life, wished Ellen were my mother. Or that my uncle Stephen were my father, because before he had kids he didn't care about things like wearing a seat belt or age-appropriate TV. Ellen was prettier than my mother, and thinner, and for a long time I believed those were the same thing and that they both meant *better.* And Ellen didn't cry the way my mother did; she didn't hit her forehead with her palms when she got frustrated. She'd never say Rachel I swear to god I swear it if you test me one more time.

But I didn't feel I could tell Ellen this. I couldn't say, for instance, *I think of you like a mother to me.*

"It was hard for us to have Sabine," Ellen said, which was something I sort of knew but also sort of thought you weren't supposed to talk about—the mechanics of my aunt's insides calling to mind the coiled uterine horn of the fetal pig I'd cut into just that spring, the yellowed ovaries stuck on the ends like tiny hats. The thought of them having sex, the intimacies conjured in words like *trying.* It wasn't like that when Jules came along and everyone delighted in the surprise. No one had ever talked to me this way.

"I thought it would never happen," Ellen went on. "And of course it hasn't happened again. But with you here, I get the family I always wanted. The family Laurent and I imagined we'd have." She drained her glass of wine and I worried she'd expect me to keep up. "Our family feels complete now, two beautiful girls to call our own."

I almost asked where Claudia fit into this fantasy where I didn't have my own parents and my own sister and my own life miles away. But Ellen had been clear, of course, that Claudia wasn't family. I was the one who'd forgotten our roles.

"Oh, I know it's not true." A self-conscious laugh, or perhaps it wasn't that transparent. "What I'm trying to say, honey." Ellen took a breath and I waited for it: the axe about to swing down. I had broken their trust. I'd abused their hospitality, overstepped my role in their home, but there was a way out of this mess I had made. If I was sorry—if I was sorry enough, and I was—Ellen wouldn't tell my mother. I wouldn't have to leave a failure, having helped no one at all.

"What I'm trying to say is that family looks out for each other. We take care of one another in ways no one else can."

I nodded. I made myself put a forkful of fish into my mouth to show I agreed. To keep my mouth too full to respond.

"I think you may have found something of mine," Ellen said, her voice gone a little tilted, a little different in some way.

I put down my fork. I was still chewing. It took a long time to push the mass down. I pictured the steps, as if I could feel what was impossible to feel: the folding of the vocal cord, each muscular contraction. It helped, sometimes, to know there were things the brain told you to do, and you did them. You didn't even have to have a say.

"I did?" A question, at last, once I'd swallowed and could think of no other escape.

"Yes, I think you did. I think you know what it is and I want you to know right away that I'm not mad. I'm not mad at all." Ellen put her hands flat on the table. "Oh, don't look like that sweetheart, you're not in trouble."

I swallowed again, even though there was nothing left inside me. "Aunt Ellen," I said.

"I'm not going to tell anyone. I'm not going to tell your mom, I promise."

I nodded. I kept nodding. I was made of string: my neck, my hands. My bobbing head. "I'm really sorry," I said, because that was all I could think of. "I promise I wasn't trying to be nosy. I shouldn't have looked anywhere."

Ellen waved again to the waiter. Again, a new glass of wine appeared, the old one whisked away. The first was still sitting in front of me. I'd been hoping I wouldn't have to finish it but now I could see that I would.

"What's done is done," she said. "But I think it's important that we have an understanding, you and I. That we know how much we love and take care of each other. The way family does. Do you understand what I'm saying?"

I did. I did understand. I made sure she knew I was following. It was a test and I'd always been good at those—inexplicably, sometimes effortlessly so. I didn't understand why Dana didn't study harder or why Morgan sometimes choked or why Ilana worked as much as she did but still did only okay. The rules were always so clear; you just had to follow them. You did what was asked and everyone was happy.

"I didn't tell anyone," I said. "I wouldn't do that. Just so you know."

"Thank you," Ellen said. "Thank you for sharing that with me."

She lifted the new glass of wine as if raising it to me, but I'd managed a second knot out of the napkin after all and was a beat too late in raising mine back.

"I didn't think you would," she added. "I know you're more mature than that. You have discretion. But it's helpful for me to know that all the same."

She leaned closer. Slight shake of her head. "Not everyone understands how long recovery after a major accident can take. Some people expect improvements to happen on a certain timeline, and they get impatient. They get impatient for life to go back to normal even when life can't go back to normal because there's no such thing as a normal to return to anymore."

I nodded vigorously, as though this was what I'd been thinking. As if I knew exactly what she meant. Was she talking about Laurent? Or my mother? Or something else, some reference to the outside world I hadn't yet grasped? *They.* I risked a glance around the restaurant. It could be anyone. There was no way to say.

"And it's easy, you know." Ellen went back to eating, using the small fork to pry the meat from its shell. "It's easy for people to have an opinion because they read one article, they heard one thing on NPR and suddenly they think they're a doctor, they think they know what's best."

"No one really knows what's going on in someone else's life," I said, and Ellen said she couldn't agree more. How important it was to know one's limitations. How some people couldn't begin to understand.

"It really is so essential not to interfere in other people's business," she said, and I knew how true this was. About her secrets, but also Laurent's, my own. It seemed, suddenly, that we had an understanding after all.

"I get it," I said. "I wish I didn't, but I totally do."

Ellen reached across the table and squeezed my hand. Her eyes were sympathetic in the soft light from the votive candles lit on all the tables. I wanted to pull away but I didn't dare break the current between us. She was so impressed, Ellen was, that I could be so young and already have this insight. So many adults would never get that far.

"Us Bryce girls," she said, using her maiden name, my mother's name that was my middle name, too. "We have to stick together. No matter where you go in life, who you meet." She paused. "Who you marry." The word hung between us. Ellen didn't take her hand away.

"You're always, at your core, the same girl you always were, and nothing changes that. It's a beautiful thing. The bond I have with my sister—it's like nothing else in the world. You'll feel that way about Julia when you look back on your childhoods and know there's no one in the world who knows you like she does. And she'll know there's no one who's known her for her entire life like you. When you think about Julia's kids, imagine how close you'll be to them someday. How close you'll want your own children to be to your sister, their aunt."

She was getting so worked up, I wondered if she might cry. Or was it the wine making her glassy. Or just the flickering candles, the glow from the pool. It was impossible to think of Jules as old enough to have a baby. It was hard enough to imagine Jules next year. Before a big game Ms. Levin always brought us into a circle to visualize scoring, visualize winning. But when I'd close my eyes I'd see only the fumbled ball, the missed shot that cost us the game. As though I could sneak up on victory. It was too much to demand it outright: to assume Jules wouldn't just live but live well.

"You know I love you, Aunt Ellen," I said with such forcefulness that Ellen stopped and stared at me, her eyes two deep pools with no way to see all the way to their source.

"I know," she said. "And I love you, too."

She lifted her hand and sat back.

She hadn't eaten all her mussels, there were still so many swimming in the broth. And the salad with the dressing the waiters knew to bring on the side. I had half the fish left but Ellen insisted on splitting dessert, tiramisu, it was her favorite but only for special occasions. "This is a good time to indulge, don't you think?" And I had to say yes. I'd have agreed to anything then. My heart was thudding out something happier than I'd ever thought possible. I wasn't in trouble. Not for anything. It was Ellen who had reason to worry, and yet she'd turned to me and me alone. Everyone needed her to be a certain kind of person—uninjured, untainted, untouchable, untouched. I was the only one she could talk to, the only one close enough, clear-eyed enough, to see the other side.

She ordered us decaf espressos. We talked about how good it was, how decadent to add a glug of cream. And the pool, what a blessing. Sabine had been wary at first but how great that now she loved it. The coffee was bitter—a whole summer of drinking it with Claudia and still I winced at the first sip—but stirring the little spoon, its clink against the white porcelain, I felt utterly transported. I would go back and knock on Claudia's door. I'd kiss her when she opened it, no questions asked. I was afraid that my flush in the candlelight as I thought it would give every piece of me away.

"One last thing," Ellen said as we finally walked out into the night toward the Jaguar, the only car left in the lot. The air was comfortable, not cool but with the first hint that it might not stay summer forever. That something else was coming, in time. She stood beside the passenger door but didn't unlock it. "I know you're curious, and at your age, I'd have been, too. But you can't take any more of them. It's not good for you if you don't need it. And I could get in serious trouble. Even Laurent could get in trouble. It's not fair, but that's how it goes. The prescription is only for me. For when I need a little extra help."

I nodded. I was so embarrassed, but Ellen made it easy. Easier than it could have been. And I was grateful, too, that nothing else had to be said. She unlocked my door, then walked around to the driver's side and unlocked her own and we both climbed in. When I tried to say again that I was sorry Ellen said oh, don't worry, don't take it that way. Just moving forward. In the future. She was glad we understood each other. She was so glad we'd shared this special time to talk.

TWENTY-SIX

Even now, a certain kind of sunlight can catch my eye just so, and in the middle of the city, despite the trash and jostling bodies and restaurants and bars and cafés and the heat wafting up from subway vents, the constant exhaust, I can almost smell the fresh-cut grass of the Corbins' lawn. More than once I've found myself on the sidewalk in Morningside Heights spitting into a trash can, trying to get the taste out of my mouth, what is it, what have I done. That coppery bite of adrenaline, as though somewhere there has to be blood.

How many mornings had I woken up at the Corbins', and yet how clearly I can recall the Monday it happened. The curtains open in my bedroom, that particular light streaming through. How thirsty I was when I woke up. The pill and a half were still in the dish where I'd left them the night before. I licked my dry lips and padded down the hall to fill the cruddy old glass from the sink.

In the end, Ellen had walked with me to the bottom of the third floor, turning off the lights as she went, kissing my cheek goodnight and whispering again how *very much* she loved me. And so I hadn't had the chance, or maybe the courage, to sneak downstairs like I'd planned. I'd lain in bed touching myself, imagining it was Claudia touching me the way I wanted, the way I couldn't quite remember through the haze of that night if she had.

In the mirror that morning, I was surprised by how tired I looked. Sleep crusted my eyes. I showered and shaved and blow-dried my hair and put on foundation, concealer, a little bit of mascara, although not so much that someone might comment that I'd dressed up for no reason. I picked a tank top Dana had once said was cute and paired it with cut-offs I liked. I spent too long in front of the mirror deciding yes, she wanted me, she wanted *me*.

And Ellen trusted me. She'd said so.

But I'd taken too long, I hadn't planned right at all. I'd missed my chance with Claudia before Ellen was up. They'd finished breakfast and Sabine was racing around with a pink cardigan tied around her shoulders—her superhero cape. She ran for Claudia, then threw her arms around her mother's legs and took off running again.

"I can take her," Claudia was saying as I came downstairs.

"Are you sure? You did so much this weekend, I know I promised you the whole day off."

"We can work out the overtime. I really don't mind."

"Morning," I chirped, as though they hadn't seen me.

Nothing had changed but everything had changed and I couldn't figure out how to stand, hands in or out of my pockets, weight rocking back and forth between my heels.

"What do you say, Bean? Haircut and then . . ." Claudia drew out the word until Sabine paused in her racing. "Out to lunch, just you and me?" She winked at Ellen.

Maybe it was all a show for the Corbins. Maybe she couldn't look at me because it'd be written all over her face.

"I don't need a haircut," Sabine said.

"But you *do* need lunch." Claudia tickled her tummy and Sabine laughed and tore off again.

"I really owe you." Ellen reached for her purse on the counter. Pulled out her wallet. Counted all those bills.

"I'll come with you," I blurted.

"That's okay!" Claudia was bright, breezy. As cheerful as ever as she cleared the table. "The appointment is in half an hour and you're probably still waking up."

"I'm dressed. I can go."

"It's just a haircut. It's not a big deal." Another smile shared with Ellen. She had it under control.

And I couldn't object. It'd look strange to insist. Even though on any other morning, Claudia would have been teasing "Come on, slowpoke! Grab a banana and let's go!"

I shrugged. "If that's what you want."

Ellen said, "Rachel, honey, once I kick this headache I've got to swing by the bank and the post office and send the world's biggest bouquet to Lori. You're welcome to come with me. I'm afraid it's a little boring, though. Really I should focus on the mock-ups for Billie, I've got to find time to go into the city this week. But Claudia, if you can? I promise I'll make it up to you."

Claudia said yes. Claudia said no problem. Claudia said she'd take care of whatever Ellen needed.

"I guess I'll stay here then," I said, and wished that when I sounded like I didn't care, someone in that kitchen knew me well enough to know I didn't mean it.

Ellen drank her coffee and then forgot all about that packed schedule she'd claimed. The plants needed to be watered, the ones inside and out, and there was a problem with the brickwork on the patio, something had chipped. How strange, later, to remember that we'd stood out there, right in that very spot between the grill and the lounge chair, examining some imperfection I couldn't see. I went inside; it was some time before she finally left. And then I was alone in the house, alone again. I took the half a pill that was left; the other pill I put in my sock drawer so Ellen wouldn't find it. I wanted to take one more, just one to have with me for later. But when I slipped into her bathroom and reached under the sink, there was nothing behind the usual hair sprays, and I had the sinking certainty that Ellen had found a new hiding place for the bottle, and it would be that much harder to find.

When Claudia came back it was two o'clock, almost; it was past time for Sabine's nap. I knew this because I was asked about it so many times by the police and then in trial prep, and at the trial itself: Where was Ms. Meadows, where was Mrs. Corbin, when did they come home, exactly. How did I know. Repeated from different lawyers, in different ways, as though they'd forgotten my answer even though it was all written down, all recorded, and everyone knew it by heart. At first I'd thought they were trying to trap me in the lie and then I realized, how stupid could I be. I wasn't the one they were after.

I remembered the time because I'd been looking at the clock on my nightstand, aching. How slow it all passed. I'd had what felt like practically the whole day and nothing to show for myself, just some cold macaroni and two beers I'd stolen from the fridge and brought upstairs to drink in my bedroom, knowing Laurent was never going to notice. (And why did no one ask where Mr. Corbin was, what *he* was doing. When did he come home and was he sure and could he repeat it louder for the jury?)

I knew when Sabine was supposed to be sleeping. I knew how bad it had been when she'd skipped her nap at the zoo. Knew, also, that Claudia and Ellen had discussed when Claudia was on her way out the door that they needed to try for a nap today, get in some rest time even if she didn't sleep.

So I knew it was around two when Claudia's car turned up the driveway. I went to the landing at the top of the staircase—would they come upstairs again, looking for me?

But Claudia marched Sabine to her bedroom while Sabine whined about how she wasn't sleepy. She didn't want to show off her pretty haircut, she didn't care about her new bangs. Claudia said they'd lie down, she'd read her a story. They'd have a little quiet time and then they could play.

I waited. For Claudia to come to me, for Sabine to say she'd only close her eyes if I was there. For everything to be as it once was.

I sat at the foot of my bed, dismayed by all the nothing that was going on around me. My heel knocked the empty wine bottles I'd shoved under there next to my suitcase. They clattered and rolled—could they hear the telltale crash downstairs? But nobody would care. I had to do something, I had to see Claudia. Now. I got down and pulled out bottles, the beer I'd just drunk and the wine and the gin with its last few inches splashing in the bottom. I shoved them into the purse Ellen had bought me from one of the boutique stores downtown, brown leather and big enough to carry my textbooks once I got to school. In between I wedged some T-shirts to stop any clinking. On top: a book, my Discman, a packet of tissues—the best cover-up I could do.

I knew I should wait for later, when the Corbins weren't so likely to come home. But I couldn't put it off any longer. Not with the housekeeper who'd be up there to strip the bed, and what if Ellen decided to come upstairs again and have another "chat"? It was my room, but it wasn't. I was justifying it to myself even as I was already doing it, as I hoisted the bag down the stairs and determined where to position myself so I could pretend to be busy, natural, just organically in the right place when Claudia emerged.

Only by the time she came downstairs, there was Ellen pulling up the driveway, walking in with her arms full of planters—peonies, she said—and more in the trunk that she had to bring in and water. Claudia said Sabine looked adorable, Ellen would love it, she wasn't quite asleep but was getting there. And Ellen said good, that was so good, she'd finish unloading the car and then—

And then what?

And then what did she say?

They each had their version to recount to the police, the hordes of reporters, and of course what wound up in court. But I was right in the middle—I should have heard every word. Later, when everyone kept asking, I should have known who was there to watch Sabine when she got up, who was responsible for her for the rest of the day.

But that wasn't what I'd been worrying about. None of it was my concern. Where the baby monitor was and who had it last and what had everyone agreed. The defense kept pestering me: *You saw your aunt go upstairs, isn't that correct?* But there was no way to explain how normal it was: Ellen busy, Claudia talking, Sabine in her room.

And the bag heavy on my shoulder, my comment to Ellen—"Oh, I just brought some stuff outside while I was reading!" Trying to be normal, normal. Trying to catch Claudia's eye.

Ellen went into her room; I heard the door close down the hall. Once again Claudia headed not for the door downstairs, but out the back and to her private entrance. I waited only a breath, the slightest hesitation, before I followed.

TWENTY-SEVEN

"Hey!"

"Hey yourself." Claudia's voice was flat. She didn't slow down.

"What're you doing?" I hurried to catch up. I didn't understand it—not her tone or her stride or the fact that she had yet to meet my eye. Ellen wasn't here. We could stop pretending.

I moved to take her hand and she jerked away from me, so hard I didn't know which of us was caught more off-balance.

"What's going on?" It was so embarrassing—the squeak in my voice, the fact that I had to ask.

But I'd watched Dana walk out on me, watched all my friends follow, and I didn't want to be that person anymore, the one who let others decide. I might have even laughed when she told me to go inside, it was that impossible. Some things were so clear: the light that morning, how it's stuck with me always. But that moment, the important one, the one where I followed Claudia outside and laughed—or maybe I didn't laugh, maybe it was already burning to ash inside me—that will always be confused. I'd been behind her, but even with the heavy bag over my shoulder I was faster, my legs were longer, and some dormant part of me remembered how to run.

I flung myself in front of the door before she could get into her apartment.

"What's wrong with you?" I tried to reach for her again—no one from the house could see us now.

But still she recoiled.

"If you think I'm upset that we, I mean—" I blushed, I couldn't help myself.

"What do you want, Rachel?"

I was afraid she was going to start running again, so I pulled the gin bottle from the bag.

"I can't keep these in my room. Someone will find them."

"Fine." She grabbed the bottle, unscrewed it, and took a swig of straight gin. My throat burned in sympathy. What was she doing? She recapped it, then dropped it behind the rhododendrons that framed the stoop in front of her door. "I'll take it in later."

I pulled out the wine bottles and set them in the dirt. Hesitating, I added the beer bottles, too. "Thanks."

"Are we done here?"

I dropped the bag. It slid off my shoulder and slouched on the stone. "Claudia." I couldn't stand it.

"Go back upstairs," she said.

I realized I was rubbing my hands together as though the motion would calm me. I wished it worked. I wished I had another one of Ellen's pills right then to help. I wished I had something besides a sinking weight inside, what I already recognized as the beginning of loss.

"Fine," she muttered again when I still didn't move. "You really want to do this now?" She looked up the driveway, as if to check that no one was coming. Then she started walking away from the house.

I wanted her to invite me into her suite so we could sit on her couch the way we'd done before, my head in her lap, her hands in my hair. But I knew she wasn't going to do that, the same way I knew my only option was to follow. We walked down the lawn to the copse of trees before the pond. Sabine had planted blueberries in the grass there: each blueberry, she'd said, was going to grow a fairy. Claudia and I had taken watering cans from Ellen's garden and promised we wouldn't let Tucker dig up her magic blue eggs. Unless that, too, was something I'd made up. Unless nothing in my life was as it seemed.

"Mrs. Corbin can't hear," she finally hissed. "This is my job, and I'm not going to lose it because of you."

I couldn't believe she thought it needed to be said. "You think I want my mom finding out about us?" *You think*, I meant, *that I don't have something to lose?*

She stared at me. "You're joking."

"You don't have to worry. I promise. She'll come around eventually, it's just—"

"Rachel, stop! You can't think that. You can't go thinking we're—" I thought she was mad I wasn't braver. Until she choked: "There's no *us*. We're not some kind of thing."

She crouched down and ripped a clump of grass from the ground. She stood and there was dirt in her hands, bits of grass falling. Why would she do that? Why would she say that to me? "Saturday night—" I started.

"It was one time."

"You wanted it."

"I was wasted, Rachel. It never should've happened."

"But you wanted it," I said again. Stupid, insistent, still so confused.

"You don't know what it's like to live here full-time. I have no one to talk to, there's no one my age. All my friends are off traveling, living their lives, and then they'll be back at school and I'm . . ." She looked across the lawn, the Corbins' land extending in every direction. "I'm sorry, okay? I made a mistake, but you have to understand that's all it was."

"You don't mean that."

"Wow." Her eyes widened. "So now you're going to tell me what I think?"

"It's only a few more weeks until the end of August. Right? My family won't find out, I promise. After that, I won't even be that far away. There's a train from Philly to New York. Or Hartford. New Haven. We can meet anywhere. You have the car. We can do this." My voice was spiraling, too high and too loud. I broke it with the smallest laugh. "I'm not saying forever. Obviously. I'm just saying we can give this a try."

"You're not listening."

"Because you keep pretending nothing happened!"

"I'm trying to tell you, in the nicest way I can—" She took a breath, recalibrating. "You're too much, Rachel. *This* is too much. You're not even eighteen—it's fucked-up just to have this conversation."

I stared at her. "You said LeRoy was older than you."

"It doesn't matter, you have to stop."

But our laughter. The things we'd shared in the dark. She was the one who'd shown me life could be different, that our future wasn't only what had happened in our pasts. I stepped closer, I couldn't stand it. Immediately she took a step back.

"I'm not a dyke," she spat, and all the air punched from my lungs.

In seventh grade I'd tried out for the middle school play, a modern retelling of *A Midsummer Night's Dream*. I was the queen but only because I was so tall. I felt it again, like I was sitting onstage in a starchy dress in front of all those people. These were our roles but only when someone was watching. So why was she still doing it when no one was here?

"I don't remember you complaining when you started it." I felt what my face was doing, the sneer. But it was only because of that word she'd used—how awful she'd made it. It was only because I was trying so hard not to cry.

"I messed up," she said. "I'm truly sorry. I won't tell the Corbins about you, as long as you let me do my job. But this, Rachel—you following me, you *stalking* me. I need your word that you're going to drop it."

I told her she was crazy. Technically we were both college-aged. And I hadn't kissed myself. I hadn't stretched myself back on that tiled floor. Ellen's pillow in the morning had been damp from my hair, but it wasn't me who'd spent the night on Laurent's side of the bed.

Why hadn't she left sooner, if I was so awful? Why'd we spend this whole summer together if she didn't like me at all?

But Claudia only repeated that this was her job, and I needed to leave her alone. If Mrs. Corbin heard anything, if Mrs. Corbin even suspected she'd been so irresponsible, she'd be fired on the spot with no income and no reference and no place to live and absolutely no protection. Her sister would kill her, her parents—didn't I understand how much power this family had?

"I thought it'd be Laurent I had to watch out for, you know men like that. But he's been nothing but perfect toward me, he'd never cross a single line. And then you come along—"

I wanted to tell her so badly. About Laurent's little habits. About Laurent's curiously specific preferences for girls who looked, well. Exactly like her.

But I couldn't say that. How would I explain how I knew?

We were so wrapped up in it, I suppose. Wrapped up in ourselves. And far enough from the house—I hadn't realized just how far down the lawn we'd drifted, Claudia still snapping at me, my face going blotchy and hot. I couldn't say for certain when the shouting started, if I'd been ignoring it or maybe I hadn't heard it at all. If I'd heard it but not realized what it meant. How long had it been going on, that cry? How long did it take us to notice that for some time now, someone had been shouting our names?

TWENTY-EIGHT

I was the one who looked up first.

I know that much. I'm sure of it—that I looked up and not Claudia. Because she'd been so busy talking over me, she was practically yelling by then, no matter what she'd said about keeping this quiet. She was that angry with me. Caught in that anger, hot with it; for a moment, until I looked up, we were the only two people in the world. Down the sloping lawn, by the trees, as though that made us hidden. Thinking we could talk like that and no one would find us.

But Sabine had seen, and now she was calling to us—that voice, those words (*Waycha*, but not like that, the *ch* was different, softer; and *Caw* for Claudia, but that wasn't it, either; it would fade so quickly, not in the way that I can no longer conjure Jules's toddler voice but all at once, with nothing to replace it). It was unmistakable, now that I was paying attention.

My eyes went to the patio, then over to the back door that was usually locked but not always.

But Sabine wasn't out there. She wasn't by the door. She wasn't on the grass and she wasn't coming toward us, even though the voice was louder now, her cry more insistent.

Claudia finally stopped her rant about the thing I was and she wasn't, the thing I should have been ashamed of, the thing she refused to believe. She finally noticed something had changed.

Some part of me, too, seemed to realize what was happening before the rest of me caught up, so that I was shouting Sabine's name before I knew where that urgency came from. In my nightmares since then, I'm never able to cry out—I open my mouth and all the sound is stuck inside. But I did shout, then or maybe it was only in the seconds that followed that I started screaming for real. My throat was so sore afterward that for weeks I was sure I was sick again, the strep had relapsed or something else, some new pollutant had clawed its way in. But when I went to the doctor they said it was nothing. Inflammation. Irritation. Rest and salt water, they said. But I'd cried so much, I'd lost my taste for salt by then.

I heard Sabine first, but it was Claudia who started to run. Up the hill, straight to the house, with me running after. That was what Claudia must have seen, in the too-slow stretch of time in which I was still trying to place it. Sabine wasn't on the patio, in the grass. She wasn't in the doorway.

Up, I had to look up. Up to my bedroom, to the window overlooking the yard and the pond and the road. The window I'd looked out day after day.

The window I'd opened when it was so hot in my room.

The window with the ripped screen, a flimsy, sagging thing no one had fixed, because I'd never told anyone they should. It had been my secret, that window. My delight, perhaps, in teasing out their imperfections. My way to still recall the outside world.

Later as I lay in my childhood bed in Cambridge, sweating, electricity in my legs so that I couldn't sleep and couldn't think and couldn't stop feeling like I had to vomit even when there was nothing to come out, when I'd sit on the toilet and will myself to empty, to shatter, in those small hours when I just wanted the time to pass, to make it to the next day, the day after, to propel myself ten years into the future, say, when I thought whatever was going to happen would have already happened and surely it wouldn't feel so bad, surely I'd be someone else altogether by then—

I'd replay each moment over and over, imagining the steps even as I couldn't imagine the steps, there was a point at which it all went blank and there was nothing to see anymore.

But first, there was Sabine waking up early from a fitful nap, or more likely she'd never fallen asleep in the first place. She'd called out, but no one came. Not Claudia, not her mother, not me.

So she'd climbed out of bed. Padded down the hall—why did nobody hear her?

It was hard to believe she'd remembered it that clearly: the room she'd once gone to on an afternoon when she couldn't sleep, or didn't want to, and found me lying in bed as if I'd been waiting. She'd never mentioned it again, she hadn't begged to sleep upstairs.

But.

The room, empty. The chair by the window. The window that was open, wide enough that maybe she could hear us after all. How else would she have known we were out there? Why would she have climbed up on the chair and started calling?

Those were the first questions.

Then there were the others.

Did Sabine start banging on the broken screen because we didn't hear her? Or did she only do that once we'd seen her, she knew we were coming, and she was excited, or nervous, or uncertain, or she couldn't contain herself, the way she'd run in circles around the kitchen island, hop on one foot to the TV and back, declaring the floor was the ocean, the floor was filled with sharks, the floor was stardust. *Run.*

How fast it happened in person. And how slow it will always replay in my mind. Sabine in the open window. Claudia calling for her to stay there, to get down from the chair. To wait.

And me, running up the hill after her. Always a few steps behind.

TWENTY-NINE

Someone with a greater sense for poetry might describe it as flying. Sabine's wings, say. As though we'd pushed her and pushed her on the swings and all she'd ever wanted was to let go and soar.

But Sabine wasn't that kind of child. She didn't beg to go farther, faster. She didn't play the seeker. She only ever wanted to be found.

Her fall was just a fall. The blunt, hard facts of impact. Blood pooled in the sunlight. Such shattering of bone. I must have been screaming but I couldn't seem to hear it come out of me. I couldn't hear anything besides Sabine's cry and then the rupture of her body against brick. A flat sound, so abrupt in its ending. The rattle of the grill top and then one last surprise: the clatter of the window screen after.

It couldn't be happening and yet I had the strangest sense of inevitability, as if it were never going to wind up any other way. In the immediate plunge of my stomach: the certainty this was somehow meant to be.

For every additional year I've lived and my cousin has not, I've never been able to locate that feeling again, or why I'd once sensed it so strongly. So many other somethings could have been and in each spinning possibility—an earlier nap, or later, or no nap at all; a closed door where one had been opened, another opened where the rest had been closed—how many wound up with Sabine starting kindergarten, starting high school. Going to prom. Staying awake in a campus library long past midnight, walking back through the snow. Never knowing what a rare and precious thing it is to taste the snowfall. The myriad ways that every *now* can become *not at all*.

The window screen had already been ripped, but I'd helped it along. Every time I'd stood by the window worrying at the tear, feeling the satisfaction of its unraveling even as I'd meted out the pleasures. There were dangers in taking it too far, but I'd thought of it only in terms of the dangers to me, by which I meant getting in trouble with Ellen and Laurent. With my parents, who'd chide me for being thoughtless in someone else's home. At the trial the defense did say what about the window, why weren't there safety features put in? Which was also something the newspapers raised, and the local channels that parked outside the gate and clumped along the hedges, training their cameras on the house, the windows, the grounds. Was it the Corbins' fault for not childproofing their home?

But my family was ready with their answer by then. It was the third floor, they said, and Sabine never went up there. Who was watching her? That was the real question, the only one that mattered. Where was her nanny, the one responsible for keeping her safe?

I alone knew the truth, the role I'd played. How little it must have taken for the tear to split all the way open, until there was nothing holding the screen in, nothing between her and three stories of air.

How scared she must have been for the final seconds of her life. A girl who hated heights. Who hated terror. Who only wanted to be with the people she loved.

Who must have felt such outrage to find Claudia and me not

sleeping as we claimed to do during her nap times, but together in the yard outside. Playing, she must have thought. Having all that big-girl fun without her.

⁂

Claudia ran inside and called 911. I ran for Sabine. Both were useless; there was no way to save her.

But I thought it meant something that I didn't look away. Even though Claudia's defense attorney said, after, that she was the only one to take *appropriate action*. To do what had to be done when no one else had the foresight to do anything at all.

Laurent was at work, of course. Ellen—who told Ellen? Claudia must have been shouting when she went inside to use the kitchen phone. For the briefest moment I was alone on the patio. Left alone to face it.

I meant to pick her up, cradle her, protect her as long as I could. This was my cousin, who loved to burrow into my shoulder. Who never could stand to be alone.

But it wasn't Sabine. Anymore. I stepped toward her but there wasn't any point.

And so when Ellen came outside, the cry coming from deep in her body, from a place even breath couldn't touch, she kept screaming how could I just stand there, why was I *standing there* as she collapsed in a heap over what used to be her daughter.

The sirens were getting louder, but there was no need to rush. I thought this type of thinking made me better. I saw reality—I faced it head-on. Only later did I wonder what Ellen had been doing all that time, why she hadn't known what was happening. The police asked where she'd been for *the incident*, and she told them she'd started a shower, which was why she didn't hear Sabine get out of bed, leave her room, call for someone to come.

And so from *Greenwich Time* to the *New Haven Register*, the public came to learn where Sabine got her haircut, what she ate for lunch, the total cost of her final day including tax and tip. And the fact—what became fact—that the mother was in the bathroom with the water running, loud enough to drown out anything outside.

I've tried to recall every detail that I can. I can say where I was standing. I can close my eyes and picture, like a photograph that never fades, the impossible stillness of it—her—*Sabine*. Blood on the grill, the brick, the flowers. I remember a handprint, bloody and wet, on the glass door—whose, I can't say. Someone, a man, had his hand on my shoulder, saying, "Miss, miss, you have to step back," and I'd wondered as if from far away who they were talking to—what girl was getting in the way.

But I can't remember if Ellen's hair was wet. If she'd changed her clothes from that morning before they were covered in red. If she had to think for a moment before she had her answer, or if it spilled out without any practice. No one went to check the bathroom to see if the tiles were damp, or the spigot still dripping. There was no way to prove why we could hear Sabine, the two of us outside, some distance from the window.

When Ellen herself, within the closed door of her bedroom, her bathroom, kept saying no, no, she'd heard nothing. Those doors were solid wood, they'd had them specially installed. The whole point of having them was to not be disturbed.

II

THIRTY

It started with a single van.

Prominent Greenwich family.

Tragedy strikes.

Tune in at six p.m. for more breaking news as we have it.

I barely noticed at first. There were too many flashing lights, strangers in uniform swarming the grass. EMTs, fire trucks, the police. *What happened?* They cordoned off the patio and kept pushing all of us back. I'd wonder why Sabine wasn't grabbing my leg, terrified of the commotion, and then have to picture it all over again: Sabine napping, Sabine in the window, Sabine—

I say *us*, but it wasn't all of us. There was no "we" like I'd imagined. Laurent sped up the driveway spewing gravel and stormed the kitchen, and that was when I realized that Claudia hadn't been led inside with Ellen and me, coaxed to take small sips of water and deep, steady breaths. She was still out there with the police. By *the scene of the accident*, as it was first called. *The scene of the crime*, it would become.

Her parents arrived, her sister; they must have left her younger brother at home. I saw them through the window. They stayed outside the house. I kept waiting for them to come in—I needed to talk to Claudia, I needed to tell her how sorry I was. Heavy boots stomped along the third floor, men traipsing in and out of my room and examining the window. *Where was Mrs. Corbin? And Ms. Meadows was with you that whole time?* My mother was stuck in traffic. The police asked who was watching Sabine, and Claudia must have said Ellen and Ellen must have said Claudia because when my mother finally made it, she stayed hovering over me, stroking my hair, saying, "Rachel, honey, can't you help us get this sorted?"

Another van down by the gate.

Another news camera trained on the house.

Laurent shouting on the phone: "I don't care, just get them out of here!"

The first thing he'd done was close all the curtains along the front windows, and I peered through the gaps until my mother pulled me away. "I don't want you in the papers," she scolded. "You don't know what they might print."

"About a random accident?" I whirled on her. I didn't know why I was angry; I just was.

"We all have to be careful right now."

And I acquiesced; I let the curtains fall and stepped back. I thought we were protecting Ellen—her reputation, her privacy. It made sense to me. Just like it made sense that everyone would review the obvious evidence of what had obviously happened and agree it was tragic, unstoppable and unexplainable, and there'd be nothing more to say. The vans would leave; the news anchors would take their somber faces elsewhere. The Corbins would fade from the spotlight even as their pain stayed fresh. I still had to talk to Claudia, to make sure she was okay. But when I asked where she'd gone, Ellen's face turned ashen. "That woman can't be here," she rasped in a voice made of cinders. My mother, more gently: "It's best to give everyone space."

We stayed at the Corbins' that night. Maybe for longer, but that first night is what I remember. The impossible silence without Sabine, her footsteps, the crackle of the baby monitor as she slept. She was supposed to have a bath. We'd pick out stories to read. I couldn't go upstairs to that room, my room—I couldn't be in there. My mother had given Ellen a sleeping pill and taken one herself. She gave me half of one and I said okay but kept it in my pocket. I didn't want to sleep in some random guest room on the second floor, I didn't want a release from this feeling. I'd have preferred one of Ellen's pills but I couldn't ask for that. (And should Ellen have taken a sleeping pill? I couldn't ask that, either.) I snuck downstairs, prepared to say I was hungry; we'd barely eaten since the afternoon. But I doubted anyone would stir. I paused to inch a curtain aside, and some of the vans had left but there were others still camped there, no matter who Laurent had called. Did they think something might happen overnight, and they alone would capture the footage? I scurried back toward the kitchen, as though someone might have filmed me just as my mother feared.

But I wasn't hungry. I was just awake, awake, and spinning. I tried the door down to Claudia's suite and this time the handle turned. Had she unlocked it, to show everything was fine, there were no conflicts here? Or had someone else come up the stairs? I opened the door slowly, holding my breath, until I remembered there was nothing to be quiet for, no one was down there. I walked right in.

It looked the same, as though she'd only left for the evening—a date in the city, dinner with her sister. For a moment I could imagine none of this had happened. My mother wasn't here, there was no caution tape around the patio, if I looked out the window toward the pond and the road I'd see nothing but night.

But her toothbrush wasn't in the cup by the bathroom sink. Shirts were missing from her drawers. And when I sat on her bed, it registered, finally, what else was missing. She'd taken her grandmother's quilt. Her family photographs were still there, and her painting in the living room. All her tapes and DVDs. I'd never know if she was able to come back for them. Never know, either, if the Corbins had asked her to leave, or the police advised it, or her family insisted she come home to Hartford. I lay down on her bed, and after a moment I crawled under her covers. I'd wonder, later, when she knew to get a lawyer. But I wasn't thinking like that yet.

I'd overheard the first part of Claudia's statement, what she'd explained to the police before I'd been ushered inside, and I kept replaying on a loop the lie I couldn't believe I'd repeated: that we'd smoked some cigarettes, Claudia and I, while my aunt and uncle were away. And Claudia had been worried about it. We'd gone outside to make sure there weren't any ashes on the patio, or a stray butt in the grass that the Corbins might find.

At first, when I'd heard it, I was annoyed—why couldn't Claudia have said it was a nice day out, sunny and warm, and we'd been talking, just talking the way that friends do?

But I saw the logic of it as I lay in her bed, my head on her pillow and the lotion from her nightstand slippery on my skin. We'd have had to come up with something to talk about, a reason we'd strayed that far from the house. And the truth was unthinkable. Even tangled in her sheets, I shoved it far back in my mind.

The Corbins retreated to a hotel, and my mother said it was time to take me home. Where there were things you were supposed to do. Shower. Put on matching socks. I stayed in my room as long as I could stand it, and when I came downstairs, I found my parents slicing tomatoes, peaches, shucking late summer corn. Jules sobbed about missing her cousin, the cousin she'd barely had time to know. None of it made any sense. I poured soggy cereal down the garbage disposal when no one was looking. Waited for the clock to make its interminable rounds until I could say I was going to bed.

Where I didn't sleep, not with sweat soaking my sheets, restlessness shooting up both legs. My skin turned puffy and dry, my eyes bloodshot from crying. I was afraid of what was happening to me, how it was possible to feel this way and keep on feeling it, minute after minute, all those hours without end. I whimpered to my mother that I wasn't okay, that there might be something wrong with me. "Give it time," she murmured, resting a hand to my cheek. "Grief comes in waves," my father added, as though he hadn't repeated the same thing just moments before. I pictured a fistful of coins, my parents slotting them into their platitude machine. Had they always been like this, and I was only noticing it now? On the phone they explained (to whom?) how devastated I was, how terrible that I'd had to see it. It was going to be, they said, a *long haul*.

In the smallest hours of the night I slid downstairs. The computer in the kitchen chimed when I turned it on and I held my breath. But no one came downstairs; no one turned on a light and said Jesus, Rach, what are you doing? Go back to bed. In the search bar: *opioid withdrawal*. Every sigh and creak in the house making me certain I was going to be caught.

But there, in the very first hit, I had an answer. You didn't even have to take that much for withdrawal to set in. And then there was the fact that I'd chewed it, that I hadn't paid attention to things like dosage or how much time to wait between each one.

It explained the shaking and the shitting and the fact that I couldn't stop crying, not just about Sabine but about anything. The brand of peanut butter Claudia had liked. That morning when the produce drawer had stuck in the fridge and I'd slammed it and slammed it until the plastic cracked.

Or maybe it didn't explain it, maybe I was just me and unraveling.

I wasn't dying, though. I didn't have to break down and tell what I'd taken from my aunt.

I deleted the search and typed in *corbin + greenwich ct.* I knew from my parents that the vans were still outside the gate, that it was impossible for Ellen to enter her own home without a picture popping up somewhere of her Jaguar creeping past the gauntlet of reporters. She was terrified someone would trail her—they'd changed hotels twice to be safe. Now I looked through the articles, weblogs, the opinions sprouting like mushrooms from the damp of my family's grief. Their loss was deemed unspeakable and yet everyone had something to say. The pictures of Ellen shimmering at fundraisers and galas and charity balls. The stoles around her shoulders, the cocktails in her hand. Were her eyes a little too glassy, they asked? Did her smile seem a little too slack? The shower was her excuse for not hearing Sabine, but in letters to the editor people said what woman had time to take long showers when her baby needed her. Maybe there was something wrong with her. Was this a case of neglect?

But where was that nanny? The responses followed, and on Blogger some writers conceded that a mother could take a shower if she had a nanny. And of course the wife of Laurent Corbin had a nanny. Laurent Corbin of the previously overlooked River Point area, itself mired in controversy but now on the brink of a massive acquisition. Expensive cuff links. Expensive teeth. The pictures looked so garish now that every mention included a little blond girl who'd died *tragically, unexpectedly,* with *questions still unanswered.* It was enough to make my stomach twist. Accidents happened, of course—but did they really? And to people like *that*? Would his investors stand behind someone so tainted? They wondered. I wondered. Every news outlet was going to keep asking who was responsible, the mother or the nanny, if they didn't take control soon. I only realized by the sear of pain that I'd been peeling the chapped skin from my lips strip by strip, peeling myself open like one of Sabine's tart, green grapes.

Grief wasn't a wave. It was an avalanche. Even once I could sleep for a few hours, have breakfast without throwing it all up again. I screamed for Jules to stop fucking touching me when it was only the edge of her elbow brushing past. Or maybe not even that, maybe it was a chair that I'd bumped into. Maybe it was my own arm, my own skin—nothing held its contours anymore. Did Claudia feel this same way, at home with her family in Hartford? Jules ran to our father in tears and I heard them talking about me in the living room, not even trying to hide it.

Afterward, a lecture on not taking it out on my sister.

A promise extracted that I'd be sensitive to what others were going through, too. I pictured shrinks. Hospitals. I heard them float the idea of delaying my start at Swarthmore. I knew there was a limit to how long I could let my insides press against the thinning surface of my skin. So one overcast Sunday, I pulled out my sneakers and pretended to go running, trusting that my parents wouldn't follow. Each day I wandered for twenty minutes, then thirty, building up to an hour and a half. Once my father rested a hand on my shoulder as he passed me in the kitchen, and I flashed to Ellen, the shower she'd allegedly taken. After that I stopped to dampen my hair in a water fountain on my way home, letting it drip down my back like sweat.

THIRTY-ONE

At the funeral, Ellen looked sculpted from wax. My mother steered her by the shoulder as though she were still a real person: "Sit there. Do you need the bathroom? Have a sip of water, I'll hold it for you." Foundation collected in the curve of her nostril; mascara clumped below her left eye. None of it made her less gray, an underlying sludge like when Sabine mixed all the watercolor paints to make mud. "It's such a shock," my mother said. "Her doctor gave her something, but even so." I wondered what the *something* was and what my aunt was taking on top of it. If that, too, explained why she was so gaunt, why her eyes roved unfocused over the pews and then, outside, the cut grass browning in that mocking August sun. If it was the same reason she kept grinding her teeth, the reason she was the only one of us not crying.

I'd seen my father cry when his old roommate Thurston died. I didn't remember the man or the funeral but I remembered my father's face, or rather the feeling it conjured: here was part of him that had nothing to do with me. He cried again over Sabine, noisily before the flowers, although I thought probably it wasn't only over Sabine; probably he was also thinking of himself in the way we were all, undoubtedly, thinking of ourselves. It could have been his daughter cold and suffocating beneath that wooden finish, and instead there she was beside him: attacking lymphocytes, growing brand-new marrow.

And me, too. I glanced over and saw his arm around Jules's slender shoulder, guiding her to sit.

I wasn't sure I'd seen Ellen cry at all since that first afternoon, even though other people cried at other parts of the day—when Laurent spoke, and the pastor, and Karen who owned the house in Block Island and called herself Ellen's best friend in Greenwich, saying she'd been there since Sabine was born but that didn't make sense because Sabine was born in New York, not Connecticut, and I'd never heard Ellen mention her—aside from the house, but that was different. Ellen didn't stand at the podium. It was Lori who got up in her place to *say a few words* about *enduring love* and how one's *community* had to *stand together.* Bile shot up my throat but I managed to swallow it down.

The casket was tiny. It shouldn't have shocked me but it did. That they had one in the first place, as though there should have been nothing left to salvage, even though that wasn't true and anyway people had empty caskets, that was a thing that must have happened. Sometimes. To other people, I meant. Not to us. Outside by the dirt pile someone put a pink stuffed rabbit in with the flowers and all I could think was how upset Sabine would be to see it get dirty. And the toy blocks, balloons, a plastic horse that would have scared her. Why did we do this to ourselves, why did we have to prove we could endure it?

Afterward there were "light apps" on the patio of a restaurant run out of a sprawling old house. Someone—Laurent, I guessed—must have rented it for the occasion. It could have been a wedding with everyone dressed up, kids running in the yard. Except for all the whispers. Every so often the voices surged, as though they'd forgotten they weren't supposed to laugh anymore, to talk about next week's tee time or plans for Labor Day. And then they'd remember, the hush would descend again, and no one would know what to say. I wished Claudia were there, whispering with me in the background. I wished I had another one of Ellen's pills.

I went outside and walked along the patio where it wrapped around the house, away from the drinks table where everyone was gathered. I didn't have a black dress and had squeezed into a shimmery purple that looked garish in the sun. My shoes pinched and I unbuckled the straps. I didn't want to hear how sorry everyone was. I was counting the minutes until we could go home.

When Laurent approached, the "I don't know" was already forming in my mouth. I was sure he'd come to ask where Ellen was, or my parents—people more important than me. But he sat on the railing beside me. "What?" I said, afraid the wood would snap under his weight. Or maybe that was exactly what I wanted, the fear distilled: for something to break and both of us to know it.

"Rachel."

He was freshly shaved, a small nick below his chin. It shouldn't have been weird to sit this close to him, but we didn't do things like that. Not before, so why start now. My ginger ale was flat and watery, the ice melting. I slurped it childishly through the straw.

"I wanted to check on you."

I sucked the bottom, that last gurgle of air. I didn't need him to be nice to me. Not so I could parrot some line about how yes, I was *talking to someone*. I was going to be *fine*. He hadn't been there; he hadn't seen it. He didn't get to walk off reassured.

"Why didn't Claudia come today?" It was probably rude to ask so directly. But I couldn't remember, in that moment, why I should care. Claudia would have rolled her eyes at how he gave everyone the firm two-handed handshake, as though anything were an opportunity for a business meeting.

Maybe she hadn't been invited. Maybe Denise had already gotten her a new job. Maybe she hated funerals or hated the Corbins or hated me or maybe it wasn't hate, not in that way, but the same blood-red flower that bloomed in my chest whenever I thought of it. Its petals, its thorns. We'd never exchanged phone numbers, email, IM—we'd never needed to when we slept only three floors apart. But I'd just assumed, as I was picking the dress and packing for the hotel and climbing into the back seat with Jules, that she'd be there. It didn't matter how angry she'd been with me, or that her family had whisked her away. How could she not say goodbye to Sabine?

Laurent wiped his palm over his mouth. His lips pressed together, disappeared, the skin around them pouchy and slack. "We'll get to the bottom of this," I'd heard him promise as he made those handshakes. "Rest assured, we'll set things right." Only to him there was no such thing as parody, and the suits nodded solemnly back, saying congratulations on the River Point sale, they hoped to be able to lend their support. I'd looked for the man from the barn, Brad, but I didn't see him. Or hear about anyone named Kip—but probably they weren't supposed to seem that close, as if they'd never spoken.

I had a thought, seemingly from nowhere, about the summers my parents had rented a beach house on the Cape, and Stephen and Anita would come, and my cousins, and sometimes Laurent and Ellen would book a better hotel room for the two of them, a top-floor suite with a balcony for their coffee and croissants. The houses were damp and stacked with used paperbacks and thousand-piece puzzles of Bavaria or water lilies or a family of tigers. We'd dump the puzzle pieces on the living room floor and spend all week hunched in frustration. Sometimes I'd think I'd tried every piece and it wouldn't fit and wouldn't fit and I'd swear one had to be missing, it was under the sofa, Jules was too little then and always careless—

And then another day I'd try what I swore was the same piece in the same spot and it would snap right into place, as though the puzzle had rearranged itself in the night, or perhaps it was I who had shifted, who'd turned what I'd been given and made it work a different way.

I felt it now: the piece in my hand. The suits. The investors with their needs for reassurance. The governor himself, as short as Ellen had said. And the lieutenant governor, the chief of staff, all the way down to Greenwich's mayor, who wasn't even called a mayor but First Selectman, even though she was a woman. What donations had Laurent made to her, or made secretly for her, in other people's names? I couldn't think like that, it wasn't fair—it was only speculation. But every time I went online there was more to keep up with: articles, op-eds, all the comments saying how does a tragedy like this happen, how do we in Greenwich keep our children safe. And then my uncle Stephen kissing Ellen's powdery cheek, saying, "You don't deserve this, you and Laurent. You did everything right, don't let anyone say a single word against you."

They wanted closure, answers, someone or something to blame. I saw that. I sympathized. But I still maintain that I didn't know what was coming. I couldn't have guessed where it would lead.

"Is this a good time for us to talk about Claudia?" Laurent said, not answering my question.

"It was an accident," I said, not answering his.

It was the word I'd heard Claudia say to Ellen, the police, the same line I'd repeated when it was my turn. Or maybe not that exact line, maybe I'd only kept intoning: "She fell, she just fell, she was napping and then she was up there and it just happened, it happened so fast" until they said I'd better go inside, I'd better get some water and calm down until my guardian arrived.

But what more was there to talk about? It was over and now everything hurt.

Only here was Laurent telling me about an investigation. Saying words like *justice* and *responsibility* and how I'd be *essential* for their *case.*

I dropped the glass. The chewed straw and the last of the ice chips went flying. My heart was a wave slammed against my eardrums but I must have said no, I must have dared enough to say that word to him. Because he went on to tell me there'd be time to prepare, they'd make sure I was ready, all I had to do was explain where I was, and Claudia, when it happened. He acted like I didn't want to do it because I was nervous, but I was thinking ahead to where Ellen was, too, and how in the world they planned to explain it.

And the showy blue gin bottle probably still lying on its side beneath the rhododendrons. That harmless lie I'd parroted to the police.

"There's nothing to look into," I said. "It wasn't anyone's fault." I wasn't sure if I was whispering or if the surge in my ears was so strong I couldn't hear myself speak. "And if it was, you know"—a little louder, forcing the words out because how could I not say them, how could I not make him see—"then honestly, Aunt Ellen was the one inside, she was the one who was closest—"

Laurent's hand landed on my thigh. Not hard, exactly. But gripping my leg. And then, as if realizing—my shock as I looked down, then back at him—his hand went to my upper arm, his palm large enough, almost, to wrap all the way around me, the gold watchband snagging on my skin. I had a vision, irrationally, of him shoving me forward, tossing me over the edge. Not that it was high; the glass had only rolled half-heartedly in the dirt. But I saw in that moment the ways that he could hurt me. There were so many different kinds of pain.

"She was too young," he said, and I thought he meant Sabine, how unfair it was. Until he said, almost a growl, "Young and careless, I'd warned Ellen about bringing her charity home. You saw how impulsive she was. That day she took Sabine to the zoo—she never even said where she was going. She was always like that, no accountability whatsoever."

My face felt hot, my chest, my skin where his fingers had pricked me. Since when did he care where Claudia went? I wanted to ask about the pills, if Ellen might have taken one or several or how it was that day. But there was no way to find out what he knew. Not without risking Ellen's trust. Without risking—I admit it—myself.

"Who went outside first, you or Claudia? Tell the truth."

"She—" I choked, I cleared my throat. "She did."

"And then who walked away from the house?"

Another pause. I knew what he was after. "She left first, and I followed."

I didn't know yet what I was giving him with that admission. How he would use it and why. But I could guess that things worked differently when you were Laurent Corbin, when you had the governor's private line and the state's attorney and probably kept a whole team of lawyers on retainer just because. It wasn't just about the money. It was the governor and the investors and every piece of that grinding machine. It was Ellen, too, and what people thought of when they heard the Corbin name. She'd need to be able to come back from this, to hold her head up in Greenwich and beyond. They must have decided any additional scrutiny would be worth it. Confirmation, even, that they had nothing to hide, they'd done nothing wrong—they were the real victims here.

Or maybe neither could say to the other that they shouldn't do this. Maybe I should have laid out every reason for him then.

He spread his palms, dark fur tufting the knuckles. His gold watch matched the thick gold wedding band—I'd never seen him wear it before. "Your aunt wanted me to tell you," he began, and I braced myself for what could possibly be so bad that Ellen wouldn't sit me down and say it herself.

His hand landed back on my shoulder. I tensed but didn't move.

"What you had to go through, Rachel. What we're going to be asking of you now." I nodded, I couldn't just sit there without nodding, but I had no idea what he was talking about.

"We've both discussed it with your parents," he went on, and I was annoyed, then, that they'd talked about me, that everyone still treated me like a child. "Your sister's treatments are expensive. And your schooling . . ."

He trailed off, and so I had to ask him what about it—was there something wrong with Swarthmore, was he trying to say I couldn't go?

"You don't have to worry." His arm slid softer around me and my spine stiffened. I wished there were someone there to translate what he meant. "Your aunt and I will take care of everything. Tuition, room and board, I hear you want to be a doctor so I'm sure you've considered the cost of medical school. You're helping so much, Rachel. We want you to know it's the least we can do.

"Whatever you need," he repeated into my silence, and I realized I was supposed to say something. Probably something better than "Oh," or "Thank you," or "Wow, that's *really* nice." It was hard to imagine my parents agreeing to such an arrangement. I'd have thought they'd deem it too much, unnecessary. Ellen had already been through enough.

But we weren't talking about diamonds, a new luxury car. I could hear Ellen's insistence: "Oh, Maureen. For once let me do something for you!" And probably it was hard to say no to her now. Just because I'd been shielded from knowing the exact dollar amount of my sister's treatment plus six years of my private schooling plus what four years of college would cost, plus whatever else went into our ongoing improvement, our sports camps and music lessons and maintaining the correct footwear per season, didn't mean I didn't have some idea. And what about college for Jules and whatever she might do after? Med school would mean loans, interest rates, payment plans that already seemed impossible to parse, and meanwhile there'd be no tuition for Sabine, no brand-new cars or trips to Mallorca or a destination wedding complete with open bar. This was nothing to the Corbins, especially now. Laurent said he'd cleared it with my parents, which meant they wanted this. All of them. They'd already decided without me.

He dropped his arm and patted the tops of his thighs as though about to stand. But not quite—it seemed he was never quite ready to let me go. "Is there anything else you think I should know, Rachel? Anything for our lawyers to look into?"

He was so calm when he said it. Not angry, not pushing. Not the person I'd seen with Ellen, with Sabine herself when he wanted his way. For a moment I even believed it was a real question—he was trying to arrive at the truth of what happened and needed insights I alone could provide.

But when I raised my eyes, when I looked at him looking at me, it was as though I could see in that instant not his tightened jaw, the shaving cut, his lips such an odd, fleshy pink, but my own self the way he must have seen me, the strappy dress and sandals, my useless rebellions. What was power anyway? All I knew was that I didn't have it.

"No," I said. "There's nothing."

He straightened his tie. "That's good," he said. "That's very useful to know." He pointed to the glass in the dirt. "You'll want to pick that up."

I could have called him back; I could have changed my mind at any time and said I had something to tell him. I had leverage—if only I'd known how to use it. But it felt like the whole thing was already done. That was what I'd keep telling myself, every second until that final moment that I'd rise and walk down from the stand and learn what *too late* really meant.

Inside, I plucked a cherry from the bowl of fruit salad and twisted off the stem.

"Where were you?" My mother was selecting a sandwich for Jules, who'd been following our father around like a much younger child, never letting go of his hand.

"Outside with Uncle Laurent."

A nod of approval. "They need you," she said. "We all need each other right now."

I dropped the cherry. It rolled under the table and my mother handed me a napkin, pointing to the trash. It seemed there was never any way to come out and say it. I could understand, in the abstract at least, how sometimes the only right answer might be to break something, to crack it so hard that it couldn't be mended. To say this is wrong and this can't happen and I refuse and so should you.

But it's one thing to stand outside of time, outside oneself, and look back or look inward or peer into another person's mind and say *yes*, that's the moment, the fissure, the time to act. It was another thing to be the one in it. To have no direction, no road map, no guide. To exist, and inside that existence, to not know what to do. Should I have ratted out my aunt? My uncle? Would my doubts have made a difference to what followed? My mother was still talking, passing me a paper plate, looking over the salads, sandwiches, miniature cakes. Going on about how this was hard, but she was proud of me. I'd pulled myself together to be there for the Corbins, who were being generous, yes, and who needed me so badly.

I picked at a brownie and tried not to think of Sabine's fingers sticky with chocolate. How, if she were there, she'd have tried to shove an entire strawberry into her mouth, and Claudia would have been the one patiently holding the green at the end, coaxing her to bite.

THIRTY-TWO

How strange that time kept going after that. I was home for one last week, shopping, mostly, for clothes, bedding, a new computer—a brand-new life. There was a chance I'd run into Dana buying her own shower caddy at Bed Bath & Beyond, or stocking up on shampoo at what used to be our CVS. But I couldn't make myself feel anything about it, or the fact that it didn't happen and I was spared some last encounter. I told myself this was progress, maturity, and I'd eventually feel the same way about Claudia, too. I tried to be hopeful, when my parents drove me down to Pennsylvania, that things were going to change.

"Hi." I stuck out my hand to meet my new roommate. "I'm Rachel." I smiled. I showed my teeth the right amount. I offered to help Alexandra—"Lexi's fine, actually!"—bring in the rest of her boxes. "Do you want the bed by the window? Or across the room?" Lexi said she was happy with whatever I wanted. She had soft, brushed-out hair and a southern lilt she'd spend the next four years trying to flatten. I was fully prepared to hate her and already annoyed that I didn't. There was still the problem of how to act, how to be, what to adopt as my normal collegiate concerns (classes, PE, rotgut vodka—Claudia had been right about that). But Lexi's friendship made it easy to pretend. Maybe the investigation against Claudia would fizzle, maybe somebody, somewhere, would tell the Corbins *no*.

Who, I now wonder, did I think that would be? I was in my room working on a problem set when the call came. I ignored it, until minutes later the phone rang again and I knew what it was about. I just knew.

I took the cordless into the hallway, and when I came back in, Lexi took one look at me, closed her Dostoyevsky, and asked what was wrong.

"My boyfriend," I blurted, touching my cheek and finding it rubbery, all the blood drained. "Ex-boyfriend. He's at Brown and says he doesn't want to do long-distance anymore."

There was no way to repeat the words my mother had just told me. Risk of injury to a minor and manslaughter in the second degree. My father had predicted it would be negligence, which was bad enough and still hard to prove. Only we should have known that wouldn't be sufficient. I should have understood there were things I couldn't reinvent myself out of. My mother didn't want to distract me, she knew I was working so hard, but I should expect a call from the Corbins' new lawyers soon. "This is horrible," I'd murmured, quiet in the hallway so no one would overhear. And I'd meant what the Corbins were after, but my mother agreed that yes, it was unforgivable what that nanny had done.

Lexi leaped up and wrapped me in a hug. "That bastard," she said. "I didn't know you had someone. He's seriously missing out."

So then I had to sit with her at the foot of my bed and make up a history, some on-again, off-again thing to explain why I hadn't mentioned him sooner, and how I was shocked that this time it seemed like he really meant it, but also shocked that maybe I agreed with him. And so actually, come to think of it, I was fine.

"Well, I'm here for you," she promised, squeezing my hand, and I nodded like I believed her, like that was all I needed, in the end.

I could have told her, of course. I could have told *someone*. But I was afraid it would make them look at me differently, to whisper and judge. To add their tidbits to the online chorus: *Their niece lives in my dorm!* And I wouldn't have known where to start.

It was easier to come up with a lie that spring, when the time finally came. My sister's birthday—her first since finishing radiation. Lexi clapped when I told her why I'd be gone. "That's so great!" she exclaimed. "That's so perfect, I'm so happy for you guys." As if it were her own sister she was celebrating, her own measureless joy.

"So I figure I should take a few days," I went on. "If I can get out of class. My aunt said she'd get me a ticket to Connecticut and drive me the rest of the way." I didn't know why I added those extra embellishments. It was a compulsion, almost. To see how close I could get and still treat myself to Lexi's beaming smile, Lexi's unimpeachable trust.

Like when she complained about the FAFSA forms for financial aid and I groaned and said, "I *know*." Or when she got a work-study job shelving books at the library and I pretended I'd missed the deadline to apply. There was no need to mention the bank account my parents had opened for me, the deposits that appeared like a paycheck on the first of each month. I hadn't known Laurent was going to give me that much, but it didn't matter—not to him anyway. Just that week there'd been an article in *The New York Times* praising the development kicking off along the Connecticut waterfront, breaking ground at River Point and initiating a corridor of *unprecedented improvement*. Kipling Holder, who'd won a "competitive" bid for the largest marina in the state. Affordable luxury that can't be beat.

When I looked up Laurent's company, beneath Flagship Solutions and Regional Markets was a new section: Real Estate Strategies. And the man himself, Senior Director and Portfolio Manager, his neck and shoulders filling out the headshot. The lawsuit wasn't hurting him. If anything, it was probably good to look like a dedicated family man, pursuing justice in his daughter's name.

When extra appeared in the next deposit, I knew what it was for. A better haircut, a French manicure Ellen would approve of, new dress pants and a pencil skirt and blazer to coordinate the set. When I did pick up the ticket Ellen had bought me, when I got off in Stamford for the district's superior court, it was as though I hadn't lied to my roommate after all. I wasn't a person who did that, and here was proof. My ticket to Connecticut. The ride from the station that, this time, no one made me wait for.

Daffodils brightened the median, and I looked out the window for something familiar: the route Claudia and I had once taken, the restaurant with the picnic tables and her face starry in the fairy lights.

But this was a different world now. There could be no going back.

The courtroom looked like a TV set, even though of course it was the TV sets that were designed to look like the real thing. The kaleidoscoping of reality made the whole scene dizzying, fantastic. The new clothes were itchy; I couldn't tell if it was hot in there or if it was me. I kept waiting for someone to announce that playtime was over, it was time to take off our personas and go home. Surely the judge would see through this. Surely there were people whose entire job it was to know when to stop.

But it had, already, a momentum all its own. When Claudia was escorted in, my mother turned to look at me; even Ellen whipped her head around. I realized I'd sucked in a breath loud enough for everyone to hear. Some part of me had almost forgotten our fight on the lawn. It was too far away, too separate from everything that came after.

But seeing her, I felt again her skin, her touch. Her fingers braiding my hair, rubbing in sunscreen, rolling a cigarette to place between my lips. My lips that felt the wet her mouth left on the paper. Her mouth that laughed and sang and whispered in my ear. The mouth that had spat at me: *dyke.*

How could she be all those people, how could we have wound up here. She kept her eyes down. She didn't turn to look at me. She was seated up front with her lawyer and his pinstripes were too wide, his suit (I shouldn't have thought this) clearly off-the-rack. Was Denise paying for this? Claudia's parents? Her hair was growing out. A flame of pimples had erupted on her chin and I worried what the jury would think. Ten of the jurors were white and two were Black and how was that supposed to be a fair makeup. *The Corbins' African American nanny*, the newspapers kept saying, showing her mug shot as though she were already convicted. Again I thought, again, again: Why didn't somebody stop this? My mother put a hand on mine and whispered not to fidget.

Someone said all rise and we rose. We could be seated and so we were. The judge was a white woman with gray hair cropped close to her temples and purple glasses hanging on a chain. The Corbins had lawyers who'd come to Pennsylvania to videotape me and play it back while I told Lexi I was at the library, the Science Center, working. But no amount of preparation could take the place of being here. The smell of the place. The theater of it. Claudia's voice when she pleaded *not guilty.* Why hadn't anyone prepared me for that?

The lawyers talked, the judge talked, the lawyers talked over one another and the judge talked over them all. There were breaks when we didn't need breaks and then no breaks when my legs were cramping and my back hurt from the seat and all I wanted, more than anything in the world, was to sleep until it was over. The state's attorney's name was Don and he had thinning blond hair and an overcompensating handshake. He and Laurent had rowed together at Dartmouth, and I wondered if Claudia knew this, if the judge knew this, but it must have been allowed because the lawyers on both sides objected to a lot of things but nobody objected to that. Don described a couple that went to church and donated to charities and wanted only to make the world a better place. I kept sneaking glances at them—when was the last time Laurent had set foot in a church? But it wasn't the kind of thing he'd have to swear to on the stand. I'd been thinking a lot about that recently, about *the truth and nothing but*. The point, Don said, his palms open to the jury, as if he had something tucked in there to show them. The point was that the Corbins had done everything right for their beloved daughter.

And look at what Claudia Meadows had done to them in return.

Claudia's lawyer was younger, with more hair, but he too had his pauses, his gestures with his hands. He'd let his eyes linger on Claudia as though to remind them—the jury, the court—that she wasn't simply *the nanny*. She had a name, a family, a home. She was a college graduate with degrees in art and French, the product of a high school program for *exceptional youths* for which she'd been a *model of success*. "Don't be fooled," he said, but I didn't know if that meant fooled by the Corbins, the state's attorney, or fooled by the court itself. Certainly he didn't mean fooled by Claudia, who continued to sit, unyielding, as if there were no emotion that would appease her captors and so she'd settled on showing nothing at all.

We ate bowls of spaghetti in the hotel restaurant. My mother went on the elliptical machine. Jules was staying with a friend so she didn't have to miss more school and each night they called and told her not to worry. Juries were made to be fair, they said, and this one would do the right thing.

There were experts brought in to establish time and manner of death—blunt cranial trauma, epidural hematoma—and the words seemed a portal to another dimension, one in which there were answers and order and none of the courtroom's byzantine rules. My father flinched at the images of Sabine on the bricks, the dome of the grill that had broken her fall. My mother kept her eyes squeezed shut and some of the jurors looked away.

But I made myself sit there, back straight, taking it in. What were a few glossed-up images compared to what I'd already seen? When it was Ellen's turn to take the stand she described her recollections of the morning, how yes it was true Claudia wasn't initially supposed to be working but then she'd a headache, there were errands to run, and so Claudia had taken Sabine for the day. "For the day?" Don clarified, and Ellen said yes without blinking. How clear it seemed then, clearer than it had been to live through it. Claudia was supposed to be watching Sabine. I could almost believe this. I could believe it because Ellen said so, and because Ellen was herself believable, dabbing beautifully at her eyes until it became impossible to see her as anyone else. Did she crush the pills, I wondered, or did she swallow them like you were supposed to? Did she take more than one, did she like it, did she need it, was it different for Ellen, Ellen whose back hurt, whose hip hurt, who no one had listened to when she said she was in pain. Ellen who kept having to do more, more, just to keep up. What would happen to River Point, the funding, the investors, the late-night calls. Laurent's name on the company website, his title and promotions, all the growth in store. What would happen if someone found out she had a secret. A secret he might have helped her keep. A secret that could have quite possibly, beyond a reasonable doubt, left her child dead.

THIRTY-THREE

I went into the bathroom to splash water on my face. I didn't want anyone to take my arm, hug me, marvel at how my aunt was being *so brave*. But I did it too much and then there were water marks on my blouse. They'd think me childish. They'd brand me a slob. Don had reassured me that I barely had to say anything, it was only to establish where Claudia was and if she'd had the receiver for the baby monitor. But it didn't feel as simple as they'd promised. "What kind of mother ignores when her daughter is in distress?" Claudia's lawyer had said, and although Don had objected—no one could say for certain what Sabine had felt when she was up in that window—the words were out there and everyone had heard them. *What kind of mother.* I tugged at the fabric in front of the mirror, eyes red even though I hadn't remembered crying. Maybe that was how I looked all the time now. Maybe that was simply who I was.

"Are you ready for this afternoon?"

I turned. I hadn't heard the door open. Ellen had been in the spotlight for hours, yet her suit looked untouched. I shut off the faucet. "I guess."

"That horrible lawyer, you heard how he twists every word. But don't worry, honey. The jury sees through it. You're going to do a great job."

I knew she didn't mean it. I wasn't one of those experts—I couldn't do anything well. I was snotty and red-faced and my clothes were a mess, and I hadn't even had to get up and say anything yet. When Ellen didn't move toward the stalls, it occurred to me that she'd followed me in there, to say whatever she didn't want to say in front of Laurent and my mother and everyone who was always crowding too close. We kept having to skirt around Claudia's family, her parents and siblings and an aunt and three or four cousins in tow (and how had Claudia never mentioned them, how in all those talks about our lives had this whole branch of her extended family in New Jersey never come up?). The papers had covered every day of the trial and protestors had begun gathering on the sidewalk, chanting that the system was racist, the system was rigged, the DA wouldn't bring such a flimsy case for a family without such connections. And then the other side, holding up signs and shouting *JUSTICE FOR SABINE*, because the nanny wouldn't be arrested if the nanny wasn't guilty, and they wouldn't rest until somebody paid.

I pulled more paper towels from the dispenser. But when Ellen reached for the wad, I passed it to her without a word. It would have looked petty, irrational, to protest this simple act of kindness: Ellen pulling the blouse taut and blotting at the stains. "I just want to make sure you're ready." Her voice was low. If anyone had come in just then, I had the sense she'd have dropped it altogether, thrown the towels in the trash, walked out gracefully as though she'd just been leaving.

But no one came in, and so Ellen could say, again, that she knew this was hard but was so grateful for all that I was doing for them. "You remember what Don told you. Answer only the question you're asked. If her lawyer asks if you know the time—"

"I say yes," I repeated, but of course that wasn't the problem.

Or maybe it was. Maybe it was exactly what my aunt was afraid of. I could say anything on the stand. So why didn't it make me feel like I had any control?

"You and Claudia—" she started, and my chest seized.

She straightened and stared at the paper towels, as though not sure where they'd come from. Her eyes didn't seem so wet anymore, not the way they'd teared so gently on the stand. I wanted to ask her how she did it. How did she get up every day without screaming.

"I know how close you were." She finally seemed to locate the rest of her thought. "But we shouldn't have trusted her, Laurent and I. I shouldn't have sent you off with someone so reckless, and I'll feel guilty for the rest of my life. This is our chance, now, together, to make sure another family never has to suffer like we have. The world needs to know she—that no one like her—can do this to somebody else. Do you understand?"

I felt so much older than I had that summer. It wasn't just college. It was how I had my own life now, and nobody got to know all about it. Not what I ate for dinner or where I lost points on a problem set or how late I slept in just because.

But as soon as I was around my family, I was a baby again. No makeup, the lawyers had coached me. No cleavage, as though I had any to show. I'd removed the diamond tennis bracelet Ellen had given me, the one that had once been a gift from Laurent. Nothing gaudy, they said. I was there to witness, which meant to attest, which I'd quickly learned was different from to see.

But the suit, bought with their money. College, summer internships, all of medical school without a single loan. "Make sure to write them a thank-you card," my mother had coached me after the second semester's tuition was due, and I'd bought a package of cards inked with birds to ensure I wouldn't run out.

I let my fingers graze her wrist. "You don't have to worry about me." I tried to find it in her skin, her eyes. Her pupils—but I didn't know what to look for. And I could have been wrong. It was like the judge said when she ruled the defense couldn't bring up the dogfight, what had happened on Block Island. What Ellen may or may not have done in another context at another time had no bearing on what had happened on the afternoon in question, the only day that mattered. And it wasn't Ellen being charged with anything. Not outside the court of public opinion, and how was it fair to have all those strangers declaring her a bad mother just because she had a part-time job, a life outside the home, because she'd hired someone else to help care for her kid? No one lamented the hours Laurent spent working, all the times his daughter went looking for him and he was nowhere to be found. Just because Ellen had taken the pills before didn't mean she'd been taking them that day. Just because I had to get up on the side of the prosecution didn't mean I, myself, thought Claudia was to blame. I wasn't judge, jury. I wasn't anyone. All I had to do was go out there and answer the questions I was asked, and what could be more reasonable than that?

THIRTY-FOUR

"To the best of your knowledge, did Sabine sleep with a baby monitor?"

"Yes."

"Had you seen it before?"

"I saw it in her room, I knew what it looked like."

"Would you know if it was on?"

"Yes, definitely."

"Were you familiar with the receiver unit?"

"Yes."

"Did Ms. Meadows usually have the receiver unit with her while Sabine was napping?"

"She always kept it with her. Like if we were downstairs in the kitchen, or outside. But we never went far from the house, because the signal wasn't as good."

"And that Monday, August ninth. Where was the receiver that afternoon?"

"I don't know."

"Did Ms. Meadows have it when you went outside?"

"I don't know."

"Had you seen the receiver other times, when you and Ms. Meadows were together while Sabine was sleeping?"

"Yes."

"Did Ms. Meadows ever keep the receiver in a bag?"

"No."

"Do you know why not?"

"I don't think you'd be able to hear it. If Sabine needed something, if she woke up. It'd be too muffled."

"Where did you usually see Ms. Meadows keep the receiver when it was on?"

"Maybe on a table, a counter, that sort of thing."

"What if there was no table nearby? What if you were moving, say, from room to room?"

"She'd carry it. It's small, it's easy to carry."

"So if Ms. Meadows had the receiver, she'd need to hold it or put it on a surface nearby, is that correct?"

"I think so, yes."

"And did you see the receiver in her hand or nearby to her while you were standing outside?"

"No."

"You're certain?"

"She didn't have it with her."

"Where was it the last time you saw it?"

A pause.

"I don't remember."

Another breath.

"I really don't know."

There was no chance Claudia's side would dispute this. Her case was predicated on her insistence that she didn't have the receiver, she wasn't concerned with Sabine's whereabouts at that moment, not because she was *negligent* or *reckless* but because she wasn't working.

Because she'd been certain, once Ellen came home, that the receiver was Ellen's responsibility. She, Claudia, was off for the rest of that day.

~

But it wasn't true, not exactly, that I didn't know the last time I'd seen the receiver. We'd had it with us while we were taking a bubble bath together. It had spent all night next to Laurent's side of the bed.

And if the defense went on to ask me where Ellen was, what she was doing for all that time in her room? If they tried to make it look like the wrong woman had abandoned her responsibilities, the wrong woman had been arrested for this crime? I rolled the words around in my mouth, testing the shape they might make. *Check her bedroom, her bathroom, her closet, her purse.* Ellen would never forgive me. But somewhere there was an orange pill bottle with her name on it. And what if that bottle, more than anything, explained why she herself hadn't known where the receiver was, why she hadn't paid attention to her daughter's cries?

Perjury was a Class D felony, punishable under Connecticut law by one to five years in prison and up to five thousand dollars in fines. I'd looked it up on a private browser at school. I could go to jail. I could go to jail for longer than Claudia, if she was convicted. I tried to catch her eye while I was on the stand. *Please.* I needed a sign, the smallest possible clue that lying about the baby monitor, about our fight, was worth it to protect her. That she missed me. Our friendship. That if I chose her over my family, my own future, we could go back to before everything went wrong.

But she'd found some spot to stare at just below my perch by the judge. I couldn't have said how I thought she should look, or what, if anything, would have appeased me. But it made me angry, suddenly—at all of them. At Ellen for doubting me and my mother for pressuring me and my father for being so absent and Jules for sucking up all the air in the room. At Laurent for bankrolling this farce and the investors and colleagues and his so-called friends who had, I was sure, encouraged him to do it. At Don for his condescension and his arrogance and his stupid little gestures, the way he flattened his lips when he said he knew this was hard but could I think back to that afternoon, could I remember, could I tell the courtroom where Claudia and I were standing and how far, give or take, would I say Claudia had led me from the house. Were we as far as he was standing from me, or were we even farther away? The jurors watched him take another step back and then their eyes swung to me and that made me angry, too, that twelve strangers should get to judge me when it was Claudia who was on trial, Claudia who wouldn't give me an ounce of support no matter how hard I was trying to be on her side.

I didn't want to implicate her and I didn't want to implicate Ellen and I didn't want to implicate myself but apparently those were the only options. So maybe I was already annoyed, on edge, when her lawyer stood up, placed a packet of stapled pages before me, and asked if I knew what it was.

"No idea," I said, handing it back. I felt bad that her family couldn't afford better counsel, that she was going to be screwed by this guy who wasn't going to ask me hard questions about my aunt and uncle's parenting if he couldn't even keep his cases straight.

But when I looked to the judge there was no shared glance, no mutual embarrassment over his glaring mistake. He told me to look again, to read from the beginning so the jury could hear. My voice was the only noise over the stenographer's keys and I sounded so strange to myself, like when I'd heard myself on the videotape and wondered who'd been speaking.

"It's a contract," I finally said, pausing once more for the lawyer to realize he'd given me the wrong document, for Don to intervene, for the judge to say thank you, I'd been extremely helpful, and I could go home.

"And can you tell what it's a contract for?"

I skimmed down and said, again, that I didn't know. But I did know; I had figured it out. I couldn't say it, though, while my chest was so hot, while everyone was watching. It was a work contract, specifically the contract between Claudia Meadows and Laurent and Ellen Corbin, specifically the one that outlined her responsibilities and her pay rate and insurance and overtime and hours off and holidays and what they, the Corbins, provided and what they did not, and finally I had to say that yes, I could see all this, I could see it was a copy of the defendant's contract (although I didn't put it like that, "the defendant," I still can't see her that way). But maybe there'd been a mistake, actually, because I wasn't part of this whole contract thing and didn't know why I had to read it.

I thought that made it better, to emphasize how little I knew. I'd envied the EMT, the coroner, their crisp responses and unruffled air. But now I was glad to be only the niece. Not a material witness, Don had assured me. No concrete bearing on the outcome of the case, which was probably why he hadn't bothered me about the contract before this, why these details weren't something I'd needed to know.

But then—then I saw the lawyer's snotty little smile as he said yes, he understood this was confusing, he understood I hadn't seen this contract before—

And I realized that probably I'd made a mistake, probably I'd done exactly what he'd wanted and expected me to do. I looked to Don for him to interrupt with one of his objections, but he was writing something down and conferring with the lawyer beside him. I didn't understand what they were whispering about, what I'd already done wrong.

"You've never seen that contract before, have you?"

"No."

"Did anyone ever, at any time, speak with you about the contract signed between Ms. Meadows and her employers?"

"No."

"Can you think of a reason why you weren't shown this contract before?"

"I'm not a nanny," I said, very slowly, as if he were the one who didn't get it. "I've never hired one, either."

That smile again. That little smirk. "You're not a nanny and you didn't hire one," he repeated. "Right, that's right. And can you remind the court, Miss Fiske—how old are you?"

I glanced to the judge. "Eighteen."

"And when did you turn eighteen?"

"September." I cleared my throat. "September first."

"So on August ninth, the day of Sabine's death, how old were you?"

It was so stupid, this whole charade. Everyone already knew the answer.

"Seventeen," he repeated after me, turning toward the jury with a broad, humiliating smile.

"I'd like you to look at a second piece, if I may." There were more pages in front of me, another contract, and when the lawyer asked me to read it aloud I did so, dutifully, because I could see no other way. Until I stopped, faltered, looked up as though they couldn't possibly expect me to go on—

But the lawyer said, "Please continue, Miss Fiske," and Don didn't interrupt and say I didn't have to and the judge didn't interrupt and say I didn't have to and of course there was nothing my parents could do for me now. And so there was no way around it. It was an addendum to their original contract, signed and dated in June of that year, after it was decided that I was going to Greenwich to help my aunt but a few days before I arrived.

"Twenty-five percent," I read, and my eyes smarted, hot and stinging and wet all over even as I told myself just answer the question, just answer the question you've been asked.

"Twenty-five percent," the lawyer repeated—why did he have to keep echoing me?—and then he asked me to say what the twenty-five percent was for, could I read the rest of the clause, and I had to say it out loud for everyone to hear.

The amount that Claudia's pay was increased for each week I stayed in Greenwich.

For each week Rachel Fiske—seventeen, a minor, a dependent, a hapless, hopeless thing—was legally in her care.

My thighs itched inside the new slacks. My palms. Heat pricked up my face. My cheeks were flaming, my lips so numb it was hard to make the words form. I didn't realize I'd been kicking the wood paneling in front of me until the judge told me to stop. I could have cried right there on the stand but I was too embarrassed even for that. I'd known Claudia's lawyer would try to discredit me, say I wasn't reliable, I had no business giving testimony about Claudia's responsibilities. And yet in every possibility I'd been prepared for, no one had thought to mention that I was an idiot, I was a nobody. I hadn't taken care of Ellen. I'd done nothing for my mother but get out of the way so she could focus on Jules. All those weeks, Claudia had been paid to hang out with me, paid to make sure I didn't complain that I was bored or unhappy or having a bad time. Paid to talk to me, paid to laugh with me, paid to sit together while Sabine was napping, paid to keep me company each night my aunt and uncle were away. It wasn't all part of her job, I knew that. I *knew* that. But then what part of it was real? When we'd stayed up smoking, when we'd shared a bed? When she'd kissed me? When I'd thought she'd changed my life—

Had she been paid for that, too?

Her attorney was still talking—"What?" I had to say. I'd missed the question. I'd missed everything. Isn't it true you never saw Claudia leave the house when she was on duty? Isn't it true you never saw her without the receiver when she was working and Sabine was asleep? Isn't it true that if you weren't responsible for Sabine that afternoon, and Claudia wasn't responsible for Sabine that afternoon, then only one other person was home that day who should have been looking out for Sabine before she climbed those stairs?

The questions kept coming, the objections, the lawyers conferring with the judge but I didn't know what it was about, if it was about me and something I'd done, even though Don had promised there was nothing I needed to worry about, it'd be over in an instant, let the lawyers take care of the rest. I knew he'd say it didn't matter—the defense couldn't discredit me as an expert when I wasn't claiming to be an expert in the first place. I saw Claudia go outside without the receiver. My testimony didn't matter beyond that.

But of course it mattered. To me. Isn't it true you don't know anything, isn't it true you're just another kid she was babysitting, isn't it true that no one likes you and they never have?

"In your statement to the police," the lawyer said, and my fingers clenched on my lap, those pale pink nails snagging into the fabric. "You stated that you and Claudia were outside checking for cigarette butts, is that correct?"

"Yes," I said. I had to say yes. It wasn't a lie—I'd said that to the police. Which was different, technically, than asking if the statement itself was true, the statement about the cigarettes in the first place. Some part of me felt proud for thinking like a lawyer, the way Don, probably, would think. Another part of me was going to be sick.

"You stated that you'd asked Claudia for a cigarette, is that also correct?"

It was harder to say yes that time. My saliva was stickier, my tongue slower than before. Had I really said that to the police? I'd been trying to help, repeating her story, so Claudia would come to see she needed me after all, and no one would find out about us.

But now I had no idea where this was going. All those people were staring at me: my family, Claudia's family, the lawyers, the judge. The bailiff. The stenographer going type type type. The court artist who would print her little sketches in the paper, which made me think of the reporters who'd swarmed the Corbins' house, and the photographers ready each time we left the courtroom. And the opinion pieces, the commentary, everyone with their constant badgering, their refusal to leave us alone and unjudged. I couldn't tell the truth, I just couldn't.

But I looked at Claudia not even looking at me, and I was angry, I was just so angry.

"I didn't—" I started, but then what was I going to say, that I'd been lying this whole time?

"Didn't what?" the lawyer asked, and I heard his pause. All that preparation and yet here was something new.

"I never asked for a cigarette. I never *asked* her for anything."

"In your statement—"

"I mean when it started."

"When what started, Miss Fiske?"

"Not the day Sabine died, I mean—"

I glanced to the judge, but the judge wasn't there for me, the judge didn't care. "Did you, or did you not, go outside to look for cigarette butts on the afternoon in question?" the lawyer persisted.

"No, I—We were already out there."

"That's not what you told the police. Are you amending your statement, Miss Fiske?"

Too long, I was waiting too long. The judge leaned closer; she was interested now. "I mean that it was also—" I looked, again, to the judge to guide me. To Don and Ellen and Laurent and my parents, all of whom were looking at me, looking into me, looking at each other. To Claudia, who still wouldn't meet my eyes, wouldn't even acknowledge that I was there, I was helping her goddammit, I had lied to the fucking police about why we'd gone outside, I was lying under oath and my god, what was I doing this for.

I could say I stumbled. I could claim it just slipped out. But there was all that time, that pause in which everyone was waiting. *Rachel is a joy to have in class*, my teachers' evaluations always said. *A quick thinker, Rachel is able to embrace new concepts and apply what she has learned.*

"I went out to give her something," I said, carefully or maybe I only wanted it to seem careful, my heart hammering, the certainty that something was happening, it was happening now and no one could ignore me anymore, no one could say I didn't know what I was talking about, I was too young, irrelevant, I'd misunderstood the whole thing.

Don turned around and looked to Ellen, to Laurent. Ellen's lips pressed together. The smallest flick of her head.

He turned back. He cupped his palm over the microphone so he could whisper to his colleague. Neither of them made an objection. They let me go on.

And this emboldened me; it made me feel better to know that someone, at last, trusted me to make my own decisions. It wasn't perjury, was it, to remember a little more once you'd had time to process? Once you'd had the space to think? I wasn't changing my story. I was adding to it. I was adding the truth.

"I went outside to give Claudia some empties for her to get rid of." I looked right at her as I said this. *Fuck you.* I wasn't the judge, the jury, the lawyers who'd built up their case. I was simply there explaining what I'd seen.

"Empties?" the lawyer asked, then seemed to regret the question. He asked the judge for a short recess, saying he needed to confer with his client. He wasn't waiting for me to answer but I was done being pushed around, condescended to.

"Bottles," I clarified, talking over him, my voice ringing out clearer now. "Three wine bottles, two beers, and a bottle of gin but that one wasn't all the way finished."

It didn't matter what Claudia's lawyer demanded, how he tried to make it inadmissible, like I didn't know what I was saying. Don had a turn to redirect and ask all the questions he wanted. And so I said it. Selectively, of course. I still had my dignity. But I told about the bottles, the gin Claudia had gulped that same afternoon. It wasn't the first time she'd supplied me with alcohol, and I hadn't told anyone because I didn't want to get in trouble. I didn't want to get her in trouble, either—what with me being only seventeen, after all, and under her care. No need to mention that my aunt and uncle had given me wine, champagne, that my parents gave me sips of their cocktails sometimes. I hadn't known what to do, afraid to keep the empties in my room where someone might find them, so I'd brought them down for Claudia to get rid of, which was why we'd gone outside in the first place, not just for the cigarettes—stumbling a little, knowing Claudia could tell her lawyer about our fight and he could bring it up in his redirect. But I didn't think so. How much worse would it look for her if they knew what else she'd done? And Don was confident that her lawyers wouldn't risk putting her on the stand. A suicide mission, he'd said, to open her up to cross-examination. Even if I told about Ellen, or found some other way—even then, it wouldn't make a difference. Some things could never be unheard.

Anyway, there was no way to prove Ellen's pills had anything to do with that day. And we could only, in that courtroom, talk about what had to do with that day. I had learned the rules by then. I was all-powerful, omnipotent, watching the private gears at work behind each person's eyes. My mother was shocked and my father confused and the jurors hanging on my every word. Claudia's lawyer was in a panic and the entire side for the state was ready to start popping champagne. Maybe that should have made me worried, maybe it should have occurred to me in the middle of speaking that this was a very, very bad idea, that telling the whole truth was still only part of the truth and none of it the same as answering the question I'd been asked. What did any of it have to do with Sabine in that window, Sabine's long tumble down?

But this wasn't about Sabine anymore. That was true when the Corbins pressed for the suit and when the state's attorney agreed to bring it and it was even more obvious the longer I talked. It was about the truth as in who got to tell it. About rightness as in who got to claim it. It was about who was going to hear me and who was going to judge me and who was going to spend her whole life acting like I was nothing more than some drunken mistake. "They're probably still there," I said. "The bottles. You can go check."

Scratch of pencils. A flurry of looks. The doors in the back opened: the state's attorney had sent someone out to make phone calls, set things in motion. No one could call me unreliable once they saw the proof that I was right. Some part of me wondered what I was doing, but the part that might have thought ahead to things like consequence was awed by this: such power. I've held a sharpened scalpel in my hands, a single cut to save a life or end it. But I've never had a moment that compares with this one since. To open my mouth and say the words that made the whole world dance.

THIRTY-FIVE

That was the end of my role, I was allowed to leave soon after. The trial would drag on for weeks and my parents, even Ellen, insisted I return to campus and focus on what was important. Which meant, to them, the problem sets I'd missed, the quizzes and essays and lab reports that had accumulated while I was gone. At first I thought that even after all that, after I'd done what they wanted and then some, it still wasn't enough.

But then Laurent gave me one of those handshakes reserved for the men who'd proven themselves useful, and Ellen slid two bottles of Vouvray into my suitcase after my mother had gone. So I knew they were pleased with me after all.

I thought I'd be able to zip my skin back up seamlessly around me: my college self, again. But it was different when I arrived, exhausted, still second-guessing the extravagant tip I'd left on the taxi from the train station, paid for with the extra cash Ellen had slipped in with the wine. Lexi was reading in her pajamas and jumped up to hug me, and I had to conjure all over again how it was supposed to feel to be this Rachel Fiske, living on the second floor of Willets Hall, considering a biology major and worried about my next calc exam.

I was two people now, leading two separate lives. What if I

was stuck like that forever? When Lexi asked how the party was, I thought it a joke, some twisted vine that had crept up to choke off the girl's familiar sweetness. It wasn't until she said it must have been a long trip from Boston that I remembered where I'd supposedly been that whole time.

"It was good," I said, rolling in my suitcase, flopping on the bed. "Fun. I have a ton of homework to catch up on, but my sister was really happy."

Lexi smiled. She had a round face, thick hair, a dimple in her chin. Sometimes I wished she'd do something reprehensible. At least moderately unkind. Stop listening when I was talking. Interrupt with some story about whatever had happened to *her* that week, so I could decide she was selfish and not worth my time.

But she beamed and said how thrilled she was to hear it. Twirling the necklace with the small silver cross she wore even to bed, going on about how much she'd missed me while I was gone.

I'd always sensed a gulf between us, the same chasm that had opened between me and everyone else on campus and that I saw now would only keep growing. I might talk and laugh and attempt to "connect," but no bridge spanned this kind of distance. Ellen had claimed we needed closure, but nothing was ending. Even if Claudia scraped out of this, if they acquitted, or agreed to time served, or whatever would put this behind her, there'd be no *behind her*, no place where that summer wouldn't follow. The posters on my wall seemed especially meaningless, and the books with their spines bent and too much highlighter. The triumph of my courtroom performance was already fading, leaving behind a sour taste like I'd eaten something rancid.

I brushed my teeth. Crawled into bed. Rote motions I knew how to complete. My stomach cramped, a constriction spreading from bowel to throat, and I wondered if I was going to vomit, if that would get it out of me, this feeling, this poison: what I'd done and the person it made me. "You awake?" Lexi's whisper startled me through the darkness on the far side of the room.

"Yeah," I whispered back, trying to keep my voice steady. Trying to put it all behind me. But of course I remembered every detail. The night I'd lain in bed with Claudia on Block Island and she'd faked sleeping, and what hadn't started that could have, and what had happened far too late that never should have been. Why did I always feel like I, too, was pretending with my eyes closed, until the pretending became real and I couldn't wake up? Lexi must have sensed it on me as soon as I'd come back, Greenwich clinging like a stench. If she asked where I'd really been, if she said she knew something was wrong with me. If she said it was okay to trust her, she wouldn't tell a—

"I had sex with Jamie DeSantos while you were gone."

I balled the edge of my comforter into my fist. "Really?"

"Uh-huh."

"Wow."

Lexi was quiet, and I thought probably that had been the exact wrong thing to say. I couldn't connect where I'd come from with this ordinary world and its ordinary appetites, its fears and disappointments and needs. My stomach gurgled, a rip down my seams that started leaking out what little had been of my center.

"Are you okay?" I asked.

"Sure."

I climbed out of bed.

I was only going to sit beside her. I could say something bland but supportive, like "I'm here if you want to talk" or "It doesn't have to say anything about you." I could just be there. The way Claudia might have in some other lifetime, in some other universe, been there for me.

But Lexi pulled the comforter down and I crawled in beside her. Right up against her in the extra-long twin bed padded with foam toppers we'd bought together our first week of school.

"Hey."

"Hey."

She pulled the covers up over us.

"Your toes are cold," I said.

She shoved them between my bare calves and I shrieked. She laughed. "You can warm them."

"Bitch." But I said it softly, without moving away.

"I didn't know it was going to happen. We hadn't even kissed before."

"Must have been some kiss."

"My parents are going to disown me."

"Who's going to tell them? Jamie? *Me?*" I held up three fingers. "I wasn't a Girl Scout but I was a Brownie in kindergarten. It's basically the same thing."

The whole truth, I'd said. As though such a thing could be cradled, certain as an egg yolk, separated from the rest that clung.

She laughed and put her hand over mine. Sort of held it and sort of shoved it away. I'd been here before, in a way, with Claudia but the more I thought about it, the more other things clicked into place, I could see the same patterns with Dana, too. This push and pull, this hesitation over what was offered and what I felt allowed to take. Wanting something and not wanting it and telling myself I couldn't have it and taking it anyway, taking and taking as though I'd never be sated, there'd never be enough to keep me full—

But I couldn't do that anymore, it wasn't an option. I'd learned my lesson and I'd learned it well.

"I kept making my high school boyfriend wait," she said.

"So? That was then." The thought came before I could stop it: *You were just a kid*. But what did I think that was meant to excuse? Had I been *just a kid* last summer, with Claudia? What about now? What about later, when I'd be older still and looking back?

"You're judging me," she said, and I had to say of course not, that wasn't what I'd meant.

"No, I can feel it. It's like this electricity radiating off you."

"That's just nerves from a week with my mom. Tell me you and Jamie used protection." I sounded like a bad high school health teacher but it was better than Lexi pressing for more.

"Condoms are for bad girls," she parroted.

"Right."

"And sex is for the sacrament of marriage."

"A toast to you and Jamie, then."

"What about when you were with Jonathan?" she asked.

It took a moment to remember what I'd told her. Nothing about the actual Jonathan, of course, but the made-up boyfriend who'd dumped me when I'd needed an excuse for the red in my eyes, the break in my voice after my mother had announced the DA's charges.

"I've never had sex," I confessed, and then, with a laugh: "So what do I know?"

A lie, I supposed. But what did it matter? Everyone has a story that's greater than the one they tell, the way the sky is more than *sky* or *blue* or what a single word can capture. Claudia had been right—one mistake didn't define us. Especially if I never let it happen again.

Moonlight slivered through a bend in the blinds and I caught the outline of Lexi's lips, the flutter of her lashes. She lifted her hand. I thought she was going to stroke my cheek, and I'd have to push her fingers away.

But all she did was take a strand of my hair—it was longer, to my shoulders—and drop it. "I wonder when it's supposed to get good."

I stiffened. "It was bad?"

"No, no. Not like that." She made a small noise, and I supposed I understood her. You could think something and never be able to say it. You could say it and still have it fall so short of what you meant.

"I bet you've never done anything you weren't supposed to." She sighed.

Envy flared up hot and aching, a pulse beneath my breastbone. What would it be like to have such simple secrets? To be able to confess them, late at night, knowing someone would be there to listen. I wished I could tell her what I was really thinking, what was happening and would keep on happening still. I wished I had one person, just one friend, I could be honest with someday.

But Lexi's eyes were closed now, her murmur softening to nothing. And anyway, I could no longer speak. If I'd never chased Claudia outside. If I'd never gone to Greenwich in the first place. If I'd never kissed Jonathan, never dragged Dana away. If I didn't know what I knew about Ellen, the way no one else seemed to know what I knew about Ellen, or at least no one who would say it aloud.

But all that meant was if I'd been a different person, if I'd had a different life that taught me how to make all different choices. Did Claudia have a cellmate? Did she tack tapestries up on her walls? Would she keep painting when she got out? Would she ever speak to me again? Outside the courtroom her sister had marched right up to Ellen, even though Ellen had left advertising and they didn't work together anymore. "How do you sleep at night?" she'd hissed. "When you look in the mirror, how do you live with what you see?" Her brother had tugged her back, warning her to be careful. But I'd seen the way she'd looked at us. No matter what the jury decided, she'd always think we were dirt.

I could have slipped out of Lexi's bed and tiptoed over to my own. But she was already sleeping, or pretending to be, and so I lay there and pretended to be, too—I pretended to be someone who could sleep at night just fine. So that in the morning we'd both wake up together, awkward but laughing, equally surprised.

THIRTY-SIX

I picked up the third time my mother called. It wasn't going to get any better. It wasn't going to simply go away. "Are you alone, sweetie? Is there someone you can be with? I wanted you to hear it from me."

I said yes, Lexi was here, even though she wasn't. She was probably with Jamie. She was always with Jamie by then.

Anyway the counseling center was free for some number of sessions, so there was no bill for my parents to expect from health services and no way for them to know I wasn't going. What was the point if I couldn't confess what I'd done, or Claudia, or Ellen herself, or any of the things I'd learned about Laurent? The only true way to keep a secret was to never tell it. I hung up the phone, insisting I was fine. And Ellen would be happy. Not happy, no, I didn't mean it like that. But it was what she wanted.

What everyone wanted, which was clarity. Certainty. I saw it as soon as I turned on my computer, opened Yahoo, and searched my aunt and uncle's names. There would be no question anymore, no risk of any stain or scent that lingered. If it was the nanny, then it wasn't the mother. Since it wasn't the mother, the father was blameless, too. Now the articles were about regulations, credentials for childcare, how to trust the person you'd hired to love your greatest asset. "Children Cannot Care for Children," read a psychologist's op-ed in *The New York Times.* "True Nannies Have Training," the International Nanny Association stated in a press release. I searched for *Greenwich*, *waterfront*, *development*, *Corbin.* River Point had sold handily, just as Laurent had predicted. Now the Planning and Zoning Commission boasted a PDF of Phase I complete with residential, retail, and brand-new office space. Kip's marina rendered in such detail, there were tiny steering wheels on every boat. How could our lives keep going, how could our plans just happen and happen, the only change that there was no Sabine? I closed the browser as dark spots floated in my eyes.

I chewed an Advil. It was only to give myself the feeling of doing something, the farce of taking something for the pain. But it was stupid and I spit it into a tissue, scraping my tongue against my top teeth to get out the taste. "Stop it," I said out loud in the small room, the windows closed, the door. My own self slammed shut. "Stop it." I said it louder. A force had come from somewhere outside of me, having nothing to do with the shake of my hands, the gallop of my heart.

"Relief and Anguish for Embattled Greenwich Family."

"Greenwich Nanny found Guilty of Manslaughter in Toddler's Death."

It wasn't the maximum sentence, what my mother had told me and the newspapers confirmed. But that was hardly something to celebrate. The jury had deliberated for days and this was the outcome: three more years in prison, on top of what she'd already served. The Corbins were "sickened" that Claudia could be found guilty of killing their child and yet serve barely more than their daughter had lived. I was sickened, too, but with a different kind of bile churning up my throat. Was this justice? Resolution? Claudia would spend the next three years at the Janet S. York Correctional Facility in Niantic,

Connecticut, while I lived on a four-hundred-acre arboretum. We'd both be released, I realized, at around the same time.

There was a sound at the door, the soft rat-a-tat that was Jamie's signature move. Like he was too cool to give a real knock but knew to stop just shy of barging in.

"It's open," I called, pulling up a Word doc, trying to look like I'd been busy with homework, reading. Normal aspects of my normal life. *Guilty*, the words from the browser still burned through the screen. I hoped the red dye from the Advil hadn't stained my teeth. I hoped it wasn't all over me, the things I'd done.

"Hey." Jamie pushed open the door. "Seen her around?"

"I thought she was with you. No, wait. Is today Tuesday? She's at MoCo." It was the a cappella group. They did silly, swoony versions of pop songs, oldies, things everybody loved.

"Right." Jamie snapped his fingers. "I should've remembered that."

"Then she has a study group for comp lit."

"You know everything."

"Because she tells me everything."

I'd never talked to him like this. I'd barely talked to him at all. But I already knew I couldn't let him leave. I was afraid to be alone again, without any distractions—afraid of what I might come up with to make the time pass. Someone, a journalist, must have found out I went to Swarthmore and tracked down my email address. I was in the court records, and he wasn't the first person to contact me but he was the first to suggest we could talk off the record. "Forward everything to our lawyers," Laurent had instructed, and until now I'd complied. Talk about what? I suddenly wanted to write this Marshall Bennett, I was suddenly itching to find out.

Jamie was medium tall, medium attractive, with medium-length hair falling into his too-small eyes. He'd go on to become a psychologist, of all things, with a focus on adolescent development. His roommate, a trumpet player, would die in our thirties from complications of the flu, and I'd read his obituary in *The Bulletin* trying to remember where I knew that name from, trying to place an old hurt that never quite healed. I can look back and wonder what I was thinking that Tuesday afternoon in late spring. But I'm sure I knew, even then, there was only one place this road led.

He tucked the limp strands behind his ears, which I saw had flushed red at the tips. All I could think was that I wanted more. I wanted to make something happen, something terrible, something large enough to drown out everything inside me. I couldn't write to Marshall Bennett, I couldn't engage. But I could do something, anything, everything I wanted. I stood and leaned against the desk.

"Does she keep trying to make you join a club? Salsa? Improv?" I laughed. I wasn't nervous. I was too numb to feel anything at all. I thought back to how it had been that summer when everything was perfect—or at least in my mind it had that crisp, idealized sheen. If I didn't think about it too hard. If I didn't let in the rot.

We joked about campus life and how much Lexi loved it. I felt bad making fun of her earnestness, how *good* she was. But it was only because neither of us had it, and if it wasn't obvious to Jamie, it was obvious to me. The way he slouched. How his eyes wandered with an unfocused need. He could have left anytime like he usually did, and I could beat myself up for all sorts of things, but it wasn't my fault he stayed.

"I'm counting on you to make this place bearable," I said.

He snorted. "I thought you didn't like me."

"Really? Why?"

A glance. The smallest pause. "You're always so quiet."

"I'm a quiet person."

"I see you laughing all the time with Lex. You only shut up when I'm around."

"Because you're hot. It makes me nervous."

Who cared if I meant it? He perched on the edge of Lexi's desk, the two of us facing each other. "I'll have you know that's a cruel way to mess with a guy." I cocked my head and he explained: "To feed him lies about himself."

He pouted, and I giggled like he wanted me to. It was annoying, but I wanted to be annoyed. I wanted to mess up his hair. In that moment, on that rainy afternoon, I wanted to mess up both our lives.

"Well, obviously I've always thought you're hot," he said. "I just thought you ignoring me was part of the standoffish, hot girl effect."

"Hot girl effect?" My eyebrow arched—a look I'd learned from Claudia but had never dared to try out until now.

He ran his eyes over me. Slowly, so clichéd, like there was any way I could miss it. Every inch of me felt exposed. I wasn't Lexi. People didn't effortlessly like me. Even if they did, for a little bit, it was never enough.

But there were options, I was learning. If you didn't overthink it. If, instead of trying harder, you went back to what you knew best.

I knew where Lexi kept her condoms. I'd made her buy them, telling her she had to take control. Now I got one from her dresser and tossed it to Jamie. He caught it, turned it over. For a second I thought he wasn't going to go for it. I'd overplayed my whole hand. He'd tell Lexi and she would slap me—that was for some reason the thing I pictured, Lexi slapping me and me standing there to take it.

And then he hopped off the desk and walked closer. Already he was tearing open the wrapper, dropping the silver foil to the floor. I'd have to remember to pick it up later. Evidence. That was how I thought of things now. I took off my shirt. He undid his belt, then remembered and kicked off his shoes, stumbling toward my bed. It was my first time, but he'd never have to know.

"Over here," I said, and led him to Lexi's bed across the room.

"That's fucked-up," he said, but he followed.

THIRTY-SEVEN

I made up the bed as neatly as Lexi liked it. I threw out the condom in the trash down the hall. It hadn't hurt, or not much, which was almost a letdown. But I felt hollowed nonetheless. I sat at my desk like I'd been before Jamie came over. If I ignored the strange, slight ache, I could almost convince myself I'd been working on a problem set all afternoon.

But the pages curled there, untouched. I watched the sun drop behind the trees that fringed our window, and then the darkness as it set in like a stain. I didn't feel thirsty, or restless, or bored. My only hunger was for one of Ellen's pills. Just half of one, just three-quarters, just enough to bring me back and send me toppling away. My face burned but it was somehow the same me, my usual skin—a little dry, with the tenderness of a pimple forming in the curve of my left nostril. When Lexi finally came back, late, from her study group, she found me bending over my dresser to try to see into the smeary, regulation dorm mirror, squeezing so hard I'd drawn blood.

"Rach!" she cried, dropping her backpack. "Don't do that."

I jumped back from the mirror. "Sorry," I said, embarrassment making me flush even deeper. "I know it's gross."

"It makes it worse." She passed me a tissue. I had blood under my fingernails. I'd scraped off a layer of skin, and for the next week I'd watch the redness swell, then scab, then fade as though the sore had never been.

"Sorry," I said again. "You ever start something and you know it's a bad idea, but you still can't stop?"

She flopped on her bed. I waited for her to bolt up again—to say something was off, she hadn't made her bed this way in the morning. Or maybe there was a hair of mine in her sheets. Maybe Jamie hadn't put his socks back on when he left and there'd be some sign of him, of us, left behind. She'd know it immediately, a perfect truth: all that I didn't dare tell her and then some.

"It feels good while you're doing it," she acknowledged. "But girl, there's such a thing as too far."

I almost blurted it out. *I fucked up.* I wanted the relief of confession, the clarity of a punishment to follow. Cause and effect, action and consequence. I'd face what I deserved.

But Lexi only reached for the worn stuffed bear she'd brought from home and asked if I had any more granola bars from a care package my mom had sent. I brought her the box from my closet, equal parts disappointed and relieved. "What's mine is yours," I assured her. "You don't have to ask."

The next Tuesday, when Lexi was at rehearsal again, I locked the door. I turned off the light. I stayed away from the door in case I cast a shadow. And when I heard the soft rat-a-tat of Jamie knocking, just like I'd expected or hoped for or feared, I held my breath until he went away.

When I was alone and sure I'd stay that way, I picked up the phone. I thought I could just call the prison, but I should have known there was a schedule. Claudia only had so much time allotted for the phone, and I imagined her using every precious second for her parents, her sister, her actual friends. "They have to contact you," the man on the phone explained, already tired of me and my ignorance.

But that was how I learned to look up Claudia's inmate number, and that I should write her a letter and ask her to call me instead. I listed my schedule for her, the times I wasn't in class, and my new cell phone so she could get hold of me anywhere. I don't know what I imagined we would talk about. How I thought the world worked, back then. But I did reach out to her, however imperfectly. I want to be clear that I tried.

It turned into something of a routine. Once a semester, a letter to Claudia saying I hoped we could talk. A thank-you card to my aunt and uncle for their generous support. Did I think I could have it both ways? Claudia herself was the only person, really, who had ever told me no. So yes, I suppose that I did. Sophomore year, Lexi was an RA and had a single, and I got a roommate through the housing lottery who barely spoke and spent every weekend off campus. I was convinced she had an older boyfriend in Philly, or maybe someone married in the suburbs nearby. Lexi was convinced she'd joined a cult, and we'd come up with ever more elaborate, hilarious theories—even well into our junior year, when I had my own single, too, and learned the girl was from Chester Heights and just liked going home. I kept sending those letters to Claudia. I called the prison every so often to see if there was any change.

My senior year, I devised a better plan. You had to be twenty-one to rent a car in Pennsylvania, so that fall was when I could finally do it, picking Columbus Day weekend because lots of people went away then. It wasn't strange for me to drop by Lexi's room and say that I was heading out to see family. I was sorry I'd have to miss Mikaela

Henning's birthday thing in Philly but we'd get lunch soon, it had been a long time.

Only when I passed through security and showed my ID, the woman behind the glass looked at it and at me and at her computer and shook her head. I hadn't known I had to be preapproved to be added to the visitor's list, that Claudia herself had to approve me. How was she supposed to know I wanted to see her if there was no way to contact her first? Laurent never would have driven four hours only to turn around without getting what he'd come for. But it didn't matter how much I argued and pleaded and reasoned and begged. Rules were rules. The woman wore a starchy blue uniform stretched tight across the long, single shelf of her breasts. Her hair was equally starched and severe in a bun—was that so the prisoners couldn't yank on it? I didn't know if this was that kind of place; if the woman was a guard or just spent her days dealing with people like me who didn't know what they were doing. Other visitors waltzed in with their tags and their pat downs and their small humiliations, and I could only wonder at how many times they'd gone through it before. I should have found a way to come sooner. There were cabs I could have taken from the bus station, the train. What was the car rental but another one of my excuses?

I sat in the parking lot under the barbed wire coils and hit the meat of my fist against the steering wheel until the ecchymosis formed. If it were me in there, who could I count on to visit? My mother, I hoped. But Lexi? Anyone else who called themselves a friend? Even my own sister would probably be too busy. Her whole life I'd pushed her away, as though it were her fault for being younger, sweeter, more effortlessly loved. And now there was no way to go back and fix it, change who I'd been. All I could do was get on the highway again. I'd trained myself out of thinking about what Claudia was doing every parallel second of the day: what she was wearing and what she was eating and who did she talk to, what did she think about, did she ever close her eyes and remember how she'd kissed me, how she'd arched her back and said yes.

But I still didn't know what to do with myself, my actions, the way the trial, that whole summer, changed shape anytime I let myself look back. Every year, on the anniversary of the verdict, a new email from Marshall Bennett asking how I was, sending clips to articles he'd written on disparities in sentencing, statistics he'd dug up on conviction rates across racial lines. I didn't read them. But I didn't delete them, either. Did he meet with Claudia? Was he allowed on her visitors list? The verdict was decided, there had been no appeal. What was there for him to keep asking questions about? Surprise, I texted Lexi, looks like I can make it to M's party after all. And so I made plans, at a rest stop off I-95, to pick her up on campus and drive together into Philly, to get dinner first and catch up.

I had somewhere to be. People who wanted to see me. By the time I got to New Jersey, the choice was so clear it hardly seemed a choice at all. Outside Trenton I found a Western Union and went inside. I wasn't sure if I should be worried—if something bad might happen to me in a place like that. But the shame of such thinking only made me more determined. I had to do something—I had to get out of myself and out of my head and out of the world I was raised in, the one where even my mother would touch the base of her throat and say Rachel what are you thinking, you're in *Trenton*. Don't you know you could be shot?

The woman behind the plexiglass was missing three teeth and it was hard to understand her. I had to keep explaining that yes, I knew where I was sending it. Yes, it had to be the whole amount. "They can't spend all that," the woman drawled. "There's limits." Like she knew personally, or maybe she'd simply done it so many times for so many people before. "Can they take whatever's left, once they're released?" I asked. And the woman said yes, so that decided it. I should have done this ages ago, not just bought some puny prepaid phone card and sent Claudia the PIN number like I'd read about in a blog for families of inmates. I had to call my bank to find out the exact amount in my checking, and then I had to okay it a bunch of times because it must have seemed like a scam, me wanting to clear out my whole account and send it to some random woman in prison two states away.

But eventually the transfer was cleared, and I felt, all of a sudden, better than I had in years, probably. Better than I had in my whole life.

"You'll want to send a note," the woman added. "So your friend knows who it's from."

But I shook my head. I didn't know what I'd write, and anyway it wasn't a gift, not really, if you only did it so the other person would thank you. I wouldn't tell Claudia, or Marshall Bennett, or anyone. I walked breathlessly out of the Western Union, back to the rental car that hadn't been broken into or stolen or vandalized in any way. *This.* This was what it meant to make things right. This was how it would feel to be a doctor—in the trauma ward, I decided right then, the most acute and frightening cases, the highest stakes of all. There was so much I couldn't make up for, but I could save a life. I could save a lot of lives. There'd be losses, too, but that was bound to happen—what was death but the definition of inevitable? It made me miss Sabine a little less to think it, Sabine who'd have been seven, almost eight by then, able to read chapter books and kick a soccer ball and play the easy parts of "Für Elise." I wondered if anyone else thought like this, if my aunt closed her eyes and saw her daughter's darkening hair, the gaps where she'd have lost her baby teeth. They'd moved to New Canaan by then, to a house that made the one in Greenwich look downright humble. Laurent was a senior vice president now and managed all the company's real estate funds, and Ellen had announced her intention to run for state senate in the Thirty-sixth District—she already had the name recognition, not to mention the governor's endorsement. She needed a new challenge, she'd said, and there was nothing to keep her from working full-time anymore. Why didn't I feel like that, like my star was rising? Why didn't anyone ever call me an inspiration for carrying on?

THIRTY-EIGHT

But I wished I hadn't texted Lexi after all. I was buzzing from the Coke I'd downed and the fact that I'd gone to a prison, an actual prison, and the realization that kept hitting me and then not hitting me and then slamming me all over again. I pulled over at an ATM to check my balance. Zero dollars. Everything was gone.

"Actually," I said to Lexi when I arrived, "I'd better take a rain check on dinner. I've got literally nothing in my account right now and I still have to fill up the tank when I take the car back."

She gave me a look, but it lasted only a second—or maybe there was no look, maybe I was only being paranoid that I couldn't pull off that breezy, relatable way other people sounded when they said they were broke. "Don't worry." She touched my arm. "You can get me back next time."

She was wearing a tight, sparkly thing and glittery makeup, flip-flops poking out of her purse for when the chunky heels came off. I saw right away my other mistake, that I wasn't dressed for a club in Philadelphia, that I'd never actually been to a club in Philadelphia and had no idea why I'd said yes. Lexi swore jeans were fine ("I'm just so happy you're coming!") and I tried to tell myself it was true. "You're too much," Claudia had hissed at me, but then why did I so often feel like I wasn't enough?

Work-study at the library must have been going well because Lexi picked a little sushi place and squeezed herself into a booth, the Saran-wrapped seal of her dress making her breasts bulge in a way I found impossible not to notice.

"You okay?" she asked. "You seem quiet."

I wanted to ask if she'd come visit me in prison, if we were the kind of friends who'd do that. But that wasn't a hypothetical you could drop into conversation without raising concerns.

"Just tired," I said. "A lot of driving."

"I assumed you were going for the whole weekend."

I lied and said my aunt was moving and I'd offered to help, but then I'd decided it'd be more fun to come back rather than stay.

"They don't have anything set up yet," I added. "I'd have been, like, sleeping on the floor."

"I love how close you and your aunt are." She picked up the menu. "Still, I can't believe you drove all the way to Connecticut and back just so you wouldn't miss Mikaela's party."

I'd managed to never give her my aunt's last name or too many details, and now I was glad she didn't have more questions. It wasn't guilt, exactly, over my omissions—I'd kept up the charade too long for that. But I wished we could order already, get down to the business of eating, which was the kind of thing people did together precisely because it gave them something else to do besides talk about each other. Something about the prison, about telling Lexi the one lie, had begun to bring forth all the others. I felt a familiar shame seep through me, a trickle that grew heavier the more of me it managed to erode.

"And also," I said, pushing away the old images: patio, brick, a sudden ringing in my ear. *Greenwich Nanny. Toddler's Death.* "I wanted to see you. It's been a while since we've hung out just us."

"Best roommates ever." She smiled.

I crossed my fingers, pretended at a quick prayer to the housing gods that I realized too late was probably offensive—I didn't know where she stood with the whole god thing these days. But she was laughing, it didn't matter, we were ordering appetizers and she insisted on sake, which came warm and tasted like rubbing alcohol but that didn't matter, either.

"And I wanted to tell you something," I said after the first swallow and then another, the thimblefuls warming inside me, thinking about when was the last time Claudia had liquor that cost fourteen dollars a person and put on too much makeup and went to a party with friends. "It's stupid," I went on. "I shouldn't make a big deal out of it, but I thought since it's just us . . ."

The soup arrived, and I knew I'd better come to my senses, I'd better rein this in before it got out of my control. But then Lexi said, "So what's your big news?" and it felt like I had to go on.

Her lips pressed together as she grinned over the soup. A shimmer of excitement to match the shimmer of her dress, her eyes, the way her very insides seemed to glow like there was always something good happening for her, something to be happy about. She had so many friends, she was being recruited for financial firms for next year, she'd had a boyfriend for the last year and a half who she was already planning to move in with after graduation. Why did some people have everything while others tried and tried and still wound up with nothing at all?

I took a breath. "I need to tell you I slept with someone."

"I knew it!" Lexi's grin widened, and I melted into the warm drink, the warm soup, the warmth of the restaurant and her smile beaming all for me.

"You're not mad?"

"Rach." She put down her spoon. "I'm happy for you. And I'm happy that you feel like you can tell me. I know you were probably nervous, and maybe you thought that I'd—you know." She twirled the cross that hung on her necklace, the one she still wore even though she'd confided in me that it was "complicated" now. "When you were kind of weird today, I figured it was because you wanted to talk about this, so I wanted to pick a quiet spot. Believe me, I'd never be mad at you."

"Shit." The air rushed out, my lungs so empty they might have been collapsing. "This is such a relief."

The gyoza came, and edamame, and I could have fallen headfirst into it, I just wanted the plates to keep coming. This thing Lexi was doing for me, all so that I didn't have to worry.

"I still feel so bad about it, and I tried to imagine graduating without ever telling you and I just—I don't know. I couldn't. I know it was a long time ago, and you guys have been broken up since forever, and you and Ben are so perfect together, and obviously it didn't mean anything and I've been with other guys since—"

Lexi had been reaching for a gyoza when, very slowly, she put the chopsticks down. "What are you talking about?"

I was mid-bite, which meant I had to go through the awkwardness of chewing, swallowing, trying to keep the other half of the dumpling pinching together midair. "What are *you* talking about?"

"I'm talking about you sleeping with Alyssa."

Pork filling fell from its wrapper. *"Who?"*

"Your lab partner? The one you're literally always with?"

"Yeah," I said, mind racing ahead. Or backward. Or I didn't even know where. The food was suddenly repulsive, I couldn't manage a bite. "Because she's my lab partner." A beat. "Why would I be sleeping with her?"

"I'm sorry." Lexi was reddening now. She picked up the chopsticks, put them down again. "I sort of thought you might be—"

The silence ballooned between us.

She looked at her plate. "I thought I'd heard Alyssa liked you, that's all." Her eyes shot up again, as if remembering where this had started, and I wished I could take it back, everything I'd ever done and certainly everything I'd said that night and probably ever. Why had I let my guard down? Why did people talk about coming clean when all it did was make a greater mess for everyone to deal with?

I'd wanted Lexi to see I was a monster, so someone could finally say it to my face because Claudia wasn't there to say it herself.

I'd wanted Lexi to tell me it was fine, it was okay, it was so far behind us, and I'd know that if one thing I'd done in the past was forgivable, maybe more of me was forgivable, too.

But Lexi wasn't Claudia. Not even Claudia was Claudia anymore, as in not the Claudia of my imagination, the Claudia I'd constructed for myself to cling to. Of course Lexi hadn't been thinking about our freshman year or guessed what I'd wanted to tell her. It was all in my head, except it didn't stay in my head if I opened my mouth and made it real.

"I'm sorry that I slept with Jamie while you were dating," I whispered to the salt-flecked sea green, the furred edamame pods.

There came another silence, the kind in which everything that went unspoken had somehow already been said.

"It was just once," I said, talking faster now, trying to get it all out. "I was in a really bad place, and it was a huge, horrible mistake I never should have done. I'm sure he thought that, too. I mean I know he did, and I—"

Lexi's mouth hinged open, a tiny bubble of saliva in the corner of one lip, and I thought she was going to ask me what kind of bad place, why hadn't I told her—if I was looking to dredge up the past, I might as well start with that. But she grabbed her jacket, her purse, and stormed out the door before I could finish. I could have called after her, I could have gone running, but what had I really expected. I sat in the booth as the food kept coming, all the rolls we'd ordered to share, this memorable night Lexi had wanted for me and my special announcement. I tried to imagine kissing Alyssa Green from CHEM048 Biological Chemistry Tuesdays 2:40–3:55 P.M. Alyssa's body under the faded flannel pajama pants she wore when we stayed up late, studying. Alyssa's morning breath, her childhood fears, the first fight we'd have, the crushing disappointments. She had slender fingers and a delicate neck that arched, exposed, when she bent over her work, and maybe it meant something that I'd noticed those fingers, that neck, that I could close my eyes and see her lips, bitten, but still. How soft. For a second, for perhaps even more than that, I ached into that softness, why should it be such an impossible thing.

But I couldn't hold Alyssa's hand. I couldn't say, "Mom, I have something to tell you," knowing there'd be no special dinner, no "I could never be mad at you!" which obviously wasn't true anyway. There were still places in this country where they'd kill you for such wanting. Where you'd always be less than, watching your back. The waitress asked if I wanted boxes for all the untouched food and I shook my head. "Just the check," I said hoarsely, and put it on my debit card, which I knew would be overdrawn but I also knew it wouldn't matter. Whatever fees I had to pay, whatever the consequence I thought I deserved, by the next month the account would refill, my gesture as empty as the way I felt when I left the restaurant and walked toward the car, a drizzle starting to fall but I had no umbrella, I never planned ahead. I didn't know where Lexi had run off to, if I should drive around looking for her, but where would I start. The idea of showing up at Mikaela's party was a joke. I was a joke. I'd seen the girls at the Swarthmore Queer Union with their butch haircuts and baggy cargo pants and they were the biggest joke of all. I couldn't believe Lexi thought of me that way. I wondered how complicated it would be to get a new lab partner at this point in the year.

THIRTY-NINE

The weeks leading up to graduation were raucous, booze soaked, a rush of dinners and parties and new hookups and last pairings as though the world were ending and everyone had to get it all done now. But perhaps the world really was ending, the only world we'd come to know. I tried to feel as hopeful and anxious and excited as everyone else. But mostly I kept checking the website where I could put in Claudia's name and birthdate and offender ID and find out what day she was being released.

My account had filled back up by then with Laurent's deposits, but the Western Union wouldn't let me send any more money to Connecticut. "Is someone threatening you?" the man at the bank asked when I tried to find a way. "Are you being coerced?" But they let me take out a thousand dollars in crisp new twenties and I left them in an envelope that I pressed with a thumb tack to the bulletin board on Lexi's door. I hadn't been over in months, not since our fight. But it was all the same: Lexi's name written in puffy paint with a heart over the i, a rainbow sticker that said SAFE SPACE, a reminder that as the floor's RA, her door was always open. *Your friendship has meant the world to me and I hope someday you can forgive me.* I'd picked a scarlet rosefinch from my stack of thank-you cards and jotted the note inside.

Already it felt easy, familiar, to take a cab to the car rental office, sign my name, hand over the deposit. It was bad timing to drive up the day before my family was set to arrive, but during exam week would have been worse. "I just want something quiet," I'd said when my mother asked what I wanted to do for graduation, and I'd meant something with just my parents and Jules. Something where the Corbins, maybe, weren't even invited. My mother had said she understood completely. It was my big day and I should have whatever I wanted. But it would be hard to tell my aunt and uncle—who'd had *such an important role to play*—that they weren't allowed to enjoy the occasion.

And if my mom's sister was invited, her brother had to be, too. If her siblings were coming, my dad's side couldn't be left out. What would happen if they discovered that I wasn't on campus right now, packing my room, cramming in those final moments I was supposed to be trying to savor?

But they wouldn't. No one in my family would imagine I was capable of this kind of surprise.

I found a hotel in Old Saybrook that was cute enough and not, I was pretty sure, the kind of place where I'd get murdered, and I ordered room service, which I'd never done before. I'd wanted a place on the water but it was June and they were filled up. I pictured the whole coastline clogged with more of Laurent's real estate acquisitions. My aunt winning her bid for state senator and casting vote after vote for rezoning laws. Maybe I should have let it go, forgotten about Claudia the way everyone else had moved on. But I couldn't shake the truth from myself. As a kid I'd just assumed there'd be an overarching logic I would one day be privy to, and how disappointing to find the world was only made by people after all.

Still, I'd take the luxury of lying in the king-sized bed with pizza and bourbon and reruns of *Friends*. The chance to imagine, for a moment at least, that none of it had happened—not the trial, not the accident, not my family's money, not how close they'd come to losing it all.

Then my mother texted with a flurry of questions about their trip, and where would I meet them tomorrow, had I double-checked the reservations Ellen's new personal assistant had made, had I finalized my outfits for graduation and the dinner after. I turned off my phone and poured more bourbon even though I knew I'd regret it the next day.

It was the first time in my life that nobody knew where I was. There was the other time I'd tried to see Claudia, but that hadn't been a whole night. A whole night and into the next morning, when I checked out of the hotel and went to buy coffee, a muffin, and told myself this was a sign of independence, which was altogether different from being alone.

I turned on my phone but didn't bother with the messages. I wasn't going to call anyone back.

I drove to the prison, only this time I didn't try to enter. I stayed in the parking lot and ate the muffin and drank the bad coffee and waited.

It was hot, the kind of hot that felt like it was already summer. I didn't know how long I'd be waiting. My stomach hurt from bourbon and grease and caffeine and I didn't know where to pee. I left to find a McDonald's, afraid I'd miss it and how would I know. But when I came back it was all the same, everything was always the same. I waited. I didn't eat lunch. I waited for longer. Think of how long Claudia's been waiting, I told myself, and after that I tried to sit without moving a muscle, not a single blink, but always I gave up too quickly and lost my own game.

I thought I might not know when it was happening. As though there should have been a sign. Some fanfare, but of course this must have happened all the time. A door opened. There were cars, three of them; I didn't know when they'd arrived or how long they'd been waiting along with me. Person after person climbed out of the cars—all of them were packed full. I didn't know how Claudia would actually be released, if there was a bus that dropped her somewhere or how any of that worked, but I'd decided that even if I got only a glimpse—even if I only waved from a respectable distance—it would be worth it. A sign that I was sorry. That she might forgive me. That both of us were going to be okay.

But I couldn't see her. I couldn't see because there were so many people surrounding her, they were hugging her and hugging each other and she was right there mashed into the center of it all. Flashes of a plain T-shirt, plain jeans, plain sneakers, her hair in plain braids—how could this be her? From across the parking lot I recognized her parents, her brother and sister, the relatives from the courtroom and others I hadn't seen before, family and there must have been friends, too, a short white girl with short bleached hair, and a bearded guy who kept holding the girl's hand, and an Asian woman—who was she?—and then another car showed up and even more people spilled out, running for her, running to hug her. Claudia was going to spend the whole day in the parking lot if they didn't let her go.

But they couldn't help themselves. Someone had a cooler in their trunk and they pulled out plates of food for Claudia, it was all for Claudia, and I couldn't see what it was but I imagined the lemon cake we'd eaten in her living room, and what would it be like to go three and a half years without tasting lemons. What would it be like to go three and a half years without hugging my mother, even though I couldn't really remember the last time I'd hugged my mother or that my mother had tried to hug me, not in that way where you never, ever want to let go. Claudia's prison wasn't so high-security, it was possible they'd hugged each other all through their visiting hours instead of only touching through glass. But how could that have ever been enough.

I wanted to get out. The whole reason to have come all that way was to get out of the car. To see Claudia—or was it to make sure Claudia saw me? I was crying in the car and I could tell everyone in the circle around Claudia was crying, but they weren't alone as they wiped their eyes and passed tissues around. Claudia's parents had their arms clasped and at one point they simply stood in the dusty lot and held each other close. Claudia, probably, was crying too—how could she not be. She hadn't cried at the trial, or maybe she did later or at sentencing, but I wasn't there. What had I done, what had I *done*. Why hadn't I been there to face it?

I was afraid, suddenly, of the circle splitting apart, of what might happen if she really did see me. My phone buzzed: my mother. I let the call go to voicemail. Then another, another. The text message: *Rachel, where are you? I thought we agreed to meet outside your dorm.* My father, too: *Sweetheart, we're here. What happened to you?*

I still have that idle, falling-asleep fantasy, the kind that sneaks up late at night and says what if I hadn't called them back that day. What if I'd turned north and sped past Boston, up the Maine coast, say; or west, to Arizona, California, where no one had heard the Corbin name. I could have done anything that morning. I still had choices open to me then.

My phone vibrated again, and this time it was a text from Lexi. *The money is under your door. You can't fucking buy having friends.* And I knew there was no choice. It was already made; I had made it or it had made me. What was the difference, in the end? No one would ever hug me the way I'd seen Claudia hugged. They'd never cry that hard over the miracle that I was in their lives. You can't ask things of people they'll never be able to give. My hands were shaking as I flipped the phone shut, as I turned on the car and peeled out of the parking lot before anyone in the circle could look back and see who it was.

FORTY

The dinner after graduation was for nineteen, and I sat at the end of the table, the guest of honor, the reason, ostensibly, why everyone was there. But most of the talk was about Ellen's campaign and Laurent's promotion and Jules's summer piano program at Berklee—how amazing she'd been accepted when she'd only just finished ninth grade. I said yes I was going home to Cambridge, yes I'd start studying for the MCATs, yes I was excited for everything to come. The waitstaff was prompt with refills, asking white or red, sparkling or still, and there was calamari with lemon aioli, salads with nasturtium, an assortment of crostini topped with whipped ricotta and a tomato jam Ellen said was divine. She and Laurent had started arguing over the wine as soon as we'd sat down, the number and variety of appropriate hors d'oeuvres to order for the table, until something dinged on Laurent's BlackBerry that he had to take care of that instant, so it seemed Ellen had won by default. Why was it vulgar to wear white at the wrong time of year but not vulgar to say "Oh *please*, you don't have a clue what you're talking about!" in front of eighteen other people on a day that was supposed to be focused on somebody else, somebody who couldn't stand wine anymore, didn't like calamari, wasn't sure she should be there at all?

"I thought they'd be divorced by now," I'd commented to my mother after learning there'd been fights, too, about what hotel to stay at, the block of rooms, the choice of breakfast venue. What was the point without Sabine, I'd meant, but that was unkind. My mother was frustrated about how late I'd been the day before, my excuse about *needing some time.* She said that was how some people related, that was how they got along, and I wanted to believe her. But wanting something didn't make it so. In the graduation tent that afternoon, after the ceremony had droned to its inevitable conclusion and everyone was clapping and throwing their hats and filing out to find their families, friends, all their loved ones cheering them on, I'd looked in the crowd and spotted Alyssa, who had recently chopped off all her hair and looked flushed and freckly and buoyant with joy. I'd wanted to go up to her, to hug her the way everyone else was hugging. To see how it might feel to be that happy.

But Alyssa had people of her own to hug—parents and siblings and a grandmother she stooped to put her arms around—and it wasn't my place to barge in. I hadn't gone so far as finding a new lab partner, but there were other ways to make a point. I could have said I was sorry, I was very sorry, actually, for being "too busy" to keep meeting up after class that semester. Sorrier than I'd realized until then.

But it was too late. My parents had run into Lexi's parents and they, too, were hugging. They barely had anything in common, but they had their daughters—who had been, they kept saying, friends for so long. Lexi didn't correct them and I didn't correct them and then we walked away, two separate families back to our two separate lives. If Lexi said anything to her parents after, I'd never know. If my parents noticed how awkward it was, I'd never know that, either. My family could have been anyone's family. I could have been anyone else on that green.

I knew why Ellen needed her husband. I knew why Laurent

would never leave. He'd probably made a spreadsheet to graph it, the profits soaring high over the costs. I wondered what everyone else was doing that night—but I had to stop thinking like that. I wasn't other people, I was only myself. I picked up a knife and used the edge to chime against my water glass. When that didn't slow the din I did it harder, and when that still didn't work I stood up.

"I'd like to say a few words," I said, the way my father might have, or Laurent himself. I flushed with satisfaction—who didn't enjoy being in charge? Eighteen faces turned to look at me, confused (my mother), embarrassed (my sister), nodding in encouragement (my aunt).

"Before we finish dessert and everyone scatters, I wanted to say thank you all so much for being here today." Polite applause, little comments that they were so proud of me, I'd done such a great job. My uncle Stephen said, "To the grad!" and everyone raised their glasses, my cousins with their Shirley Temples, the adults however many bottles into their wine.

And then they began talking among themselves like it was over, just because Stephen had said so.

"And also," I said, louder, projecting over the table and the noise of the restaurant, the other large groups and clinking dishes, cocktail shakers rattling at the bar. "Thank you especially to Aunt Ellen and Uncle Laurent for all that you've done for me."

More clapping, happy murmurs, and then Ellen, another glass raised, basking in the table's attention. "Darling, it's been our pleasure and we're—"

"So please don't think I'm ungrateful," I pushed on, interrupting her in a way that probably no one (besides Laurent) had interrupted her in quite some time. Her glass faltered but only a little, as though she knew it couldn't be the way it seemed. "I know what a difference it's made for me and my family," I said, and I was aware that I was stalling, testing to see if I was really going to go through with it.

But then my mother touched the back of my hand, whispering my name as though I were embarrassing myself, the way she sometimes hissed *Leonard* when my father's voice got too loud, and I said, twisting free from her, still standing at the head of the table where everyone was watching: "You need to stop paying me now."

The table hushed. All of them at once, leaving only the other diners and their silverware, the swish of the distant front door.

"What?" Ellen said, a touch of a laugh, as though I'd just walked up to them and farted.

"I refuse to take your money anymore."

At last Laurent looked up from his phone. For a second I thought Ellen didn't know about the deposits, but the look she was shooting me wasn't one of confusion. It was that you didn't do this. You didn't say no, not ever. And not so publicly. Nakedly. You certainly weren't allowed to phrase it like that.

"Rachel." My mother's voice came harsher, both hands on my arm, not just touching me but grabbing to pull me down. I was a child climbing on a jungle gym and it was her job to bring me to safety, to stop me from climbing too high. I didn't know my own limits. It was dangerous to be up there, alone.

But I shrugged her off; I didn't topple. "No, Mom. Let me say this." To Laurent, to Ellen again: "You need to take the money you were going to spend for me on med school, an apartment—all of it—and give it to Claudia instead."

Ellen put down her glass too hard. Wine sloshed out and onto the tablecloth. I flashed forward to hours from then, when we'd all be gone and the restaurant quiet but for the people whose sole job was to clean up after us. Jules had dropped a plate of cherry tomatoes she'd taken from the graduation tent and I thought, too, of who must have come by later to pick up the trash. Of course they were being paid for it, but what about the plates strewn by the wind, the perfectly good tomatoes she'd left there to burst on the ground?

"I know I can't force you. I'm not holding a gun to your head." A laugh, but no one laughed with me. I wondered the last time any of them had spoken Claudia's name. Jules's jaw hung down, my cousins starting to whisper. Laurent and Ellen were silent. His ashen stare could strip me down to bone.

But I didn't stop. I wouldn't let him. "However that works. However you were going to do it. Whatever you were going to pay me, it has to be hers."

It wasn't an apology or turning back the clock or undoing what one family—what *my* family—had done. But money was money. Everyone needed it, artists most of all. I can't force you, I'd said, but Ellen would know that wasn't true. And Laurent—I'd never told anyone what I'd overheard at the barn, or that night in his study. But it wasn't too late. How many emails had I accumulated from Marshall Bennett by then? He'd been nominated for a Pulitzer for a series on how juries exercised their discretion, not in situations with a mandatory minimum but when they could make some kind of choice. I hadn't read past the headlines but I got the gist. All I'd have to do was hit reply and say interestingly, yes, upon further reflection I did have some observations pertaining to how this trial came about and what might have influenced its outcome, and perhaps it was finally time for us to meet.

There came an eruption of talking. My mother tried to get me to sit. My father rose from his seat and went over to Ellen and Laurent to say sorry on my behalf—a laugh, ha ha, it was an overwhelming day and I didn't know what I was saying. He pressed a hand to Laurent's back, his smile unnaturally broad: "Best to leave business until after the brandy, kiddo," as Stephen said, "Come on Len, she's a college grad now! It's good to let them have convictions." The waitstaff hovered with dessert plates until Laurent signaled them to come, there was nothing worth waiting for. My father sat back down but I could tell he didn't want to. The kids scrambled for their spoons—there was chocolate cherry cake and an ice cream bombe and something with vanilla crème, I wasn't sure exactly, I'd had nothing to do with the ordering; I seemed to have nothing to do with the whole of my life. They were already moving on, as if what I'd said had never been, and I pushed back my chair, dropped my napkin on my plate, and reached for my purse. It was one Ellen had bought me and I couldn't believe myself, I just couldn't believe myself sometimes.

"Rachel," my mother said, as if that were the only word she knew. But the tone had changed, more incredulous than sharp. No matter the things she used to say about her sister when it was just my father and Jules and me to listen. There was never an excuse to be impolite.

I kissed her cheek. I used to wish she'd take more care—learn to use foundation, a simple eyeliner, at the very least pick up an under-eye serum and antiaging cream. But now I wanted to inhale her lotion, her drugstore shampoo. What difference did her little statements make when all their choices, hers and Ellen's and everyone else's, turned out to be the same? She should have gone to Connecticut that summer to see her sister. Even with Jules sick, even with me begging to go. She shouldn't have left me to handle it alone.

"Thanks so much for this," I said. "I've got to go back and pack."

"We're not finished yet. You haven't touched the desserts."

"We have to drive you," my father added. "You've no way to go."

"I'll see you for breakfast tomorrow." I touched Stephen's shoulder, Anita's, rumpled my cousin Georgie's hair. I wanted to do the same to Jules, to pull the sleek tail of her braid through my fingers and say sorry to have done this but you'll be fine, I know you will. But she sat there with her back rigid, ignoring me as she spooned vanilla crème. I brushed my lips to the top of her head. "I love you," I whispered, so only she could hear.

I didn't know how Ellen and Laurent would arrange it, if you could do that for someone who wasn't family. If they could keep it quiet enough that the Marshall Bennetts of the world wouldn't sniff out the transfer and start asking why. But of course you could; there were ways of doing anything. I'd seen such a look on Ellen's face—had she thought I was about to tell her secret? But it was my final card to play, and I intended to hold on to it. I was grinning as I left the restaurant, grinning as I stepped into the street. It was late, the dinner had dragged on a long time. The air was thick and still warm. A light rain misted and I felt the immediate effect on my hair. I was lifting, everything lifting in the early summer night. Ellen and Laurent would pay Claudia because I'd said so, I knew how to bend them to my will. Still grinning as I stuck my hand out for a cab—

I couldn't do that anymore. There wouldn't be another deposit next month, or the next month, or the month after. I lowered my arm. I went back inside, hoping no one from my family would come out and see me. How silly they'd think I was, changing my mind at the very first stumble. But they were still eating their chocolates, perusing the coffee and aperitifs list. Talking about me, no doubt—how this was a difficult time in a young person's life, full of transitions, and I was acting out but there was no need to take it personally. Once it had seemed intolerable to be the source of gossip, to be misunderstood. But now I wanted to be talked about. I wanted them to ask about the details—"Why," Stephen could say, or Anita, or one of the kids, maybe even, someday, Jules herself. "Why would she call it a payment, why would she put it like that?"

Back inside the restaurant, I asked the hostess where the nearest SEPTA station was. She drew me a map on the back of a cocktail napkin. It was a bit of a hike, she warned. Would I rather the restaurant call me a cab? But I was still smiling, still thrilled with myself. I followed the route, and there was a moment when I did begin to falter, afraid I was lost, I'd made a horrible mistake—

But then there was the station, there was someone who told me how to get a ticket, where to transfer, I was on the right path after all. All I had to do was sit and be taken away. I gripped my purse to my chest. In my wet shoes and wet dress I knew I stood out, but the smile popped up anyway. People tried to look dour, unapproachable, and there I was. Floating over them all.

I couldn't go to Cambridge, not with the way they'd looked at me across that table stained with wine and aioli and crumbs. But who wanted to move home anyway, only to have Laurent deciding on my apartment, Ellen selecting the décor? "You're so lucky," my mother had told me just that morning, after my parents had stopped in my dorm room, a single, with my graduation dress up on its hanger, my books partially in boxes but mostly still unpacked. "You don't know how many of your classmates would kill for what you have." She promised she'd see me as soon as the ceremony was over. And I had thought, as I'd watched them walk down the hall, my very own parents, that what my mother meant was that *she* would have killed for what I had, the education and prestige but most of all the lack of worry, the way it was all allowed to fall into place. "It's not luck, Mother," I could have said, but they'd have told me not to be testy, nervous, it would ruin the photos of my big day.

I could move somewhere else, though. Why not? People got jobs. Apartments. If it took me longer to study, so be it. Med schools didn't frown on work experience. It might even make me look better than the lucky girl who'd never had to try. I imagined it on the long ride out to Swarthmore: my future. Someday, I thought, I'd tell Claudia what I'd done for her. When the timing was finally right.

SIXTEEN YEARS LATER

FORTY-ONE

I came across the advertisement on the subway. Minding my own business, standing wedged between a man who smelled like popcorn and a man who smelled like worse. But who knew what they thought about me. I'd come from the OR, a woman whose appendix had burst, the inside yellowed like mustard—it felt like I'd never come clean. Her boyfriend had told her the pain was probably gas, and I was thinking about that, about pain and how we bear it, about who tells us what can hurt and what cannot. Which means I was thinking, as I sometimes did, about my aunt and whether she was still taking oxy. She'd won her state senate seat handily, and then had set her sights on more. Now she was in her second term as governor of Connecticut, her husband the groundbreaking executive of his own firm. But I tried not to let my mind wander. Most days, it was better not having to know.

There came a jostle, or maybe I just lost my balance. I still wonder what might have happened if I hadn't looked up. I found myself caught—not by *her*, but a picture. A recent ad, only barely scummed by subway grime. I'd have recognized that face anywhere. Glossed and knowing, half smiling down on us all.

Popcorn man grumbled, I must have bumped him, but my

apology came out a croak. Everything was stuck inside me, all the words I'd ever reached for clogging up my throat. In the headshot Claudia still had the smallest side dimple, but it wasn't the same, it didn't mean whatever it used to. Whatever I'd once thought. I pulled out my phone to look up the venue—I'd never been but I knew what it was, a place for lectures, shows: *NYC's premier cultural voice*. The shock of it had me frightened, legitimately scared, of how hard my heart struck against bone. I'd never had a panic attack before, but it wasn't impossible. Or maybe it was a coincidence and I only happened to be dying of some unrelated affliction, my chest seizing, my extremities numb.

She was headlining their fall lineup, in conversation with a woman named Sandra Price, and I didn't know who that was, why it should do such things to me to read it. I'd turned thirty-eight two weeks ago, my coworkers bringing donuts with a candle for my shift. What I mean is that I had a career, a life, things I could be proud of. I'd googled Claudia ages ago, just enough to know about her MFA, her first piece accepted into a small LA gallery show. She'd moved on, I'd told myself, and successfully, which meant that I could, too.

Now, though.

At home I dropped my bag, went out again. The apartment was stifling, the air, summer always lasted too long in the city, even into September the nights stayed cloying and hot. I'd stopped drinking after college, although that seemed like the kind of thing I should do, what the movie version of myself would do if I were somebody else, somebody sitting at home watching my life and frowning at my choices.

But I only walked and walked, and when I finally returned to Amsterdam Avenue and climbed the creaking stairs to my studio apartment on the fifth floor, I showered again and watched TV that passed one episode after another until at two thirty in the morning

I opened my laptop. *Greenwich*, the subway ad had said. And now here was the write-up when I found the website, when I clicked the link for her talk.

Come hear artist and noted activist Claudia Meadows discuss her latest series, Greenwich, *a kaleidoscope of collage, watercolor, and more, that deftly expands and contracts from the individual to the family, the workplace, the state, and back again, exploring class, power, and labor in what Meadows calls "our racialized world." On display at Kym Howard Gallery, Chelsea, Sept 14 through—*

I added one ticket to my cart and pressed Buy.

I could have looked up her email, her agent, surely she had a publicist—there were ways to get in touch. But that wasn't what I wanted. I wanted to sit in the darkened theater, beneath the lights that lit her up in all her spectacle, and find out what the fuck she thought she was doing.

But by the time the night arrived and I took my seat, I kept having to swallow. My saliva had a sour taste. I'd thought I was prepared—I'd seen her picture on the subway, online, in the program I kept curling in my lap. But when she strode onstage to the roar of applause, the paper ripped in my hands. Whatever happened to those California galleries, maybe teaching somewhere, the exhilaration of an occasional sale? The audience clapped and clapped, cheers ringing like a thousand silver bells. She herself was made of silver, of light, her hair long and vibrantly curled, pulled partway back to show off large silver hoops that matched, of course, her silver belt, silver shoes, the silver stitching of her crimson blouse. It made no sense. How she, Claudia, could be the person raising her hands to the crowd while I sank even lower in my seat.

She couldn't profit, I didn't think, from what had been deemed her crime. She was too smart to court a defamation suit. But there were things she could talk about, things she must have been saying for years. About Greenwich. My family. *Me.* Sandra took the microphone and launched into her introduction, but I barely followed. I missed the first question altogether. I kept thinking about Sabine lying in my lap, and Claudia lying in my lap, and were you ever close to someone, really close to them, if it turned out you'd never known them at all.

"The series actually came out of these small doodles," Claudia was explaining, leaning toward Sandra as though they were lounging in her living room, sharing an inside joke they'd laughed over for years. "Those little, everyday things that you start to realize maybe aren't so little after all. For a while I was approaching it like my real work was elsewhere, and this was just the outlet where I could let myself feel whatever I wanted—where I could be angry, or whatever, in that way you always know you know you're not supposed to show."

"Like in the piece *Denise Makes Coffee*," Sandra prompted, and I put the program down before I tore it to shreds. I'd seen the painting on the gallery website: a woman in silhouette, flattering heels and a pencil skirt morphing up, up, into a grotesque caricature spilling forth from the top of her blouse. A stream of coffee poured from the carafe and overflowed the mug as she smiled—no, grimaced—at the viewer. At me.

"It started because my sister Denise—who worked with Ellen before she was Governor Corbin, by the way—was always expected to make the coffee for meetings. Or she'd have a client waltz into her office looking for the white woman with her title, since obviously it couldn't be her."

A blond woman in the row in front of me nodded, but what right did she have to nod, to act like she knew how it was? The price of the painting was like looking at Ellen's dresses, realizing there was an entire world out there I didn't know, a world that didn't include me and never would. I couldn't believe Claudia's voice, how smooth through the microphone, how certain she could sound.

"I didn't intend, I don't think, to focus on Greenwich in the beginning. The thing you have to understand is that even after you're released, you have to keep checking that box that says felon. You're never truly *out*, you know? And that's the point, obviously, but I didn't want that to be the only story I get to have. Except it was like with the anger, with all the times you're told to make the coffee. What happens when, instead of running from it, pretending it's just this blip that has nothing to do with you, with your actual life, your humanity, you start to say—okay, fine, world. You want this to define me, so what if it does? The white women had their *lean in* moment." (Titters.) "Nina, my wife, was the one who first said, well, what if I lean into this?"

She went on, the audience nodding, laughing, hoots of approval, it was less a lecture hall than a church. But my ears were ringing. My tongue felt furred. *Wife*. I pushed out of my seat. "Sorry," I whispered to the woman beside me, to everyone as I stepped over their legs and purses and folded programs featuring Claudia's dimpled grin. I couldn't run, it would draw too much attention, but I kept my head down, my phone in my hand as though an emergency had just come up.

"Honestly"—her voice carried, it echoed, it pulsed through my skull—"when I started putting that first ink wash down I told myself, it's only for me. It's only what I want to say, and if it doesn't go anywhere, that's okay. But people connect, I think, with the ways the paintings play with size and scale—to show how we can be reduced, or demonized, or transformed in someone else's eyes. That moment when you see yourself the way they see you and realize you've trusted all the wrong people. You haven't been having the same conversation, you haven't even lived in the same world. I'm hoping the series will encourage people to be more, you know, attentive to the things they say, the ways they view others as a means to their own—"

The doors swung shut behind me.

I crossed the empty lobby and went into the humid night. I sat on the steps of the building with my head between my knees. The air was heavy. My lungs burned from what I'd held inside. You weren't supposed to feel your pulse move, you were supposed to be free of certain kinds of knowledge. But I felt each electric impulse fired through my heart. Claudia had a wife and solo gallery shows and subway ads and featured speaking events and art I'd never be able to afford, and I should have been happy for her, I *was* happy for her. But the program had announced she was donating all proceeds from sales and speaking engagements related to *Greenwich* to charity, without a single mention of why she didn't need a thing.

Maybe she'd have been able to get this far on her own. Maybe her family would have recovered from the costs of the trial and everything after. Maybe Nina would have supported her—I had no way to know.

What I did know were the years of receipts I'd accumulated, every month a confirmation from an offshore bank about a transfer into Claudia's account. Meanwhile I had student loans and interest and residency had paid so little, not to mention fellowships, all the licensing fees, on top of New York rent and New York bills—everything harder than I could have imagined at my college graduation when I'd thought I was taking a stand.

Someday I'd make more, I'd come out ahead. But *someday* still felt so impossibly far away.

Sirens ran up Lexington Avenue. *When you've trusted all the wrong people*, Claudia had said. I breathed in, out, and had the strangest feeling of Sabine sitting there on the steps with me, Sabine at three years old taking both our hands and begging us to play.

FORTY-TWO

I should have left. Part of me wanted to, the part that always longed for things to be easier. That still wanted, more than anything else, to be liked.

But I wasn't a child anymore, I couldn't act like that. I had to wait a long time on those steps, off to the side scanning the crowd as audience members streamed out, just like I'd waited such a long time to catch sight of her once before. While I waited I looked up her glowing reviews in *The New Yorker*, Artnet. My life was my work and my work was my life—there was so much I hadn't kept up with. It seemed different, now, what people thought of the case. And her. And my aunt, who was still popular—but not with everyone. Not in quite the same ways. There was more than one interview where Donald S. Thayer, now Connecticut's chief state's attorney, was pushed to defend his record, including his role in "the Nanny Trial" from 1999. Miscarriage of justice. Abuse of the courts. Marshall Bennett had won his Pulitzer, finally, tracing how prison growth was foundational to local economies—*follow the money*, he'd said. Who did Laurent golf with these days? Who was on Ellen's list of tennis partners? I pressed my palms into the sockets of my eyes until the darkness popped and burst into stars.

I was afraid there was some other exit, an alleyway or nondescript door so the luminary—so Claudia—wouldn't get mobbed. But after a time the doors opened again and there she was, her strappy silver sandals clicking smartly with each step. She laughed, hugged a woman—white—who told her she was fabulous, flawless, then wished her a good night and went back inside. I stepped into the lamplight. She could have shouldered past me like I was just another stranger on the street. But she stopped, and I thought this meant something, that with all the possibilities in the world, she still stopped for me.

"Hi," I said. I shifted my purse from one shoulder to the other. I felt, suddenly, dumpy, ridiculous. I hadn't known what to wear—how do you dress to see a sort of but not quite ex you'd helped send to prison nineteen years ago? I was in flats and she was in heels and standing on a higher step. I wasn't used to being shorter and found I didn't like it, such imbalance.

"It's Rachel," I said into her silence, as though that were the problem, the reason for her stare. "Rachel Fiske."

Up close I caught the smoky touch of her eye makeup, the faint grain of the lines around her mouth. A few silver hairs coiled around her temples and it gave her a gravity my own dull, dyed grays had never offered. I wished I could tell her how good she looked, but I was afraid how it might sound. "I know who you are," she said, finally looking away from me, past me, out toward the rest of the night.

My breath singed between my lips. "I heard your talk," I said.

"You mean the part before you left."

How had she seen me? How did she know?

"I had a work emergency," I lied.

"And yet you're still here."

"I found someone else to take care of it. At the hospital," I added. I wanted her to know I'd done it, everything I'd wanted back then. Everything she'd encouraged me to be.

"You were brilliant," I went on. "I saw the subway ad. I couldn't believe it was you—I mean of course I did, of course I believed you'd go on to do great things." I sounded like a high school guidance counselor. I hated myself right then. "I can't wait to see the show," I added after a pause in which she, again, didn't nod, didn't say anything, certainly not that it was good of me to come.

"Have a good night, Rachel Fiske."

I rushed forward before she could leave me. I wouldn't dream of touching her, but she flinched anyway. "Please," I said, drawing back. Leaving space. "Five minutes. Just five minutes of your time. I wanted to tell you that I'm sorry, Claudia. I'm so sorry. Hearing you tonight, knowing how you've been impacted by the Corbins, everything that happened—I mean of course I know you'd think about it, but that it's such a part of your life." I must have sounded so stupid, my voice spiraling, the way I was rambling on. "I know it's too late, but I really am sorry. If there were any way to do it differently—" I paused, she had to know what I meant. "I wish I could take it all back."

She stared at me as though I were a zoo animal, a curiosity, no telling what inexplicable feat I'd perform.

"You have to believe me," I said.

She smiled. I couldn't understand what there was to smile about. She said, "I don't, actually, have to do anything."

"We were kids, remember? We both made a lot of mistakes."

"Is that how you see it?"

The flush. The burn down my throat. At least this time, I knew when to stop. "I didn't come here to argue."

Her smile spread. "Of course you didn't. You thought you'd say 'sorry,' and I'd say 'me, too,' and we'd hug it out and you'd go home feeling good about yourself, like all that weight's been lifted. Right, *Rach?*" A spin to my name that said she didn't mean it, none of the closeness it implied.

Tears pricked, such rising heat. I didn't know if I was more shocked by what she was saying or by the fact that I could still feel this kind of shame. I wanted to tell her it wasn't my fault—it wasn't, any of it, what I'd wanted for myself or for her or our lives.

But it felt, suddenly, like I'd stumbled too close to a campfire, dangerous enough to feel my face burn. It may not have been what I'd wanted, but I had to know it was still what I'd done.

"What do you want from me?" I said—not angry, just pleading. "Tell me honestly—what can I do?"

She held up her palms. "You're the one who came up to me."

"To apologize!" But it was too loud, I didn't mean it like that.

"Yeah," she said. "Might want to work on that."

"Just listen. Please." Here it was. My fists clenched and unclenching, my voice struggling not to break. It was my last chance, maybe ever, to turn something around, to steer against the course that we'd been set on. Nothing of that summer, the trial, would have happened without me. But this wouldn't have happened without me, either.

"The money from the Corbins," I continued. Not *Ellen and Laurent.* Not *my aunt and uncle.* "You should know—it's from me. It's always been from me."

Her nostrils flared. "No, it's not."

"It is. I should have found a better way to tell you, but I'm the one who made them do it. This whole time, I've been—"

"Stop, Rachel. Just stop." Her palms still raised as if to push me back, even though I hadn't moved, I hadn't done anything but stand there. "I meant it's not from you because it's not your money. I know you're the one who had them send it."

I sucked in a breath. It felt like I might stumble after all, not toward her but back, back, toppling down the steps. "You knew?"

Her hands went to her hair. "Oh my god. You think I believed those people would—what? Make it up to me? Out of the goodness of their hearts? I don't owe you, if that's what you're after. You've made your choices. I don't feel bad about mine."

The door opened. A woman headed down the steps. Nina—who else could it be? Who could walk that assuredly toward Claudia with the conviction that comes from knowing someone is yours? I wanted to say what about forgiveness, what about her apology to me. Was she not even going to say thank you?

But my mouth had gone dry. My throat ached. Nina wore slender heels, slender jeans, with slender dreadlocks piled on her head. She linked an arm through her wife's and smiled with unspeakable ease. "Sorry, hon. The line was still long."

Claudia said, "That's okay, let's go," before I could introduce myself, say who I was or the fact that I'd known Claudia all those years ago—far longer than her. Claudia turned with such finality. They walked past me down the steps.

I was still standing there, frozen, dismissed, when Nina glanced back at me.

"Who was that?" Her voice carried as they walked away.

"You'll never, ever guess." And then a sound I can't get out of my head, a sound that tore out something new, or perhaps only something forgotten: she laughed. Not a laugh like anything was funny. But a sound that carried the words she didn't have to say, because her wife already understood.

My feet unstuck and I took off after them. They were heading down the avenue, toward the subway or to hail a cab crosstown, and I raced to catch up. How could she laugh like that, how could she walk away when there was so much still unspoken. I couldn't believe she'd known all this time and never called, emailed, never said a single word to set things right.

I was almost upon them. I didn't know what I'd say, but we weren't done yet, this wasn't over—

And then Claudia leaned her head against Nina's shoulder. And I stopped.

I stood in the middle of the sidewalk. I watched them strolling, arm in arm, each one holding up the other. Their silhouette, the shape of them: together. The simplest thing, and yet I felt it like a punch beneath my solar plexus, in the cage of my ribs that housed what was supposed to be my heart.

"Watch it, bitch," some man spat as he jostled past me, but I still didn't move. There was nothing to run to. There was nothing left to say. I'd held hands with people, sometimes, sure. But not like that. I'd never known a world like that, one that couldn't be bought, or won, or demanded, or owed. One that wasn't automatically mine. Down the block they disappeared into the night and were gone. Not gone, of course—I could have caught up. But gone from me in every way that mattered.

I turned off the avenue. I didn't know where I was going, only that the sprint had left a sharp split in my sides and everything hurt. The soles of my shoes were too thin for walking, my toes pinched, a blister was forming on one heel. But I didn't want a cab, the subway, a bus. I couldn't stand the thought of other people. I pulled out my phone and opened up my contacts, scrolling down to *E* as I walked on as though I had somewhere to be. Someone waiting, someone wanting only me.

One word to my aunt would end this. Claudia's smile, that laugh, whatever it had meant. Everything I'd given up for nothing. This was my chance to get it all back, to reclaim all that should have been mine to begin with.

It didn't matter how long it had been since I'd last called Ellen, I knew she'd pick up for me. Our special bond, she'd once said, and time hadn't changed that. If anything, I'd proven myself worth their investment: my silence, my support. "Give me back my money," I hollered ridiculously to the yellow of a passing cab. Needing to hear it out loud, to trust I could make the words come.

Trees rose against the strange blue of the city's night sky, its perpetual illumination, our imitation stars. I looked up from the phone and saw I'd reached the edge of Central Park. I thought of the copse of trees on the Corbins' front lawn, and who lived in that house now, who seeded the grass and watered the dahlias and lamented the rabbits, the groundhogs, the deer. What did they take from there. What was the cost. What had I ever truly had to pay? I imagined my aunt laughing at me with that bell of a laugh, like nothing could touch her. *Sweetheart*, she'd say, the same way she used to. *What took you so long?*

I closed my contacts list and opened my email. I'd blocked Marshall Bennett years ago, tired of his little missives, the reminders of my own inertia. I didn't have that Swarthmore address anymore, and my personal email was private. I'd told HR an old boyfriend had been stalking me, I was worried he might come to my workplace, and so they kept my full name off the hospital website, and my photo, any contact information. I hadn't heard from him in years, but it was easy to remember his email, first name last name @nytimes .com. Even if he'd moved on from the original case, this was the governor of Connecticut we were talking about. I could give him a scandal—a story—no journalist in their right mind would dismiss.

Because if I was going to make a call, if I was going to undo anything from that time, then how could I not think about this. There were statutes of limitations, probably, but that wasn't the point. My aunt's negligence, my uncle's corruption—didn't it still matter? Nothing simply went away. The public had a right to know who they were voting for. And after state senator, after governor, what would Ellen set her sights on next? What new financial coup would Laurent court? I'd once wondered who would come along and stop them, and only now did I have an answer, the same answer that had been there all along. Somewhere there'd be a paper trail from Ellen's first, legal prescriptions. And what about all those gifts, political donations, rigging the bid in Kip's favor? Bennett knew what money could buy. Look for what year Kipling Holder got a new hot tub, I'd say. See what he donated to the governor's campaign. And Brad Whittier, I'd add, because I remembered him, too. Check the construction costs for the work at River Point. See where all those numbers happen to line up a little too well. Try to find out just how far this goes.

I wiped a palm on my slacks and then the other. What would he say if I began to steer him in the right direction? Ellen's career would be over. Laurent's, too. The Corbin name and everything it represented. I had to think, though, about what part of this would blow back on me. One touch to reach my family, another to tear it apart, and no one but myself to make the choice—

I stumbled on a crack in the concrete, and that made me look up, startled back into myself. I dropped the phone into my purse as though it burned.

I didn't know where I was going. North, maybe, deeper into the park. I walked. I walked. Even now there was still the stray runner out, and young men, a couple, holding hands and walking their dog. I kept my eyes down. Do you know, I could have asked them, how lucky you are? I walked. I walked. I couldn't do these things I was thinking. I passed a meadow, dusty baseball fields abandoned in the dark. By morning the grass would be full of people picnicking, throwing frisbees, doing whatever made them happy until the leaves changed and winter came and the city transformed again. Why couldn't I be like that, too? But it wasn't transformation, not really. There were so few ways to truly change.

The skin rubbed all the way off my right heel, wet seeping from the wound. A dog barked from somewhere in the shadows. A woman laughed. I felt the sharp edges of Claudia's laughter ricochet inside me. I missed Sabine the way I hadn't missed her in years, I missed being seventeen and thinking it was love. But this was the laugh of someone happy, for whom there was no need for more.

I touched my purse, the weight of it, knowing what it held. I had to make a decision. I had to feel that I was someone after all.

The dog, again. The laughter. Claudia and Nina would have arrived wherever they were going by now—their hotel, a nightcap, perhaps there were children back in LA and they'd call home to hear their milk-soft voices through the phone. A babysitter, a family member, someone watching them with care. Good, I thought. Let someone be happy. Let them be safe. I kicked my heels out of the shoes and stood pressing the backs down, night air biting my bloodied Achilles. I spun in a circle, disoriented, intentionally lost, like a small girl in a private game, the rules unspoken and all of her own making. But all games ended eventually. I put the shoes back on. I walked. I pulled out my phone.

ACKNOWLEDGMENTS

Acknowledgments TK

ABOUT THE AUTHOR

Kate Broad holds a BA from Wellesley College and a PhD in English from the CUNY Graduate Center. She is a Bronx Council on the Arts award winner for fiction, and her writing appears in *The Rumpus*, *No Tokens*, *The Brooklyn Review*, and elsewhere. *Greenwich* is her first novel.